The Crazy Widow Lady's

Grand Experiment

Kat M. Walker

Applemont Books
Cumming, GA

Applemont Books
Cumming, GA

Cover Design by Angela Masters Lamb

Library of Congress Cataloging-in-Publication Data
Walker, Kat M.
The Crazy Widow Lady's Grand Experiment
1. Title 2. Fiction
Applemont Books: September 2019
ISBN 978-1-7331763-0-9
Trade Paperback
Library of Congress Control Number: 2019908464

The Crazy Widow Lady's

Grand Experiment

Prologue

The late spring sun hung around in the early evening, allowing people to enjoy the art walk. They strolled along the city sidewalks—alone, in pairs, more often in groups filled with chatter and excitement. No one paid attention to the older woman sitting on the wooden bench studying the crowd.

If they had, they would have seen her fiddling with something in her purse as her gaze lingered on each person who strolled by. The woman's blue eyes filled with sadness. She sighed, stood and followed a couple in their mid-thirties until the end of the block.

At the corner, the couple turned left, but the old woman stayed put. She peeked in her purse, then patted it like a dog that had performed a challenging trick.

She hadn't known the couple, so why follow them? Was she waiting for someone? A husband? Friends?

The woman didn't appear to be homeless. Her gray hair was clean and cut in a stylish pageboy. Dark jeans paired with a paisley sweater spoke of good fashion sense. Her makeup had been applied with care, although her mascara-less eyes were a tad bloodshot from crying.

As a family hurried by, the mother doing her best to corral two young children, a boy and a girl, the older woman watched them. When they crossed the street, she did the same.

"Molly, stop." The mother held onto her daughter's arm. "You have ice cream on your face."

After digging for a tissue, the mother pushed her bag over her shoulder where it bumped against her back. The old woman hid a smile.

While the mother wiped her daughter's cheek, the father held fast to the boy's hand as they both stared at the drone display across the street. Seizing the moment, the older woman quickly reached into her purse. She removed the item she needed and slipped it into the mother's bag.

Excellent, she thought. *Another victim.*

Mission accomplished, she eased back into the crowd and continued along her way.

Easter Dinner

Lee died on Epiphany. January 6. Today is Easter Sunday. My first Easter in fifty years without him. So many firsts this year—Valentine's Day, Ash Wednesday, St. Paddy's Day, what used to be The Darkest Day—and so many more to go.

The thought of facing yet another day without him makes me not want to get out of bed ever again. I now know why some husbands and wives pass so close together. When you've been with someone that long, the idea of that person not being there is too much to bear.

I will get up, but not because I want to. If I'm not awake and dressed and at least pretending to be normal when June or Dolores or one of my other friends arrives to check on me, they'll drop by even more often. A blessing and a curse to have several friends who care about me.

"Busybodies," Lee used to grumble on the way home after one of the many social gatherings. "Don't they have their own problems? Why are they always talking about everyone else?"

"We're women," was the only response I could give.

"You're a woman," he'd say. "You're not like that."

3

The comment made me smile and snuggle close, plus he knew he'd be rewarded again later that night.

Now, I have to imagine him saying those words. I won't get to hear him, or see the sly wink he'd give me, or feel his strong arm draped around my shoulder and experience that glow of love and affection that was our mainstay.

Even on the darkest day, when our sweet Cassandra Marie came into the world early, and stillborn, that glow held us together. I didn't want another child, prayed hard not to get pregnant, and both God and my husband seemed to understand.

Would it have helped to have someone to share this grief? Any child we might have had would be long grown by now. Even Cassie would be nearing forty with a family of her own and maybe even living in a different state. Or she'd be like my friends, sticking close the first several days and then taking turns checking in on me.

Of course, Cassie would be grieving, too, having lost her daddy. And Lee would've been one of the best. At least they're together now, and that thought brings comfort.

"C'mon, old lady," I muttered. "Time to stop woolgathering and get ready to face the day."

As usual, I managed to do both. Lee used to joke that I was the "thinkingest" woman he'd ever known. Could I help it if my brain wouldn't ever turn off?

I once considered that particular trait to be a good one, but recent events have me reconsidering. My mind used to throw me the craziest ideas sometimes, and it might keep me up at night or jar me awake at 2 AM with puzzles to solve. These days all it wanted to do was traipse down Memory Lane and I was more than willing to follow along, forgetting about the house and friends and even myself.

Even today, while taking a shower and getting dressed, my brain brought snapshots of Lee and how he left those little hairs in the sink after shaving. I could picture him—tall, stocky, short dark hair wet against his head, grizzled chest above the towel cinched at his waist, shaving cream covering his face as he stared intently at his reflection. If I caught his attention, he'd turn and wrinkle his nose at me, deep brown eyes glinting with amusement.

Oh, how I miss that man!

The pain of loss mixed with the pleasure of memory made me want to crawl back into bed.

"No!"

I refused to let myself sink back into depression. I had to keep going. I'd promised Lee, and I promised myself the same thing.

I was not going to be one of those old women who couldn't make it on her own. Myra O'Malley had gumption. Myra O'Malley was strong. I'd seen hard times before and made it through every one of them, which meant I could do it again. I'd already made it through the last three months, and I'd continue to make it, too. No stopping Myra O'Malley.

"Aw, shit." I slumped onto the bedroom bench.

The phone burred and I went to pick it up, wondering which of my friends would be on the other end of the line this time.

"Myra! You're up."

June.

"Don't sound surprised. It's almost noon."

"You weren't at 10:30 mass," she said. "It's Easter Sunday."

"Oops." I grinned as I pictured her puckered face. June tended to take her religion a little too seriously. "Guess I'll order me a handbasket."

June sighed. "Henry wants to know if he should come get you."

"Whatever for?"

"Easter dinner." June paused.

So I'd be getting the sermon today even without setting foot in St. Anthony's.

"I'll look past skipping church on this holy day, but I cannot forgive missing dinner. We are celebrating the resurrection of our

Lord and Savior, Myra. Besides, I host every year and my girls couldn't make it, but *almost* everyone else is here. I'm not letting you slide. Henry's on his way to fetch you."

I remained silent, not sure she was finished.

"Well?" she prompted.

"Guess I'll see you soon."

"You bet your butt you will. Luv ya."

And with that, she hung up. Guess it was a good thing I'd managed to get myself out of bed and cleaned up, if not dressed up. My old jeans and ratty brown sweater would earn another homily from Mother June, but I just didn't have it in me to get all gussied up for dinner with friends. I decided to swap the sweater for a pretty pink blouse and dab on a little make-up to look and feel more presentable.

When Henry arrived, he engulfed me in a bear hug. I wasn't sure if it was because he knew I was still hurting or if he was apologizing ahead of time for June. Either way, I'd take it. One can't ever have enough hugs.

"Come on, then," Henry said when he let go. "Best not keep the lady of the house waiting."

I smiled and nodded. Ever the gentleman, he held the door open to his newish Ford F-150 and made sure I was comfortable before getting in himself.

"Who all is there?" I asked when we were on our way.

"Let's see." He hesitated. "Mabel and Roy. Susan and Sal. Betty and her girl and I think that's it. Dolores and Jim went to see one of their boys and other folks are out of town or doing their own thing."

As the names were mentioned, I pictured everyone in my mind. Mabel, with her dark hair and pixie cut, so perfect for her petite stature and heart-shaped face. Roy, blond of hair with a stern face and paunchy frame. Betty, who looked like a grandmother should with her long gray hair and ever-present smile. Her daughter, Jean, although still slim, was a carbon copy of her mother. Dolores, gray hair in a short bob and a perpetual scowl while her husband Jim loved being the life of the party.

Henry cleared his throat. "Steph and Kim couldn't make it this time."

"June told me about the girls. Sorry."

He shrugged.

I wanted to say there would be other years, but you just don't know. Last year my Lee had been at the event, looking as healthy as a horse, and now he was gone. Was the cancer eating at him even then?

"How you holdin' up?" Henry asked.

"It's been rough," I admitted. He could take the truth. "One day at a time."

"All you can do." A quick nod. "When you've had your fill today, and I don't mean food, let me know. I'll get you out of there."

"Thank you."

Another quick nod as he pulled into the driveway. I let him open my door again, and I also let myself lean on him as we moseyed up to the house. The front porch featured two Easter lilies on either side of the steps, and a large pastel egg with the words "Happy Easter" hung on the front door.

Henry squeezed my shoulder and pushed the door open. "Juney girl, look who's here," he called as we stepped into the foyer.

I remained in the entryway while Henry continued into the rest of the house. Someone would be upon me before I knew it, so I took a few seconds to breathe and get my bearings.

Luckily, June's house had a long foyer, with the fancy dining room to the left and the sitting room to the right. These were rarely used, which meant the group didn't gang up on me all at once. They'd be clustered in the back in the kitchen or family room.

"You made it!" June wiped her hands on a bunny-covered dishtowel as she walked toward me. She flung it on her shoulder and embraced me. "Bout time you got here."

I hugged her back in silence, her lily perfume tickling my nostrils. Unexpected tears sprang to my eyes as I let go and trailed her to where everyone else waited.

"Hey, Myra," Mabel said when we got to the kitchen. "Good to see you. June, did you want the carrots in circles or lines?"

"Circles," June said. "Myra, help with the pie. You have the right touch with the crusts. Yours are so light and fluffy."

I nodded absently and grinned at the scene before me. The women were all in the kitchen, keeping an eye on pots on the stove or cutting up veggies or sitting at the table calling out instructions. The men were all in the family room, huddled in front of the TV.

No matter how much the times changed, some things stayed the same. Was that good or bad? Guess it didn't really matter. It was nice to be among friends.

"Betty, shove on down." June nudged the woman with her hip. "Myra will handle the crust. You can do the apples."

"Granny Smith?" I asked.

"You know it." June handed me the wooden rolling pin. "Best pie apples in the world."

"Those new honey crisps are good, too," Betty's daughter Jean said.

"I like pink ladies," Susan chimed in.

"Wrong time of year," Mabel said. "Best apples are in the fall. Everyone knows that."

"Apple pie's good any time of year." June peered in the oven. "It's Myra's favorite, so we're having it."

That shut everyone up. I was pleased June remembered my favorite dessert, although I could've done without the pitying side glances. It made me want to apologize to Jean because I'm sure we did the same to her when she moved back in with her mama after the divorce.

The silence only lasted a moment before everyone started gabbing again. I concentrated on the pastry and let the chatter wash over me. I threw out a comment now and again so I wouldn't get chastised later, and I had to admit being here was better than being at home pining for Lee.

"You doin' okay?" June whispered as she took the last crust. "I'm glad you came."

"I had a choice?" I teased. "And yeah, I'm doing okay."

She didn't notice the lie in my words, but I did. When you repeat the question in the answer, more times than not you're telling a fib. Forget where I picked up that nugget—some book, probably. Books were my lifeline.

"When are we gonna eat?" Henry called from the family room. "You been cooking all durn day, lady."

"You have snacks," June responded.

"Snacks?" Roy scoffed. "Veggies and dip ain't food."

"Well, it's all you're getting right now," Betty told them.

"Another hour, guys," Susan said. "Then you'll be sitting down to Thanksgiving in April only with ham instead of turkey."

I couldn't help but laugh. I hadn't ever thought of it quite that way, but the girl had a point. Not that this crew needed an excuse to eat, and you can't have a gathering without food. Why, that would be as sacrilegious as skipping sunrise service on Easter Sunday. Gave myself a mental pat on the back for that gem.

My observations earlier about times not seeming to change came back, too. Some things were different in today's world. Everyone dug out their phones to show off pictures of grandkids or to check a recipe online, and Jean kept tapping away at her screen for some reason or other. At least here people still looked at each other instead of their phones while chatting. We were old enough to understand the importance of connection.

"Aunt Myra, you're staring into space," Jean said. "You okay?"

I nodded.

"Don't mind her." June handed me the Corningware pie plate. "Gathering wool is her stock in trade."

9

I stuck my tongue out at her.

Jean giggled. "Y'all are crazy."

"As foxes," Betty said and we all giggled.

Between rolling out the dough and talking with loved ones, I found myself relaxing almost despite myself. Company was preferable to a big lonely house, at least for the moment.

After my pie duties were over, I washed up and went over to visit with the menfolk. Sal and Roy barely glanced up from the TV, but Henry gave me a nod. Both of us glanced toward the corner of the flowered sofa right next to Henry's recliner. Lee's spot. You know you've been best couple friends when your hubby has a spot on the couch.

I moved my gaze to the television and my jaw dropped. The men were watching soccer. Soccer!

"No ESPN?" I asked.

"This is ESPN," Sal said.

"Baseball game ended." This from Henry.

"But soccer? You guys always said—"

"Atlanta has soccer now," Roy said. "We gotta learn."

"I see," I said, although I didn't. Maybe to men, as long as there was a ball of some kind involved, and one team tried to prevent the other from scoring, all was right with the world. I left them to it and returned to the land of women.

What we were missing was the children. Jean was the closest we had, and she was in her thirties. Her kids must be with their dad, which made sense. Poor things would've been bored out of their gourds having to spend time with all these old people.

Not that I felt old, mind you, even if I did know how long I'd been around.

"Pies smell good," Mabel said.

"That mean the ham's out of the oven so we can eat?" her husband shouted from his place on the sofa.

"Man can hear that but can't hear when I ask for help with the groceries," Mabel muttered.

Selective hearing did seem to be a problem with men that grew worse as they got older. Even my Lee, God rest his soul, could drive me up the wall when it came to what he really heard and what he pretended to hear.

"Well, are we eating or not?" Roy asked.

"Hell's bells," June cursed. "Come on then. Everything's ready even if it's not on the table."

Betty handed out plates while Susan got the silverware. June tried her best to direct traffic, to establish some semblance of order, and ended up standing by the sink with her hands on her hips and a scowl on her face.

"Easy, muffin." Henry put his arms around her waist. "Folks are happy. We've got good food and good company."

She sighed.

"Let it be," he said. "Come join the party so folks won't think you're a bad hostess."

June smacked him with the bunny-themed tea towel, but his joking had put a smile on her thin face as we all went into the dining room. I missed that—the ability to change someone's mood for the better with only a few words.

That little scene must have triggered something else because as soon as I sat down, grief washed over me. That's the thing I forget about mourning. Grief comes in waves. I'll be doing fine, and then a wave smacks into me. Sometimes I know the cause, and other times it comes out of nowhere and knocks me flat.

"Henry, say grace," June commanded from the head of the table.

I bowed my head with the rest of them, and then put a brave face on as everyone dug into the meal. The food smelled wonderful. I really wanted to dig in, too, but my appetite refused to cooperate.

"Not hungry?" Betty nudged me. "Or just done?"

I looked at her, wanting to respond yet unable to speak.

"I'm on it," she whispered.

Betty stood and headed toward the kitchen like she forgot something. On her way back, she said something to June, who nodded.

I stared at my plate, the pink of the ham a contrast to the yellow corn and green spinach. The smell got to me, too, and I pushed my chair away and shut my eyes.

Henry was at my side in seconds. He whisked me outside and then let me stand on the front porch breathing in the fresh air.

"Let's get you home." He strode toward the truck, stopping when he realized I had not moved.

"June Bug'll handle it." Henry shepherded me forward. "Everyone knows you tried. You lasted longer this time."

I supposed that could be interpreted as a positive sign, but I was tired of trying. All I wanted was to be home, curled up in a ball on the bed and surviving the latest wave. They were getting smaller and shorter and farther apart. It had been a few days since the last one.

"Ready?" Henry asked.

I nodded.

"Radio or silence?" He asked when we were in the truck's cab.

"Silence."

The ride was a short one, and we'd be at my place in a song or two at most, so not listening to anything was preferable. Henry patted my back once we arrived, then waited until I opened the front door before driving away.

Now I was alone with my sorrow, which is where I'd longed to be. Only faced with the greater quiet of an empty house, I wished to be back among my friends. Why couldn't I make up my mind?

"Lee, why aren't you here?" I whispered.

Not that I expected to hear my dead husband speak out loud, although I did sometimes hear his answer with my heart.

With a heavy sigh and heavy tread up the stairs, I decided to grab a book and try to forget about life and death for a while.

Book club was scheduled for the week after next. No time like the present to get started on the selection,

A few chapters in, I wasn't really connecting with the work. However, I vowed to finish this book and all the others I had piled up around the house. Even being home by myself, I wasn't alone if I had good story to lose myself in.

Chapter 2

I woke to incessant pounding on my front door. What in the world? The sun hadn't even finished rising. Cursing the person on the other side of the door, I rushed down the stairs and yanked it open.

"Took you long enough," June huffed.

My best friend stood on my front porch in a floral top and white capris, a ridiculous grin on her face and a briefcase-sized leather bag draped off her right shoulder.

Irritation seeped out of me as confusion took its place. She seemed so certain, all ready to go…somewhere. Had I forgotten an outing? I could not recall discussing one when we talked a few nights earlier.

"We're going to Gibbs Gardens!" she announced.

"Ummm…were we supposed to?" I shook my head and rubbed my eyes, hoping that might clear my head.

June set her bag down and placed her hands on her hips. Oh, lordy. I was in for it now.

"You need an outing." She jabbed her right index finger at me. "Get away from here for a day. So we're going to see the last of the daffodils at Gibbs Gardens."

Drat. That *did* sound like fun.

"Get dressed. I'll smoke."

"I thought you quit. Again." I leaned against the doorframe. "You're allowed to come inside, you know."

"You'll hurry if I wait out here." She lowered herself onto the top step. "And I have a ciggy every now and then."

"When Henry won't find out."

She pursed her lips and studied the sky. "Get ready."

"Yes, ma'am."

I hadn't really planned for or wanted to go anywhere today, but it was easier to comply with June than try to argue. And it might be good to spend the day away from Atlanta. Daffodils were my favorite flower, and the ones at Gibbs Gardens were truly amazing. Plus the views were breathtaking and it was always a lovely place to visit.

By the time I put on lipstick, I found myself impressed by June's ingenious plan. She'd chosen the one place I wouldn't refuse, and she sprang it on me so I wouldn't have time to find an excuse to back out.

When I stepped back outside and hugged June, I delivered the shock this time. I could tell she wanted to ask about my change in mood, but for once she remained quiet.

"Let's go," I said. "Time's a-wastin'."

"Glory be, Myra, that's an old one." June led the way to her Accord. "Was that the Carter family or with Johnny?"

"Don't quite recall." I shrugged. I didn't want to admit that I'd forgotten June Carter Cash sang that song. "Probably both."

"I just love those old songs," June said when we were headed north. "Gets me thinking of being young again."

"Bring back the good old days." I smiled. "That's either Carole King or the other one."

"Which other one?"

"One of those really good female singer songwriters." I sighed, irritated I couldn't bring the name to mind. "Who did the one they say is about Sinatra?"

June tapped her fingers on the steering wheel.

"Carly Simon!" I shouted. "She's the other one."

"Well, what about Loretta Lynn?" June asked.

"She's good, too. Patsy Cline."

"Dolly Parton," June offered.

We kept ourselves occupied for the next hour or so naming female musicians and some of their songs. Got me thinking about how people tended to say how wonderful it was these days that there are so many women in the music industry when in reality they've been there all along. All you had to do was look.

"Hey, where's everyone else?" I asked, a little guilty I hadn't thought of our friends earlier. "Don't they deserve to get out of town, too?"

"Thought you'd have more fun with it just being us," June said. "Less pressure. That okay?"

"That's fine." And it was.

Easter dinner this past weekend had been a bit overwhelming. Since that night, I'd holed up in the house reading, only venturing out for necessities. Barring today, I couldn't remember the last time I'd left the safety zone of my neighborhood. Lee and I had been rather insular through the final stages of his cancer, and I stayed with that pattern after he passed. No wonder June wanted to take me to Blue Ridge.

"Look at that skyline," June said. "Everything seems more beautiful in the mountains, doesn't it?"

"Yes, it does."

The parking attendant gestured for us to turn left, and the next attendant pointed to the spot they wanted us to take. Stepping out of the car, I took a deep breath and inhaled the clean mountain air. My spirits lifted along with the altitude, and I felt a smile take over my face.

"This is my treat," June said as we followed the path to the main building. "Don't even think about trying to pay."

"I'll get lunch then."

"No." She grasped my arm as I went to open the door. "The entire day is on me."

Her gray eyes were serious, and her stern lips echoed the sentiment. I didn't like to accept gifts, but I'd have to let her have her way. I'd learned over the years that sometimes people needed to take care of you, and sometimes you needed to let them do it. This was one of those times for both of us.

"Yes, ma'am." I pulled open the heavy glass door and motioned for June to enter first.

While she paid for our passes, I browsed the gift shop. Lots of flower-related item and also some jewelry, clothing, accessories like scarves and purses, and books about the area or local history. A nice little collection.

"Ready?" June handed me my paper ticket.

I nodded.

We pushed our way through the next set of heavy glass doors and found ourselves outside once again.

"Have you been here before?" The guide asked. She was close to us in age and her welcoming smile was genuine. "It's a lovely place for a stroll."

"Haven't been here in a couple years," June told her. "Today we're here for the daffodils."

"Certainly." The woman opened the map and detailed the best places to see them. "We also have several other wonderful exhibits. You could spend the whole day here without getting bored."

I returned her smile and took the pamphlet she held out. Unfolding it to show the map, I thought she might well be right. I'd forgotten how large the place was, and how many different flowers and trees there were to see. Gibbs Gardens even had live music on certain nights. Lee would've loved an outdoor concert.

"Let's move." June hustled off.

June, on the other hand, liked to accomplish things. She was not one for strolling among the flowers, even if today's trip had been her brainchild.

"Thank you," I told the woman before heading after my friend.

One of these days, I was going to be the one in the lead. For now, I was content to follow. At my own pace. I let June bustle along while I took the time to enjoy the sun, the light breeze, and to read through the literature in the pamphlet. I'd either catch up to June eventually or she'd slow down long enough for us to walk side by side for a little while.

"See, isn't this better than being holed up at home?" She asked when we were next to each other.

I uttered a noncommittal grunt, not wanting to give her the satisfaction of being right. The sun warmed my face, the scent of spring grass and flowers filled my head, and I could almost believe I'd soon be happy again.

Then we turned a corner and came face-to-face with rows of daffodils of different sizes and colors. Tiny white blooms. Lemon yellow. Buttercup. Goldenrod. Almost too many to take in at once.

"Ohhh," was all I could manage.

I bent down to a canary yellow blossom and cupped my hands around it, stroking the soft petals.

"My mom thought daffodils in a wedding bouquet would look dumb," I said, caught up in the memory. "I fought hard and won. Lee wore one with his tux. It's still pressed in our wedding album."

The tears hit me hard, catching me off-guard. June placed her hand on my back, which was nice even if it could not stop the flood. Why couldn't he be here to see all this beauty? Why should I have to experience it without him? He ought be the one taking me to the gardens, not June. It wasn't fair.

"I miss you, Lee," I whispered to the flower.

I wanted to believe he could hear me. I wanted to believe we'd be together again someday. I wanted to believe…

"Oh, god." I put my hands over my face and continued weeping.

When I'd finished, June offered me her hand and helped pull me to my feet, then she handed me a tissue. All without saying a word. Overcome with emotion yet again, I gave her a giant hug.

"Did I do right or wrong bringing you here?" she asked when I released her.

"Good." I laughed and wiped away a final tear. "That was the good kind of crying."

"Okay." She drew out the word like she didn't quite trust my response. "Should we keep going?"

"Not just yet." I consulted the map. "We're right by the café. Let's have a quick bite, catch our breath, and go from there. How's that sound?"

"I packed snacks in my bag," she said. "They'll keep, though."

"We can have those, too," I said. "There's seating at the café, but no rule that says the food has to come from there."

"Let's see what they have," she said.

"They used to have a divine apple crisp cookie," I told her.

"I'm sold."

We linked arms and followed the path back to the little hut that passed as a cafe. Wrought iron tables and chairs surrounded the building, allowing visitors to continue to enjoy the scenery.

After selecting my chicken salad sandwich and brownie—only cranberry walnut or chocolate chip cookies were left—I went to grab a table while June paid for the grub. When she rejoined me, the look on her face triggered warning bells.

"What you need is a hobby." She placed the tray on the table.

Ahhh, my instincts proved correct.

"Hear me out." June unwrapped her sandwich. "You need something that's going to take your mind off things. Get your spirits back up."

"But—"

"He's gone, love," she said softly. "Lee wouldn't want your life to stop because of him."

I tried to form an argument, but the words running around my head refused to be corralled into coherent thought. I concentrated on the feel of my toes inside my shoes, trying to center myself in the present moment.

"You needed time to mourn, and you've done that."

"We were together fifty years," I managed to say. "High school sweethearts. You don't get over fifty years in a day. Or a month. It takes time."

"You've had time."

"Not enough!"

I pushed my chair back with a squeal, and some of the other patrons glanced our way. I blushed. I'd already broken down once today, no need to make a scene as well.

"Sit down, Myra," June hissed. She took a deep breath. "I'm sorry."

"Grief doesn't have a time limit." I sat back down and crossed my arms over my chest. "I'll never get over Lee, but I'm learning to deal with the loss."

"I know, I know." She held up her hands in surrender. "I didn't mean it like it sounded. What I meant was that you need to start living again. I hate seeing you suffer and I want to help make things better."

"And a hobby will make everything better?" I opened my bag of potato chips. "That's your solution?"

June nodded. "If you focus on something other than Lee, you might start feeling better. Ever tried fishing?"

"Fishing? Can't say that I have." I took a sip of water. "The last time I spent more than an hour in the woods, I got poison ivy."

"Forgot about that." June chuckled.

While she thought about her next suggestion, I concentrated on eating and drinking and enjoying the sunshine.

"I know." She snapped her fingers. "You should write a book."

"A what? Me?" Was she joking?

"Why not you?" June grinned. "Everyone seems to be doing it these days."

"Everyone?" I repeated.

"Well, yeah." June popped a chip in her mouth.

"Name one person you know who's written a book."

"That hussy whose family owns that big hotel chain." She gave me a haughty stare, daring a comeback.

I rolled my eyes. "And when's the last time that floozy broke bread in your home?"

"Okay, then, smartypants, that nice girl who was on that show."

"What show?"

"The one about the mother and daughter, took place in some small town up north somewhere."

"She been to your place, too? Are you having dinner parties with celebrities and not inviting us regular folk?"

"You're impossible." June took a bite of her sandwich.

I looked at her, waiting for the next volley. June was building up steam, not unlike a teapot. And if you paid attention to the signs, you'd also know when each one was ready to blow.

"If not a book, what about painting?"

"Are you forgetting how much I hated that painting class you talked us into last summer?" I shuddered. "Or the time I tried to help the girls build a solar system?"

"That was science, not art," June pointed out. "There has to be something."

"I'll ponder while we tour the grounds," I promised.

Chapter 3

Somehow, I managed to stave off June for a few days. Maybe because I told her I liked the idea of finding a hobby. Maybe because I really did need time to think about it. She was right on one count—I needed something to focus on, something that got me out of the house.

Would clearing the house of Lee's things count as a hobby? And why did we tend to say it that way? His "things," like they're leftover food or stuff you have lying all over the house that you meant to get rid of yet somehow never quite found the time for.

In all honesty, we all have those items. Lee's basement office and my sewing room upstairs are full of junk we accumulated over the decades.

When was the last time I sewed anything? 1982? Definitely not this century. I tried needlepoint one of those times when it was in fashion, but all I ever made was a mess. Same with knitting and crochet. Or were they the same craft? Let's just say that anything with needles and fabric was not my forte.

Mabel and Betty made their own clothes. Betty designed most of Jean's dresses while she was growing up, and now she creates all kinds of clothes for her grandkids and everyone else's to boot.

I enjoyed ceramics, although the last time we'd done that must have been thirty years ago. Possibly more. We still had the glazed ceramic nativity scene in the attic along with the decorated Christmas tree and scary Halloween pumpkin.

Now if reading was ever considered a craft, I could earn a ribbon at the county fair. While Lee was alive, I finished off a book or two a week, often curled up on the loveseat with him while he watched his sports. I never ran out of books, and the man always managed to find some sport to watch. Even bowling or the one with the big scoopy things. Who would ever believe there was major league lacrosse?

Lee said even the boring or unusual sports were worth his time because he learned something new. The tedious and the weird books were like that for me, too. Plus, we got to spend time together most nights. We also had nights where I read in bed before dropping off and he puttered around his office. That was his sanctuary, the office, and I rarely bothered him when he was in there.

Now, though, I wondered if he kept anything in that room other than items signed by his favorite players or the boxes for the stuff that he retired or simply had no space to display. I could wait to find the answer to that question.

On the other hand, he no longer had any need for whatever was in there. Perhaps Henry or Roy might like something, or even a stranger might have use for the items.

"None of this is solving the problem," I muttered aloud, which made me chuckle.

Funny how the mind wanders when you're alone.

"Okay, focus."

If time and money were no object, what would I do? Lee asked me that very question a few months before he went into hospice. I couldn't answer him then, and I couldn't answer him now.

He knew his answer: travel to Vienna, Austria. We'd been to lots of other European cities and countries, but not that particular city or country. The why was a little crazy yet had significant memory and meaning for us.

Vienna had been on the itinerary for our very first European adventure. Munich, Prague, Vienna, Budapest. Then about six weeks before we were set to leave, Lee and I were washing dishes after dinner…or trying to, but when a good song came on the radio, he'd take me in his arms and whirl me around the kitchen.

I shut my eyes and reveled in that feeling of being loved, of being held close by the love of my life. The heat between bodies. The softness of skin under my hands.

When one song ended and the next began, Lee refused to let go. He stood there, feet on the linoleum floor and his chin resting on the top of my head. I breathed him in as slow piano introduced the next song, and I did my best to concentrate on the words to keep from exploding with sheer contentment.

"Let's not go to Austria," I said as the song faded.

Lee nodded. "We'll take it as a sign," he said and sang the next part, "Vienna waits for you."

"For us," I said as he dipped me.

Who knew a simple Billy Joel song could have such an impact? We took those *Vienna* lyrics to heart, declaring we would let the city wait for us. We would save it for later, for years, as our very last overseas journey.

That we never got to take.

"Oh, my." I wiped at my eyes. "Where does the time go?"

And how do I get myself out of these clouds when they come up? Lee was the one who brought me back, and I wasn't used to doing it on my own. One more thing I'd have to learn.

I needed to take care of someone, or something. Plants despised me, but animals adored me and vice versa. But how could I take care of a dog or cat when I barely seemed able to take care of myself these days? No wonder my best friend claimed I needed a hobby.

Good idea. No idea how to execute on it. Nothing I thought of felt right, and the mere act of coming up with ideas sent me down Memory Lane.

Betty had conned me into hosting book club tomorrow night—I'd ask the group for suggestions. Together, we could come up with at least a few viable options, and June would be pleased because we could talk about something other than her not having read the book.

"Everything looks great." Mabel gave me a quick hug, then lowered her voice. "I'm so happy you're hosting again."

"Wine, water, or tea?" I asked as I stepped back.

"Hot tea, please. With lemon."

"Coming right up," I said.

I disappeared into the kitchen, knowing Mabel was familiar enough with the house to make herself comfortable. Before the water finished boiling, Susan and Betty arrived. Betty went for the wine while Susan also opted for tea. Everyone dug into the snacks.

Even though this was the first book club I'd hosted this year, I'd been the hostess often enough for folks to have unofficially assigned seats. Mabel and Betty shared the loveseat, Susan perched on the fluffy chair, leaving the couch for June and Dolores and the other poofy chair for me.

As usual, we were all seated and enjoying the cheese, crackers, and crudité when June blew in.

"Sorry, ladies." She hung her pocketbook on the newel post. "Had to train the new girl. You wouldn't think answering the phones was a challenge, but apparently it is for some people."

"New girl?" Dolores's eyes widened. "Are you retiring?"

"Fat chance." June started making herself a plate. "They'd be lost without me. No, I'm cutting back my hours. Henry wants to travel before he's too old to get around."

I stood and brushed invisible lint off my dark gray pants. "June, would you prefer wine, water, or tea?"

"I'll grab something." She waved me away. "Y'all keep talking about the book."

"Did you at least read the summary online?" Dolores asked.

"Or the book flap?" Susan threw in.

June ignored them as she slipped into the kitchen. The rest of us erupted in laughter. June not reading the selection had become one of our traditions, which also gave us the excuse to turn to other topics after awhile. We wouldn't want her to feel left out now, would we? That would be downright rude, bless her heart.

All kidding aside, we did spend time talking about the book. I'd done my best to slog through it, but never could get into it. Not sure what the millions of people who made it a bestseller saw in it.

"I loved it." Mabel leaned forward, elbows on her knees. "The author made me feel like I was right there in the story."

"You say that every time." Dolores grumbled.

"But it's true!"

"I'm with Mabel," Susan said. "The three women were all different, yet I felt a part of each story."

"What was the book again?" June asked.

"*Where Are the Girls?*" Mabel leaned back in her seat. "I bet they make it into a movie."

"I think they are," I said.

That comment took the discussion off on a whole new track as everyone did their best to cast the various roles. Since I couldn't even recall the last movie I'd seen—in a theatre, anyway—I left the ladies to their debate.

Even though June spoke up more in this debate, I noticed she kept giving me the eye. She had food, drink, and friends, so I was hard-pressed to decipher what she wanted.

I should've known she'd get there eventually.

"Ladies," she said during a break in the chatter. "I'd like to propose a new topic."

Pregnant pause.

"Yes?" Betty broke the silence.

"We need to find Myra a hobby."

A groan escaped. Was it even worth trying to protest? There was nothing this group enjoyed more than problem solving, especially for one of their own. And I had been planning to bring up the topic myself, so why fight it?

"I don't need a hobby." I had to at least pretend to resist.

"Oh, honey, you most certainly do." Susan's hazel eyes wrinkled with concern.

The other women nodded, and I snuck my hands under my legs to keep from wiping the smirk from June's face. Yes, she did it out of love and worry and all that happy crappy, but I would've preferred being allowed to broach the topic on my time and not hers.

Once the proposal was on the table, the ladies pounced and tossed out suggestions, which I quickly dashed.

"Gardening," Mabel said.

"I'm allergic to almost everything green in the state."

"Jewelry making." From Susan.

"All thumbs."

"Scrapbooking?" Dolores suggested. "My daughters have the ones I made from their baby pictures. Might be a good way to put some memories together of you and Lee."

"No arts and crafts." I sighed. "I've proven glue guns are practically lethal in my hands."

"She has a point." June chuckled. "Remember when she hot-glued her fingers together?"

"Oh, dear," Mabel said. "That was a sight."

"What about when we did crocheting and she got tangled up in what was supposed to be a baby blanket?" Dolores laughed so hard she snorted.

"Now, now," Susan said. "Myra did bring the yarn so she gets credit for participation."

"Thanks, everyone." I stood and collected plates. "I'll figure something out on my own."

June grinned and shook her head. "Not a chance. If it were up to you, you'd never decide."

"Hold on," Mabel said. "Myra knows what she wants."

"Ha." June scoffed.

"Well, I think she does." Mabel huffed and crossed her arms.

I admired and appreciated Mabel's loyalty, and everyone's willingness to provide assistance. Still, it got us no closer to a conclusion or even a different topic.

"You could try yoga," Betty said. "Jean swears by it."

"Have you done it?" I asked.

"Err...no." Betty blushed. "Okay, yes. I didn't enjoy all those weird moves. Walking is good enough exercise for me."

We all murmured agreement. I seized on the temporary silence and went to the kitchen to retrieve dessert. June followed, naturally, and brought the plates and silverware while I carried in the lemon cream pound cake. I did enjoy baking, and watching the pleasure people took in enjoying the end product. Did that count?

"You could teach a course at the community center," Susan suggested.

"How about helping with the cooking classes?" June shoveled in a big bite of dessert. "You're good with people."

"They always need folks to do mock interviews with job seekers." Betty placed her empty plate on the end table. "You'd be good at that."

"Just volunteering in general," Mabel said. "At the library or the animal shelter or a school. Lots of options."

Wow. Once the ladies got going, they came up with some really excellent ideas. I should've brought the cake out earlier.

"I've got it." June shot to her feet. "Like I said at the garden place, you should write a book!"

The others all nodded, but I had to laugh. What did I know about writing a book? Even if I had something to say, who in the world would read it?

"No one reads actual books anymore," I finished aloud.

"Don't need to," June countered. "Everyone has one of those fancy devices nowadays."

"You can also read on your computer," Susan said. "Or phone."

"Jean loves her Kindle," Betty said. "Takes it with her everywhere."

"I think it's a great idea," Dolores spoke up. "Think of all you've lived through, all you've seen and done. You could write about overcoming the loss of your spouse. Memoirs are in right now."

Okay, things were getting out of hand. I opened my mouth, but Dolores kept going.

"You can change names and places and make it a novel. I think writing a book is perfect for you."

June gave me a smug look.

"You have the best insights at book club," Mabel said.

"I'll bet they have writing classes at the community center," Betty said. "Or the college. Online, too."

"Thanks for the suggestion." I stood and cleared my throat. "For all the ideas. I'll...think on it."

For some reason, I felt tears stinging my eyes and dashed off to the kitchen again. The support was nice, but trying to wrap my head around all the ideas simply overwhelmed me. I craved peace and quiet to absorb what everyone had said. How could I ask them to leave when they'd been so kind?

Being friends for decades has its benefits. The women knew how I felt and gathered their belongings while June and Mabel brought the cake and plates to me.

"Thanks for hosting, Myra," Mabel said. "You're the best book club hostess."

She put the dishes in the sink and gave me a big hug. June winked and set the cake on the counter. I stood in the doorway and watched my friends get ready to head home. I waved them all goodbye, then closed my eyes and enjoyed the silence.

While I cleaned up, I reflected on all the ideas my friends had put forth. I could see myself volunteering somewhere. I might even be able to imagine taking a cooking class. I just could not fathom being an author.

What would I even write *about*?

Chapter 4

Three o'clock. AM. 3:14 to be exact. How I dreaded those nights when I couldn't sleep. I'd be fine for days, even a few weeks. Then, for no reason I could discern, the cycle would start again and I'd wake at 3:14 for several mornings in a row. No matter what I tried, there was no going back to sleep, at least not right away.

The restless nights began two months after Lee passed. I'd had plenty of sleepless nights leading up to his death, and some afterward, but at least then I'd wake at different times. Now, it was always the same time.

Other than knowing these three numbers were recognized as *pi* in mathematics, they held no significance for me. We'd lost Cassie during the late morning hours and I said my goodbyes to Lee just before midnight. If I was going to wake myself at the same time every day, wouldn't it make sense to be closer to the precise moment a loved one left me? Math and I weren't friends at the best of times, so that definitely was not it.

After several rounds, I knew what to do. I'd get a book from the rec room and curl up on the couch to read a few chapters. Or I'd boot up the computer and browse the Internet or respond to emails. I was smart enough not to send the messages. Some people check the time stamps of when they were sent, so I'd set them up to go out later in the day.

What I should've been doing was sifting through Lee's stuff. Well, I'd tried once, but just couldn't do it. The moment I entered his closet and touched one of his shirts, I'd swear I could smell him and that would cue the tears.

Dolores thought I should be brave and just bite the bullet, get rid of items I would not need or use. Mabel read somewhere that you should wait a year after a loved one died before making any major decisions.

In reality, none of us had a clue what to do. I was the first to lose her husband. Funny that. I would've said I was much more of a follower than a leader. Lee called me a peacemaker, said I followed along to keep everyone happy and together while still finding a way to be my own person. Maybe I was still doing that.

"Oh, Lee." I sighed. "I miss you so much."

None of this would get me back to sleep, so I decided to read for a bit.

Lee's office was right off the rec room so I decided to peek in there first. I stood in the dark for a moment, breathing in his scent and that of the room. When no tears came, I flipped on the light. How I longed to see him sitting at this executive desk, smoking a cigar and giving me a wink and big grin. Instead, the room remained silent and appeared to be waiting for its occupant to return.

Did any of the pictures or other items have any real value? Would Henry know? Or one of the other men? Roy loved sports even more than Lee did. Maybe he was the one to ask.

And what could be in the boxes stacked against the walls? If it wasn't important enough to display, was it any use to anyone? After all, the office had tons of space and Lee was always talking about building more shelves. I kept boxes in my sewing room, too, but they were all neatly labeled and most were supplies with little chance of ever being used again.

"What were you storing in here?" I asked my absent partner. Curiosity got the better of me and I carefully pulled the flaps apart on the top box.

Baseball cards?

That's what was in the box? Baseball cards? I don't know what I expected, but it was not little squares of paper with men's photos on the front and a bunch of statistics on the back. How many years had he been collecting them? There had to be hundreds in this box alone and there were three boxes along this wall and another four on the side wall.

"Okay. Hold on a moment," I said to calm myself. "Lee loved his sports. He used to say his collection would be worth something someday."

Could someday be today? I didn't really need the money the items might bring, but I also didn't want the stuff, either. Sports memorabilia might hold value for Lee or Roy or the others, though. And they'd know if the cards were actually worth anything.

Also, the guys might like to have one or more of the signed jerseys or baseballs or footballs as a memento. I'd ask them what they wanted when I inquired about the value. What they didn't want, I could potentially sell and give the proceeds to the local shelter.

I'd been a regular contributor at the no-kill shelter for years. I also donated to organizations that fed the hungry or helped people find work. Maybe, besides donating, I could volunteer. One of the women mentioned that as a possible hobby, so if I did help out at the shelter, maybe that would be enough to get my friends to quit nagging me.

Helping others certainly held more appeal than writing a book. Really, what would I write about and why would anyone want to read it?

What if I combined the two and wrote about other people who volunteered at animal shelters? It certainly takes a special type of person to invest so much time and love to find cats and dogs their forever home, or even to foster animals. Then again, it takes a special type of person to donate their time. Most people would rather give money and let someone else invest the blood, sweat, and tears.

Hmmm….nobody would read a book with profiles of essentially the same person each time, just a different name and slightly new story.

Now story, that's what I enjoyed about spending time with other people. I love hearing all the varying stories from people's lives, get to know them a bit and maybe share in the drama, give some advice and hope things turn out for the best. Finding out what makes someone tick and what they believe is an incredible buzz, as the kids said once upon a time.

Speaking of long ago, Associated Press or NPR or one of those news outlets published a book several years back with people contributing an essay on what they believed. That's the kind of thing I enjoy reading, and I wonder if I kept it around for that very reason. Time to dig through my own boxes upstairs.

Huh. Twenty minutes later, I actually found it. This I Believe, an entire book of folks writing an essay on what something meant to them, what they learned about the world.

Famous people were invited to contribute something to the compilation. While it was nice to hear what they had to say, I prefer hearing from *real* people who live in the *real* world. Folks who have to struggle for what they want, folks you wouldn't know to trip over them. What better way to peek into someone's life for a few minutes?

One of the best parts about traveling somewhere new is all the people you get to meet. Heck, I could take an entire vacation to London and do nothing but ride the Tube all day. Some of the best conversations I've had abroad and some of the most interesting people I've ever chatted up, as they say over there, were all while riding the English subway.

Sadly, I could not say the same for the United States. Lee and I rarely took trains or subways while visiting American cities. Instead, we met fun people in local bars or at festivals. Funny, the conventional wisdom has the Brits being buttoned up and Americans being friendly, yet Londoners on the Tube will divulge their life stories without a thought while many people in the States only start opening up after a drink or two.

I doubted there was a book in comparing people from other countries, although it would be a fun read. At least for me. It would be a hoot to read what people believed and what lessons they'd learned in life, too, and much more educational than what celebrities had to say.

If I wrote a book, that's the type of thing I'd want to write about. Somehow, even if I did manage to put something like that together, I couldn't see a regular Joe version of This I Believe ever getting published. Sad.

"Is there another way to get there?" I mused aloud.

I couldn't exactly go around asking strangers on the street what they believed, now, could I? They'd be calling the police or the men with the little white coats if I even tried.

A tiny voice in the back of my head reminded me that the celebrities had not been asked to speak about their beliefs. They'd been asked to write about them. Which might work…only no one writes much anymore.

Or did they not write because no one asked them to?

Could I make that request of someone? If so, how to do it? Would someone even respond to a crazy widow lady wanting them to write what they'd learned about life, what they told themselves to get through it all? And, perhaps the most important question of all, even if someone agreed, how did I turn the responses into a book?

This idea was perfect, but I was going to need a sounding board to help me turn it into reality.

Chapter 5

"Myra, that's fantastic," Mabel gushed after I told her my idea. "I would love to read something like that." I'd invited Mabel and Roy to dinner so I could run my thoughts past her while he rummaged through Lee's baseball cards and other items. Mabel tended to be less excitable and less judgmental than June, and Roy was definitely the biggest sports collector among the husbands, so they got tapped for both duties.

"So, are you going to do it?" Mabel prompted.

We'd sent Roy to the basement office while we stayed upstairs to make the salad and garlic bread to go with the chicken parmesan baking in the oven.

"Myra," she whined.

"I'm still working out the how," I admitted. "I'm not sure anyone would want their thoughts published for all the world to see."

"Are you kidding me?" She took a knife from the drawer and sliced the cucumber. "Have you watched TV at all in the last few years? People are falling all over themselves to be on camera however they can."

"Maybe." I broke up the head of lettuce and washed the leaves. "Television is different, and it's not like I'd be paying these people."

"Well, what if the book was only for you?" Mabel dropped the cucumber slices into the glass bowl and grabbed a tomato. "There's no law that says you'd have to share what people told you, or what they sent you. How are you getting these essays again?"

I took a knife from the block and sliced the bread. "Um…I don't know."

"Well, you can't exactly go up to complete strangers and ask them to tell you their innermost thoughts." Mabel frowned. "I like the idea, though. Only you would come up with something like that."

"Yeah, something that can't be accomplished." I sighed and went to the fridge to get the butter.

"Now, don't give up that easy. We'll figure it out."

Mabel continued putting the salad together while I prepared the bread. Our chatter stopped while we pondered and worked on our tasks. Why in the world did I decide to tell someone about my idea? Good thing I'd opted for Mabel, who wouldn't blather on about it to the others if we ended up not finding a way to make it work.

In this day and age of mobile communication and instant gratification, would anyone even take the time to write an actual essay?

"What if we put it online?" I retrieved the garlic powder from the pantry.

"Like a blog?" Mabel pressed her lips together. "I think people read those and comment. I don't think the audience is supposed to contribute."

"Oh."

She patted my shoulder. "I'm no internet whiz kid. I could be wrong."

"Doesn't matter. I haven't even bought a computer this decade and I hate reading a screen. Give me pen and paper any day."

"Buy yourself one of those fancy tablet things."

"Still a computer." I slid the bread pan in the oven. "Ten minutes."

"I'll set the table and let Roy know." Mabel wandered off, allowing me more time to consider my harebrained scheme.

I took courage from the thought that at least one person liked my idea, which meant others would, too. But going from hypothesis to finished product was more of a challenge than I imagined. Still, if there was a way, we would find it. After all, even Rome wasn't built in a day.

For the moment, I would concentrate on what Roy thought of all the sports memorabilia and enjoy a nice meal with friends. We could send the man back to the basement while the women plotted and got dessert ready.

Just like at Easter, I marveled at how some things never seemed to change.

"What are you smiling at?" Mabel asked upon her return to the kitchen.

"Life."

She gave me a side hug. "It's good to see you smile. By the way, my husband is grinning like a little boy, so he must've found something good down there."

"Smelly cards and dust balls." I sighed. "Signed pictures of grown men who get paid to play a kid's game. Seems silly."

"I agree," she confided. "No matter how many times I've tried to watch sports with Roy, I just can't see the point."

"Lee felt the same way about my reading," I said. "He couldn't wrap his mind around the fact that I could read the same book more than once. Yet I loved to cuddle next to him while he stared at the TV and whatever sport happened to be on."

Mabel nodded. "I do my knitting while Roy gets his fix."

The timer went off, and we sprang into action. Mabel carried the salad to the table while I pulled the chicken and bread out of the oven. On her way back, she got out the long plate and shorter trivet. While I laid out the meal, Mabel went off to get Roy.

"Damn, smells good," he exclaimed on his way up the steps.

"Chicken parmesan," I said. "Should we have wine with dinner?"

"Yes, ma'am," Roy said.

I grabbed a bottle of Cabernet Sauvignon and let him open and pour. I also filled a pitcher with ice water and placed that out as well. While I enjoy wine, after a glass or two I prefer to switch to water.

"To good food and good company." Roy raised his glass.

Mabel and I repeated the phrase and everyone clinked glasses. I couldn't help but smile, reveling in the glow of friendship.

"Okay, let's eat." Roy pulled out Mabel's chair, then mine. "I'm starving."

I don't know why, but meals taste better when shared with others. I needed to remember that fact when I struggled with the urge to be anti-social.

"Did you find anything good in the office?" I bit into a piece of warm garlic bread. "Or was it mostly junk?"

"Junk?" Roy sputtered. "Junk? Myra, there's a goldmine down there."

How in God's green earth could a bunch of cards, balls, and pictures of men in sports costumes be a treasure?

"Really?" Mabel asked.

"Oh, yeah." Roy nodded. "Some of those items are worth a pretty penny. I had no idea Lee had that much stuff, and we've been looking at each other's collections since we were kids. Tony will flip his wig when he sees it."

"Tony at Sports Town?" I asked. "I am not inviting him over."

"Thought you wanted to get rid of it all." Roy sipped his wine. "Ain't that why you had me check it out? See if there was anything worth selling?" He paused. "You're not planning on keeping it?"

I shook my head.

"So make some money off it!"

"How much do you think it's worth, hon?" Mabel put her fork down and looked at her husband. "Couple hundred?"

Roy guffawed so hard he started to choke. Mabel stood and whapped him on the back a few times, then rubbed his shoulder blades until he recovered.

"You crazy?" He drank more wine. "There's probably ten thousand dollars of memorabilia down there."

"Are you shitting me?" That slipped out before I could stop it.

We all have our pet phrases when something truly shocks us, and I'm a little embarrassed to admit that one happens to be mine. And there must be something powerful in the verb, because Lee's phrase was "shit the bed, Fred". He was the only one I ever knew who used that phrase, and he couldn't recall where or when he picked it up.

"No shit here," Roy said. "Might be more than that. Tony'll know."

"What would you do with that kind of money?" Mabel asked.

I shrugged. The thought of my husband's collection being worth that much was beyond my wildest expectations.

"You could take a trip," Mabel suggested.

Vienna popped into my head and I dismissed it just as quickly. I would never go there now, and I was perfectly okay with that. In truth, I couldn't picture myself going anywhere at all, not for a long time.

"Maybe I'll donate the money to charity." I pushed my food around my plate. "Maybe several charities."

Mabel smiled while Roy nearly spit out his wine.

"I'll think on it," I said, using my go-to response.

"Want me to talk to Tony?" Roy offered. "I can take everything to him if you don't want him to come over here. Might be easier."

"Do you want any of it?" I asked. "Would any of the other guys want anything? I'd rather y'all have it than a stranger, and it'll give you something to remember him by."

"There are some cards I'd like, but I'll pay you for them," Roy insisted.

"Not a chance." I batted the idea away like a pesky insect. "Lee would want you and Sal and the other guys to have them."

"Okay," he agreed. "I can divvy up part of it and take the rest to Tony."

That sounded like a solid plan. I gazed down at my plate as Roy patted my shoulder. Silence took over for a few seconds, and then we tried to return to our meals. Whether it was the money or the thought of Lee being gone, or just all of it together, none of us seemed able to finish our meal.

"I'll start putting them in some sort of order." Roy pushed away from the table.

"Thanks, hon." Mabel smiled at her hubby. "We'll call you when dessert's ready."

He nodded and returned downstairs. Mabel and I cleared the table, neither of us quite ready to break the mood. I rinsed the plates and loaded the dishwasher as she went back for the last round. When we had nothing left to do, I filled the kettle with water for tea.

"You could use the money to pay people who sent in essays," Mabel suggested. "Ten thousand would buy a lot of responses."

I considered the suggestion. "Nah, I'd rather have people send it in of their own free will. Just gotta figure out how to even ask them." I paused. "Too bad I can't just hand out flyers on street corners."

"Well, why not?" Mabel asked.

"If I didn't get arrested, some youngster would video the whole thing and put it on the internet somewhere."

"So put the flyer up in shop windows instead." She grinned. "Or put it on car windshields like they do with other ads."

I gawked at her. Mabel had been joking—at least, I think she'd been making a funny—but her words intrigued me. I could imagine it in my mind's eye. Me placing a letter on a car or slipping it into someone's bag while they weren't paying attention. No one would guess the culprit, and their curiosity might just be enough to engender a response.

"Mabel, you're a genius." I removed the whistling kettle from the stove. "Now I have to figure what to say. Can you get the cake plates?"

"You're really going to sneak people a letter?" She handed me the dinnerware. "You think that'll work?"

I took the cake from the fridge and placed it on the counter. "Good way to remain anonymous. I don't want anyone to know who's behind the letter or they might send the fuzz after me."

She laughed. "I doubt that'll happen, although you might end up on the news."

That might actually be worse than a padded cell. I shied away from the spotlight, even among friends. The attention I was getting as a result of being the first widow was more than I could handle. Having the media calling or camping out on my front lawn would be the worst kind of nightmare.

"I need to remain anonymous," I reiterated to Mabel.

"Then how are these people supposed to send you their essays?" she asked. "You can't use your home address."

She made a good point, which while irksome, was the reason she was here instead of one of the other women. They didn't give Mabel a lot of credit, but I found her smart, logical, and able to keep a secret.

"I suppose you could get a post office box," she continued. "And you'll need to set up a separate email account for the ones who don't want to mail it in."

"You think so? How do I do that?"

"No idea." She chuckled. "Betty's Jean will know, or one of her girls."

This little experiment of mine was really taking shape. More than that, I could see it becoming reality.

"This might work," I said aloud. "Thank you, Mabel."

"You had the thought," she said. "All I did was consult. So… does that mean I get to read the responses, too? I might die of curiosity otherwise."

I could barely wrap my head around someone sending in a letter and now she wanted me to share it? A little voice in my head whispered that the respondent would never know. That was the point of being anonymous. I wouldn't know them, and they wouldn't know me, so why couldn't I share the essays?

"Don't see why not." I searched the junk drawer for the cake knife. "I just wonder if anyone'll respond."

"They will," she assured me. "Oh, this is so exciting." She bounced on the balls of her feet, "Let's take Roy his cake and let him eat in the basement while we keep plotting."

I laughed out loud and cut the first slice.

"Seriously, Myra, he's in hog heaven down there." She slipped the wedge on a plate and scuttled off. "I'll be back in a flash."

Her "flash" could well turn into several minutes, so I cut my own piece of lemon pound cake and dug in. Myra and Roy's visit gave me two things to mull over. What to do with the money from the sports stuff, and what to say in my letter to potential responders. At the moment, I had no clear path for either one.

While extra money is nice, Lee's life insurance and retirement plan—not to mention my own retirement plan—had me pretty well taken care of. Donating the money seemed the best path. But should I give to human or animal endeavors? I generally leaned more to the animal side, since they couldn't take care of themselves. Lee preferred human, his argument being that some people couldn't care for themselves, either.

Maybe I'd split the money between the two and make both sides happy. That seemed like the best approach.

"Okay, he's good for the moment," Mabel said as she climbed the steps. "Now, where were we?"

"Trying to figure out if anyone will even respond to this crazy invitation." I handed her a piece of cake.

"You're not chickening out?"

"Heavens, no," I assured her. "I've got to have something to keep me busy so June will leave me alone. Maybe that could be my new hobby, getting her to stop pestering me."

"That'll be the day," Mabel scoffed. "Are you sharing the essays with her, too? With everyone? They'll want to read them, too, y'know, once you tell the girls what you've decided to do."

I helped myself to another slice of cake. "I can't think of that right now," I said. "I'm still figuring out how to make it all work."

"You'll be fine." She waved away my concern. "All you have to do is write the letter and start handing them out. Ooh, we could help you. Give us each a location to scout. More people, more responses."

I hid my face behind my hands and sighed. Why had I invited her over again? She asked too many questions, but she gave my experiment form and for that I could only thank her.

"Perhaps," I said.

"That's halfway to a yes," she sing-songed. "This is going to be so much fun! Should we start local or think big?"

"Let me write the invite first." I held up a cautionary hand. "I'll think about the best places to start sneaking them to people, and if need be I'll recruit others. On the other hand…I could ask the people who write in to give the letter to others."

Mabel's jaw dropped.

"Like that old shampoo or perfume commercial," I said. "She told two friends, and she told two friends, and so on and so on."

"I love it." Mabel did a little dance. "You're a genius."

"Well, let's not get carried away before we even get started."

Before Mabel could respond, we heard a crash in the basement and hurried down to make sure Roy survived. When we opened the door to Lee's office, Roy stood there with a box in his hands and a sea of baseball cards at his feet.

"Damn bottom fell out." He put the broken box aside and knelt by the cards. "Sorry about the mess. I'll get 'em in new boxes before carting them out of here."

"Sounds good."

"I called Tony. He's real excited to look at everything." Roy put the cards in piles. "Should I start loading my truck?"

I opened my mouth to say yes, and a wave of sadness hit me. When all of this stuff was gone, part of Lee would be gone, too.

"Let's give it a day or so and come back," Mabel said, sensing my mood. "It's been a long day and I'd like to get on home. Myra, is that okay?"

"That'll work," I managed to say.

"As you girls wish." Roy pushed himself to standing. "I'll talk to the guys, see what they want, too, before hauling the rest off."

"Thank you."

The three of us stood there, not sure of what to do next. Mabel took charge, hugging me and thanking me for dinner. Roy did the same, then handed me his empty cake plate and napkin. I nodded and followed them upstairs to the foyer.

"I'll call tomorrow to check in," Mabel paused before opening the front door. "Figure out a good time for Roy to stop by again."

"Okay."

After another round of hugs, I watched them head out. When they drove away, I turned off the porch light and trudged back upstairs. I finished cleaning the kitchen and returned to the living room to plan the first phase of my experiment.

I liked having everyone handing out the letters, or sneaking them to people, and I also knew I would ask the respondents to do the same if they opted to send in an essay. The one thing I hadn't figured out was what to say in the flyer. Only one way to tackle that assignment.

Hello there,

Congratulations!

You've been selected to take part in an anonymous social experiment. Participation is completely voluntary. The experiment should be fun. Please read the rules carefully before deciding to take part.

> *Rule #1: Write a 500 to 1,500 word essay that explains what your personal life philosophy is and why. It's fine to give examples of how you live this philosophy and how it manifests itself in your life.*

> *Rule #2: Essays can be typed, emailed or hand-written and may be slightly under or over the expected word count.*

> *Rule #3: For those who decide to take part in the experiment, please email the response to crazywidowlady@gmail.com or send via regular mail to PO Box 379, Smalltown, GA 30067.*

> *Rule #4: You have 30 days from the time you receive this letter to write your essay and respond.*

> *Rule #5: If you enjoyed participating, you get to choose the next victims. Choose up to 5 random people and provide them with a copy of these instructions.*

Thank you for taking the time to read this letter. To satisfy your curiosity, the person conducting the experiment is not a professional. I am a recent widow with a keen interest in what keeps people going. Any responses are welcome diversions and a learning experience for me. I appreciate your time and willingness to participate.

> *Crazy Widow Lady*

Chapter 6

After reading the letter aloud to my friends, I continued to stare at the paper rather than face their responses. I hadn't been able to wait for the next book club meeting and asked everyone over. Of course they all came. Only now, no one said anything for several long moments, and finally I raised my eyes.

June pursed her lips, Dolores gawked at me, Betty grinned, and Mabel stood and hugged me.

"Perfect," Mabel whispered.

"I love it," Susan said.

Someone patted me on the back, so I let go of Mabel to get a little breathing room. Dolores had been the back patter. June remained where she'd been sitting, her lips still pressed together liked she'd bitten into a lemon.

"No one will respond," she said.

"You hush." Mabel waggled a finger at June. "You're just jealous that she didn't tell you first."

"The hobby was your idea," I reminded her.

"Getting letters isn't a hobby." June scoffed.

"You don't know that," Dolores returned to her seat on the couch. "This kind of thing could keep Myra entertained for years."

June hmphed.

"Oh, stop being a sour puss." Betty rolled her eyes. "Or you won't be allowed to come to the reading parties."

"Reading parties?" I jerked my head in her direction.

"You *are* going to read us the responses, right?"

Hmmm, hadn't really considered that option. "I suppose I could..."

"We'll have reading parties," Betty said.

My little idea was taking on a life of its own and I hadn't even given out a single letter.

"I love it!" Mabel bounced on her cushion. "Let's have our first one next month."

"Or next week," Betty said.

"Let's wait until..."

I tried to break in, but they were off in party planning heaven. Only June stayed quiet, arms crossed and feet firmly planted on the ground like she wanted to take root. Whoever made the jealousy comment was correct, but June would come around once the essays did. She couldn't stand to be left out.

"Y'all!" I raised my voice this time, and everyone quieted. "Let's shoot for next month. If I give out the first round of invites this weekend, we might have a response by then."

"If anyone sends one in," June commented.

"Oh, they will," Mabel countered. "I can't wait."

"Do we get to give out invites, too?" Dolores asked.

"Of course," Mabel said, then turned to me. "Right, Myra? You can't be having all the fun."

What had I gotten myself into? And how had it blossomed so quickly before it even began? I shook my head in wonder and smiled.

"Yes, you can hand them out." Most of the women cheered, but I silenced them when I held up a warning hand. "But only after we've received three responses."

"Why three?" Mabel asked with hands on hips.

"Because that will mean people are interested."

"That makes sense." June relaxed her arms and sat forward. "Might as well make sure this is going to work before we get too invested."

Dolores rolled her eyes and I chuckled. Still, better to have all four friends caught up in the grand experiment. We preferred to be an all-for-one group whenever possible, and for the most part over the years we'd succeeded.

As we continued discussing plans, it hit me that I hadn't thought of Lee for several hours. That had to be a good thing, right? Isn't that why I was supposed to be getting a hobby in the first place? Not to move on, per se, but to at least have something else to focus on for a while, and it sounded like this activity would keep all of us occupied.

"When are you going to start?" Betty asked.

"I'm aiming for this weekend."

"Are we going to do it around here?" June asked, which proved she was hooked.

I shrugged. "I don't know. Probably not. The goal is to find out about strangers and I'm pretty familiar with everyone in Riverview."

"Good point," Mabel said. "Let's go downtown. We never go downtown."

"I'll be doing the first round alone. Remember?"

Dolores and Betty snuck a glance at each other, and Dolores gave a quick shake of her head. Mabel's bottom lip quivered, and her body slumped. June blinked twice, then yawned. I stood and explained myself.

49

"Everyone will get a chance to hand out invitations once we receive three essays," I assured them. "But I'd like to do the first batch on my own. In a place of my choosing."

"So only you will know location zero," Susan said.

"Well, yes."

"But we're a team," Mabel whined. "We're going to share the essays, why not this, too?"

I didn't mind having the ladies in on reading the responses, or even getting the chance to widen the pool of candidates later on. What was the fun of a grand experiment if you couldn't have your friends join you? Once it got underway, that is. I wanted to kick it off myself, to be alone when I sent this particular ship sailing into the night.

"A gaggle of old women will draw attention," I said. "If we each do our round alone, the people won't even notice us."

"That's true." Betty sighed. "It took thirty minutes last week before one of the clerks at Penney's even bothered to ask if I needed help."

Susan nodded. "You think that's bad? When we went out to dinner a while back, the hostess took two other couple's names before asking for ours."

"I've got one," Dolores began.

"Back on topic, ladies," I said. "So, we'll get to choose where we want to do our round, and the only rule is we can't tell anyone where we did it. Sound good?"

That did the trick. The women were giddy at the idea of having a secret all to themselves. I left them to their thoughts and went to bring out the blackberry crumble I'd made for dessert.

For once, I was allowed to go into the kitchen by myself to gather the pie and other items. This little idea of mine was already paying dividends.

I woke with a feeling of hope I hadn't experienced in months. I'd almost forgotten what it felt like, although I also felt a twinge of guilt for my first thought not being of Lee.

"I know you'd be happy for me, my love," I whispered and closed my eyes to imagine his wonderful face.

While taking a shower, my thoughts turned to the plans for the day. Specifically, where I wanted to part with the first set of letters. And how many did I want to disperse?

Three?

Five?

Yes, five. One in five had to provide better odds than one in three. Or maybe I should stick to a nice even number like four. One in four was twenty five percent, and that type of response rate sounded good.

After all, I only needed one person to respond for the first round to be a success, regardless of how many flyers found their way to a new home. Plus, this opening salvo could take place in more than one locale. I was making the rules here, which meant I could hand out as many slips of paper in as many locations as I wanted. Oh, was I ever going to have a blast!

Now, where to go?

I considered Ball Ground, or Gibbs Gardens, but people wandered the grounds and didn't really stop unless they got a bite to eat at the café. I needed a downtown area, like someone suggested, only not Atlanta proper. While it would offer diversity, it was also noisy and crowded and hard to find parking.

No, I needed somewhere smaller. Maybe Decatur or Roswell or Marietta. Yes, that was the one! Marietta Square had that lovely fountain, the adorable gazebo and, more importantly, lots of little shops.

People walked around the square, too, but they also sat in the restaurants or rested on the benches or strolled along slowly enough for me to sneak a folded sheet of paper into a large purse or stroller pocket without (hopefully) getting caught. Plus, they were always having events there on the weekends. A perfect time for the kick-off of the grand experiment.

Once upon a time, I might have used the telephone or scanned a newspaper to check on upcoming happenings in and around downtown Marietta. Today, I used the computer and the Google. Although not nearly as much fun, the answer came much more quickly.

And it turned out the community was holding an art walk this Friday. I could kick things off under the cover of darkness. What could be more perfect? And how in the world was I going to wait until then?

I did have Roy and the divvying up of the sports stuff to keep me occupied for a couple of days. I could also take the time and attempt to go through even more of Lee's belongings. The sorrow would still be with me, but the excitement of this new adventure might just be enough to see me through. Hope might not be a strategy, but it sure was a reason to keep going.

Friday afternoon, I headed to Marietta Square early to get a good parking spot and to scout the location. I made a pact with myself not to buy any of the art, but I still knew I'd be carting a painting home, or a pair of earrings at the least. Even if I had an alternate mission, you can't go to an art walk and not make a purchase. Artists need all the support they can get, especially monetary, and what better way to do that than purchasing their wares?

Arts and crafts and people-watching. Oh, and a mission. What a wonderful way to start the weekend!

One of my favorite things about living in the Atlanta area is the diversity of the people—ages, colors, genders, religions, accents—all melding together in a picture-perfect example of how to get along.

I wanted to hug everyone and give them an invitation so I could find out their thoughts on life.

"Easy, Myra," I cautioned. "You only have so many flyers."

Oh, my, talking to myself again. I really *was* turning into a crazy widow lady. The thought made me grin, and a young mother walking past returned the smile.

Unfortunately, she moved too fast for me to even put my hand in my purse, much less pull out the piece of paper. That inspired a new plan. I dug into my bag for the paper and folded it until it was small enough to fit in my hand. Next time, I would be ready.

I scanned the crowd, looking for my first victim. One of the painters working the stands along the street? Or one of the patrons perusing the goods?

A woman checking out a collection of landscape drawings caught my eye. Late thirties, maybe. Brown hair, friendly face, in jeans and a purple jacket. I rather liked the deep purple jacket. Here was a woman who enjoyed color, who wasn't afraid to stand out in a crowd. My kind of girl.

"How do you choose your subjects?" Purple Jacket asked the artist, a younger woman in faded yellow overalls.

The fact that my girl even thought to ask this question proved she was an excellent choice. I sidled closer, pretending to study the pictures while looking for my opening. I didn't see a purse, and there was no way I could slip something into the jacket pocket without being noticed.

"Can I help you?" The artist asked me.

"Just looking," I said. "Your drawings are amazing."

"Thank you. Let me know if you have any questions."

I nodded and returned to plotting. Purple Jacket said something to the stand owner and ambled away. Drat. Now I needed to follow or I'd lose her.

After half a block, the girl stopped, removed her jacket, and pulled a smart phone from her front jeans pocket. While doing so, the coat dropped to the ground. I darted in, picked up the jacket and slipped the paper into the side pocket.

Score!

"Oh, thank you," Purple Jacket said when I handed her the piece of clothing. "I should've left the darn thing in the car."

"Weather is getting warmer."

"Yes, it is."

She smiled and continued on her way, phone pressed to her ear and jacket grasped in her hand. With a little luck, she wouldn't even notice the paper until later when she'd forgotten all about our encounter.

Halfway back to the landscape artist's booth, reality smacked me upside the head. I'd done it. I'd really given someone the invitation. The experiment had begun!

"Oh my word." I placed a splayed hand on my chest.

"Ma'am, are you okay?" A nice young man asked, his hand lightly touching my shoulder.

An inappropriate giggle worked its way into my throat, but I managed to choke it back and nod. That satisfied the good Samaritan, who removed his hand and continued on his way. I hadn't quite fibbed, even if I wasn't exactly "okay". Instead, I felt ecstatic, in control of life and the future for the moment.

Speaking of which…should I keep a list of people I'd invited to participate in my little experiment or was it better to be surprised? The latter fit with the grand scheme, especially since I'd have no way of knowing who my invitees might have passed the message along to.

I planned to stop at a booth, but my mood was far too ebullient and I could not bring myself to stop. I had all night, or at least until 9 pm when the art walk shut down. And there was no rule that said I had to hand out all five flyers tonight.

When I came to the end of the block, I turned right. My burst of excitement had started to fade, and I was able once again to slow down and browse the various booths. At the end of this street, one of the local shelters had set up an adoption station.

"Hello," one of the workers said as I paused. She had spiky black hair, piercing green eyes, and a chubby face. "Are you enjoying the art walk?"

"Very much so," I said.

One of the other volunteers came up, and she excused herself. Although I knew better, I decided to pet some of the dogs and cats.

Lee and I loved animals. Ironically, he was the cat person and I was the dog person, so at times we'd had one or more of each. When Mitzi, our thirteen-year-old terrier mix, passed away five years ago, Lee decided that was it for us. I honored this decree even if secretly I wished for another animal.

One of the dogs whined for attention, and I bent down for a closer look. The poor thing strained to get to me through the cage, and I forced my hand through to stroke its fur. The large block head made me think there was pit bull in there, but the thin legs and black coat made me wonder if lab was also part of the mix.

"She's a sweetheart," the girl who greeted me earlier said.

"Pit bull and lab?" I asked.

"We think so," the girl said. "Someone found her wandering outside the Woodstock Target so we don't know for sure."

"Oh, poor baby." I scratched at her ear, and the dog leaned toward me. "How long have you had her?"

"Six months or so. I can let her out of the cage if you'd like."

"Please," I found myself saying.

What in the world was I doing? I was here to search for guinea pigs, not adopt a dog.

"Her name is Grace."

"Well, hello, Grace." The dog's entire body wriggled with excitement as she came out of the cage to greet me. "I know, I know."

After licking my face, she sat and cocked her head, tongue lolling out of her large mouth. What a sweet, gentle creature. I scratched her head and she closed her eyes and grunted with pleasure. I spent the next several minutes giving her attention and reminding myself of all the reasons I did not need a pet.

"She really likes you," the girl said.

"The feeling is mutual," I admitted. "How old is she?"

"The vet said maybe six or seven, but he also said she's in great health."

Six or seven, black, and pit bull in the mix. No wonder this girl was so pleased I seemed interested. I knew enough about animal adoptions to know those were three very big strikes against this pooch. She was lucky to have been taken to a no-kill shelter.

I stood and Grace butted my leg, requesting additional petting. I stepped back instead, and the poor pup sighed and stretched out beside me. Okay, I needed to get back to my mission before I took her home with me.

"Thank you," I said to the girl.

"You're very welcome." She handed me a business card. "We're here until 8:30 or you can stop by the shelter any time."

I thanked her again and with a final pat for Grace, I turned and walked back into the main crowd with some difficulty. Time to focus on the real reason I'd come out tonight. I took another paper from my handbag, folded it, and started scanning the crowd for my next target.

A man walked by, in his mid-twenties with dark hair in a buzz cut and dressed like he came from a business meeting. He stopped in front of a restaurant and checked his watch. That gave me the opportunity, only I doubted I could slide the paper in his suit pocket without him noticing. A girl called out to him and the two hugged before heading into the eatery.

Two women about my age passed by and then lingered at a jewelry booth. Even though that gave me an opening, I already knew what women like me thought about life. I heard those stories from my friends all the time. I needed more variety.

"No," I heard someone say with force. "You've already had two hot dogs. You cannot possibly be hungry."

A harried mother grasped her daughter's hand while another daughter stood close by with arms folded. I'd put the younger one at six and the older one at eight, although they could have been older or younger. I found the older I got, the more difficult it became to accurately predict someone's age. Everyone seemed young to me.

"Can I have cotton candy?" The six-year old asked with huge eyes.

"No." Her mother sighed. "They don't have cotton candy here."

"Yeah, dummy," the eight-year old added.

"Don't be mean to your sister," the mother said.

Why was the woman alone with the kids? Where was the father? Maybe he was home while the girls had a night out, or maybe he would be meeting them somewhere before they returned home together. These days, it didn't pay to jump to conclusions.

"I'm hungry," the little one whined.

"Mom just said you can't be."

"Girls, give Mommy a minute." The woman let go of her daughter's hand and, placing her hands at her hips, blew a breath skyward.

As she did so, I noticed the large shoulder bag she carried. This woman certainly seemed like she needed a diversion. The kids started pushing each other. Before it could escalate, the woman intervened. As she pushed the bag behind her to pull the girls apart, I stepped forward and slipped the letter into her purse.

"Okay, kiddos, let's get moving," the mother said. She took the little one's hand in hers, placed her other hand on the older one's shoulder, and steered them forward.

She hadn't even noticed me. Another potential respondent selected. I gave an internal whoop of excitement. The art walk had been the perfect choice. The noise and the activity and the distraction allowed for easy access. These people should be happy I wasn't a pickpocket. Rather the opposite, I thought with a secret smile.

On to the next victim!

Thirty minutes passed and although I found several likely targets, none of them allowed me the opportunity to slip them the invitation. Guess I wasn't as good of a reverse pickpocket as I thought.

I slumped onto one of the benches along the street. Well, no one said I had to give away all five invites tonight, even if that was what I really wanted to do. And no one said I had to physically slip the invite to someone either, I thought as I stared at the parking deck at the end of the street. I could put the flyers on car windshields.

My mood lightened, and I hurried into the garage. I walked up and down the first row, studying the cars. Lots of SUVs, but still a good mix of older and newer models. Lee preferred American cars, so I chose a black Ford Explorer with an infant seat in the back. I tended to like foreign sedans, and gave an older, slightly beat up gray Mitsubishi Mirage the next invite.

Okay, only one left, at least for the initial round. I almost wanted to save it, to continue enjoying the thrill of deciding who should get the paper. It was more fun seeing the person. It was also getting late, almost eight o'clock.

Knowing the time made me think of Grace, and the adoption place being open another thirty minutes. If I went back there, I could sneak the invite to the girl and visit the dog one more time.

Or you could bring the dog home, the voice in my head whispered. Now why did that voice sound like Lee?

"Are you trying to tell me something, hon?" I asked.

No response. Just like Lee. He'd had his say and didn't need to answer my question when I already knew what he'd say.

Grace gave a happy bark when she noticed me.

"You're back," the girl said. "Does that mean..."

I nodded. "Yes, I'd like to take her home. What do I need to do to make that happen tonight? I'm Myra, by the way."

"Heather." She extended her hand, and I shook it. "Here, you tell Grace the good news while I get the forms and a leash. I just *know* you'll be happy together!"

Marietta Square held magic tonight. I'd planned to take something home from the art walk, but had not expected it to be an animal. Grace was the perfect piece for my home. Much better than a painting.

While walking back to the car, the lab-pit bull mix happily plodding along beside me, I couldn't help but think what a wonderful night this turned out to be. All five invitations had been handed out and I had a new friend to love on.

For the first time in months, something stronger than hope returned to me. Time. I could look beyond the minute, the day and see ahead weeks and months. Getting to know Grace. Waiting to read all the different essays. Finding a hobby was indeed the right move. I couldn't wait to see what happened next.

Dawn

Dawn didn't mind being single. In fact, she relished it. Most of the time, she loved the freedom. Doing what she wanted to do, when she wanted to do it. Being able to watch what she liked, be in her own mood, good or bad, and not have to worry about how it might affect someone else.

She'd done well for herself over the years—owned her own home, paid off her car, had a great job as a dental hygienist for a successful practice with an equally great salary, and maintained a substantial "rainy day fund" and stock portfolio. She'd visited England, Ireland, France, Italy, and passed through several smaller European countries and had also visited most of the 50 states.

The dentist liked to try to fix her up with his friends and colleagues, which got on her nerves. Every once in a while, her father might ask if she'd thought about settling down, but she'd learned to laugh it off. She told Dr. Goldfarb, her father, and other well-meaning friends and family the same thing—she enjoyed being single.

Oh, she'd dated and had the occasional steady boyfriend over the years. It was a rare individual who made it to thirty-eight without having had at least one relationship, and Dawn was not that rare of a girl.

There'd been Scott in high school, although he turned out to be gay. They were still friends and met for lunch now and again. He and his boyfriend Pete were good people, and well-matched as a couple.

College brought Dave, the die-hard Chicago sports fan. He'd grown up outside the city and was a wonderful boyfriend on the days when none of his teams played. Dawn tried, but could not bring herself to care enough for the sports, the teams, or the man, and so parted ways with Dave after a few years of being together.

A long break followed, but then Kevin came along, an electrical engineering major, during their senior year. Dawn had been drawn to his quiet, serious nature as well as his boy-next-door looks. He'd lasted nearly five years, enough time for them to settle in Atlanta and start a life together. The word "marriage" had even been mentioned, but then her mother passed away and he transferred to Baltimore and that was the end of that.

The remainder of her twenties and thirties were spent building a life as a single woman. She thrived on her own, buying the house and making money. Singlehood was a blast, and until recently she would've said she planned to stay that way.

The weird thing was that she couldn't put her finger on what exactly had changed to make her question the future. Seeing Scott and his boyfriend so happy together? Hearing about Dave getting married? Maybe, although she had no desire to marry him herself, move to Chicago, and raise little sports fans.

Was it the big 4-0 looming on the horizon? That seemed the more likely culprit since it had her thinking about life in other ways, too.

Did she want to be a dental hygienist for the rest of her life? Did she want to stay in Atlanta or try somewhere else in a few years?

Spend more time getting to know her nieces and nephews before they grew up and started their own lives?

So many questions, and she hated not being able to come up with the answers. Dawn tended to know what she wanted without second thoughts, but lately she seemed to be full of not only second, but third and fourth thoughts as well. The ambiguity was driving her batty.

How else would you explain driving the hour from Cumming to Marietta to meet some old family friend of Pete's? Apparently, the friend had moved back to Georgia after several years in Seattle and wanted to reconnect with his roots. That was all well and good, but he better not expect her to connect with his root.

Dawn arrived early and decided to wander around. With her hands in the pockets of her purple jacket, she meandered along the main street. Marietta Square had a nice feel to it. Friendly, but not overly quaint. A good mix of the traditional and the new, so a cutesy cupcakery was next to the long-established bookstore.

Tonight coincided with an art walk in the square, which allowed for plenty of sensory input and window shopping. After several minutes of taking in the sights, she decided to head over to The Magic Bean, the coffee shop right off the square. She wasn't really a fan of coffee, but it was only supposed to be a quick stop before determining if it was worth the effort to include dinner as well.

"Dawn," someone called. "Are you Dawn?"

She turned to see a tall man with sandy hair and blue eyes studying her. He was cute. Score one for Pete.

"I'm sorry, I thought you were someone else," he said and started to turn.

"No, no." Dawn touched his arm to keep him from walking away. "I'm Dawn. You have the right person."

"Oh, good. Now I won't get called into Sheriff Brown's office for accosting women on the street." He drew a hand across his forehead in an exaggerated gesture. "I'm Paul."

"Good to meet you."

"Same here." He smiled and nodded toward the coffee shop. "Shall we?'

When they arrived, Paul held the door for her, which she considered a nice touch. Not all men practiced chivalry these days.

The coffee shop was smaller and darker than expected. The walls were painted dark brown, the floor was a dark hardwood, and the tiny bistro tables were painted beige and ecru. Were the owners trying to go for the feeling of being a part of the cup of java you were drinking? Because Dawn certainly felt like she was in a coffee mug.

"What's your poison?" Paul asked.

"Would it be sacrilegious if I asked for green tea?"

He threw his head back and laughed. "I'm sorry. If I order that, they might well ask us to leave."

"Darn." She snapped her fingers.

"I'll try, though," he said in a serious tone. "Why don't you find a table?"

With only six tables in the place, that could be a challenge. Dawn turned to see if any were available when an older lady jumped up and ran out of the shop. The woman's tablemate shrugged and followed the woman outside. Dawn wondered what was going on there, but went ahead and commandeered the empty table while she had the chance.

"Here we go." Paul set the mugs down a few minutes later. "Green tea for the lady."

"Any trouble?" Dawn asked.

"The barista is expected to make a full recovery."

He was funny. She liked funny.

"So you're a friend of Pete's," he said. "Good man, that Pete. How do you know him again?"

"I'm good friends with Scott," Dawn explained.

"Ah, yes. I have not had the chance to meet The Boyfriend yet." Pete lowered himself into the chair while giving Dawn a stern look. "He's good for Pete, this Scott of yours?"

"The best," Dawn said. "They've been together for three or four years now. How have you not met him?"

Paul blew out his breath. "Been in exile on the left coast for the last ten years. The authorities just let me back in the Eastern time zone a few weeks ago."

"And what did you do?" She waited for his response.

"Pete didn't give you the whole sad story?" He seemed surprised. "What *did* he say?"

"Old family friend, just moved back and needs to meet people," she said. "Any of that true?"

"Two and three are spot on. The first," he held his hand out flat and flipped it back and forth. "I suppose it's close enough."

"So how do you know Pete?" She sipped her tea.

"We dated for a few years right out of college."

Dawn swallowed hard and started coughing. She had assumed Paul was straight. Pete had made this sound like a date, anyway. It wasn't like him to leave out such an important detail. She goggled at Paul, trying to regain her breath and her composure.

"My bad." Paul reached over and squeezed her hand. "That was meant to be a joke. I expected you to laugh."

Okay, maybe funny wasn't such a good thing.

"What?" she managed to squeak out.

"It is funny if you know the whole story," he insisted. "I just assumed Pete would tell you, given our history."

"But—"

"Oh, not that we dated." Paul shook his head. "We didn't. I'm into girls, I promise. Pete's my second cousin. My mom and his mom are cousins and we used to spend summers here in Woodstock at my great-grandparents. Then they died when we were like ten and there was some big fight at the funeral and we never came to Georgia again after that. Pete and I stayed close, though, and when my mom passed last fall, he said I should come back home so I did a few weeks ago." He paused. "I'll stop talking now."

"Thank you."

Dawn needed to process all that information, which sounded involved and complicated. What she got out of it was that Paul was related to Pete and that Paul had lost his mother. Her own mother had died several years back, so although sorry for his loss, she was also envious of the extra time he had with his mom.

Her thoughts rambled much like his speech. No wonder Pete felt like they'd be a good match.

Paul averted his eyes, but she sensed he was itching to tell her more. He could have his turn in a minute.

"Look, maybe this was a bad idea," Paul blurted. "We should've talked on the phone or something first."

"No, no, this is fine." Dawn tried to put some spirit in her tone. "Most of the guys people set me up with are boring as hell and I'm ready to climb out of the bathroom window after the first five minutes."

"And you're not with me?"

She shook her head. "Not yet, anyway."

"Have I frightened you with all the family drama?"

"You haven't told me what the family drama is, so I really can't say. But I have to ask. What happened?"

"Clueless." Paul shrugged. "Pete and I have been trying to figure that out for nearly thirty years. Grandma and Grandpa were fairly well off, but they divided everything equally among the three kids. Our moms were the grandkids. I'm not sure if they got anything or not. Pete and I didn't go to the funeral. We didn't see what happened and none of the relatives talked about it, including our moms."

"Weird."

"Yup." Paul downed some coffee. "Please tell me your family is closer to normal."

Dawn nodded.

"Oh, come on, there's more to it than that." He leaned forward, placed his chin on his hands. "Spill."

"Mom died when I was twenty-three. Dad hasn't remarried and has no plans to. Two much older brothers, both in New York. Dad's still in Florida. Fairly normal."

"Sorry about your mom," he said.

"I'm sorry about yours, too."

"Yeah." He drew out the word. "So, do I pass the test? Are you brave enough to have dinner with me?"

She gave him a long look, smiling while he pretended to sweat it out. "Why not?"

He grinned. "That's the spirit. What are you in the mood for? Drive or walk?"

"Let's walk," she decided. "And you choose."

"Good old Southern cuisine it is," he said. "Believe it or not, there's a really good gastro pub a few blocks over."

"Works for me."

And it did. She wasn't quite sure if Paul was boyfriend material, but he was definitely friend material, and she could see spending more time with him either way.

He held the door open for her again on the way out, but did not take her hand or put his hand on the small of her back. Instead, he waited until she was beside him and kept pace with her as they made their way down the sidewalk.

"Here we are." Paul stopped outside a brick building with a black sign saying "Paisley" in dark red cursive.

The restaurant downplayed its name, although the waitresses wore tartan skirts and the napkins sported argyle patterns. The place had wood paneling contrasting with lighter wood booths, but was well-lit and gave off a friendly vibe. Only a few TVs and those were by the bar, and a section in the back for pool tables and dartboards. It wasn't too noisy or crowded, but Dawn imagined that would change as the hour grew later.

"Hey, Paul," the greeter said. "Back again, I see."

"Joyce's having fun," he explained as they followed her to a booth. "I joined the darts club last week. This is like the third time I've been here."

Darts club? That was a thing? Did that mean he was also a sports fanatic? Might as well find out sooner than later.

"Are you a sports fan?"

Paul shrugged. "Not really."

"Your waiter will be along shortly," the greeter said.

"Thanks, Joyce." Paul turned to face Dawn. "I like sports and I like going to a game now and again, but I don't really follow the teams like some guys do. I'll stick to darts. What about you?"

She wrinkled her nose. "No on sports and I don't think I've ever played darts."

"Keep it that way. Gets in your blood." He winked. "I won't force you to play until at least the seventh date."

"If we make it that far." That one slipped out.

He chuckled. "Fair enough. I'll let you peruse the menu."

In following his suggestion, she found herself surprised by the options. Paisley had the standard burgers and sandwiches, but also offered dishes with herbs and vegetables and some things she wasn't sure which category they belonged in.

"Good variety," she said.

"You wouldn't have seen a place like this here when I was growing up."

"Is that good or bad?"

"Good. Definitely good. What are you going to have?"

"Steak and mozzarella salad."

Yes, it was a bit of a cliché for a woman to have the salad on a first date, but the steak part was unexpected. The pumpernickel croutons intrigued her, and since she didn't know if they'd be back, she opted for what she wanted.

"Not bad," Paul said. "I'm having the chicken cordon bleu sandwich. I had it the other night and it was quite tasty."

Two hours later, Dawn wondered when the last time she'd enjoyed a first date so much might have been. She hadn't been tempted to escape even once, and neither she nor Paul checked their phones until they were leaving the restaurant. And then shared a laugh when they discovered they each had a text from Pete wanting to know things had gone.

"You tell him you hated me and I'll gush on how much I liked you," Paul suggested. "That'll confuse the heck out of him."

"I'll tell him when I get home. Make him sweat."

"That's my girl."

Paul did not hug or kiss her goodnight. Instead, he walked her to her car, gave an exaggerated bow, and stepped back. She wasn't quite sure what to make of that so she waved and drove off.

At the last stoplight before heading onto the highway, she squirmed out of her jacket. Tossing it onto the seat next to her, a sheet of paper slipped out of one of the pockets and onto the passenger seat. Where in the world did that come from?

The light changed so all she could do was wonder. Could Paul have snuck it in there? Would he have had the time or the opportunity? Her curiosity would just have to wait until she got back home.

Pete's curiosity did not share the same patience. She received two more texts from him, and one from Scott, which was an apology for Pete, before pulling into her driveway.

She texted Scott: *Tired. Will update Pete later.*

Scott: ☺ *I'll hold him off until morning.*

Thnx!!

Dawn found she truly was tired. She'd enjoyed herself beyond all expectations, but the drive and conversation wore her out. After a long, hot shower, she made herself a cup of peppermint tea and opened the envelope.

She read the letter again. And again. The words did not change.

What a strange experiment! Who was this crazy widow lady wanting to know her personal philosophy? For a second, Dawn's mind flashed on the two older ladies at the coffee shop. She hadn't gotten more than a glimpse, but they'd seemed normal enough.

Could this be real? Was there any harm in participating either way? It's not as if they were asking for personal data like date of birth or Social Security Number. They weren't asking for a credit card number or any type of money, either, just what she, Dawn, believed.

All she had to do was write an essay. She hadn't done that since college, and it might be fun to think about her personal philosophy. The letter did promise anonymity...

Maybe she should discuss this with Scott. Or even Paul. Did this sort of thing happen in small towns? She'd certainly never heard of it happening in Atlanta. Well, if it really was anonymous, who would tell? It's not like she was being invited to share her thoughts with the world, just one lonely old lady.

Her phone buzzed and she silently cursed Pete. What had happened to Scott keeping him at bay until morning?

Had fun. Hope yr home safe. Do it again soon?

Ooh, it was from Paul. Much better.

Dawn: *Sure.*

Cool.

Wow. Contact within 24 hours. She must have made an impression. A man she was interested in and an invitation to participate in an intriguing experiment. Not a bad day's work.

Dawn's internal alarm clock had her up and working out at seven a.m. She rarely slept past nine, which allowed more time to get stuff done, and she'd lay down for a little bit in the afternoon if the mood struck.

Scott and Pete tended to be late risers, so she had plenty of time before they hounded her for a debrief of last night's date.

After the usual breakfast of scrambled eggs and rye toast, Dawn retrieved the letter and re-read it. As odd and unexpected as the request might be, she really wanted to take part. Something about the idea appealed to her, even if she had no clue what to write.

Heck, what was her personal philosophy? She didn't believe that love conquered all. If that were true, she wouldn't have lost her mother so early, and the cause of the feud between Pete's and Paul's moms wouldn't matter.

Love is all you need? While a wonderful Beatles song, she didn't think it was something you could build your life on. Love was important, but not all someone needed.

The golden rule—do unto others as you would have others do unto you? Again, a philosophy she agreed with, just not one she considered her own. The Beatles were correct again and kharma was going to get you, which is why it was important to remember and try to follow the golden rule. Still, not her personal philosophy.

Hmmm....perhaps she didn't want to take part after all.

No, she'd come up with an answer after thinking about it some more. A good long walk outside might trigger something.

Her cell phone buzzed when she stepped back in the house and she answered before checking the display.

"I can't hold him off much longer," Scott sounded winded. "Can you meet us at Heartland for lunch like now?"

Dawn chuckled. "Give me an hour."

"Forty-five minutes. See you there."

Scott hung up. Fine, she could get ready and be there on time. It was just the boys. No need to look her best for these two.

Even with the deadline looming over her, Dawn found herself thinking of and then rejecting options for her personal philosophy. She also decided not to tell anyone about the invitation to keep them from asking about her response. This was between her and the crazy widow lady.

"You're late," Scott said when she walked into Heartland. "Are you okay? You're almost never late."

"Did you have that much fun with Cousin Paul?" Pete leered.

She hugged them each in turn and responded to their questions. "You didn't give me much time, Scott. And as for you, Petey Boy, you have a sick mind. Your cousin didn't even kiss me goodnight."

Pete rolled his eyes. "Such a prude."

They followed the greeter to a table, allowing Dawn a few moments to further compose herself. She ordered a Coke before turning back to the boys.

"Why didn't you tell me you were related to the man you fixed me up with?" she asked with fake rancor.

"More fun this way." Pete grinned like the Big Bad Wolf. "I couldn't have you going in there with preconceived notions, now could I? You might not have ended up liking him as much as you did!"

Scott punched his boyfriend on the shoulder.

"And why do you think I like your cousin?" she asked.

His grin deepened. "When you don't like something, you say so right away. When Scotty here said you hadn't mentioned what you thought of Ol' Paul, I knew he was in."

She silently appealed to Scott, who ducked his head and refused to meet her gaze.

"You're impossible," she said.

"Which one of us?" Scott asked.

"Both," she clarified.

The waiter saved her from further embarrassment, and the three of them placed their orders. The interrogation started the moment the waiter left.

"When are you going to see him again?" Pete asked.

"Don't know."

"But you are going to see him again?"

"That's the plan."

"I just knew you'd hit it off."

"That's not a question," Scott pointed out.

Pete huffed. "Didn't I tell you they'd make a good couple?"

"You did," he agreed. "But I'm not the one you're interviewing."

Dawn glared at Scott. He stuck out his tongue, then took a very long drink of his water, his eyes on her the entire time.

"Okay," Pete said, getting warmed up again. "Where did he take you to dinner?"

"Paisley."

"That dive?"

"Hey, I liked it," Dawn said. "My salad was excellent."

"And after?" Pete asked.

"We said goodnight and I drove home. I told you, no good-night kiss."

Pete made a face. "Bore. Ing."

"It was only the first date," Scott said in her defense. "We didn't kiss on our first date, either."

"Fine."

"Can we talk about something else now?" Dawn pleaded. "You can quiz me again when the food comes. Or better yet, give me the skinny on cousin Paul."

Pete sat up straight and placed a splayed hand over his heart. "Dish on a family member? I would never."

"Yes, you would." Scott draped an arm on the back of his chair. "But tell her about the kitchen remodel first."

After a few minutes of trying to listen to all the details involving cabinet choices and drawer pulls, Dawn let her mind drift back to her response to the letter. She had thirty days, but liked to plan and get things done early. The charge of overachiever had been thrown at her more than once, even though she didn't agree. She just liked to check things off her list and move on to the next task.

What about kindness? That was a trait or a behavior, not a philosophy. And it was pretty much an offshoot of her earlier thought around "love is all you need" and the golden rule. No, she had to do better than that, dig a little deeper, if she was going to find a response that resonated with her.

"So green or teal?" Pete's question intruded on her musings.

"For?"

"The backsplash," he said in a tone that questioned her basic intelligence.

"Can you do a design with green, teal, and some blue?" she asked.

Scott shot her a look of respect as Pete smacked the table.

"You're a genius!" Pete got up and walked over to hug Dawn. "Oh, look, food is here."

Scott and Dawn turned to see the waiter arrive with the plates. Her burger and fries looked delicious and she dove right in. The men briefly allowed their target to eat in peace before the questions started again. For this round, she instituted a new rule. For every question he asked, Pete had to tell her something about his cousin. And it had to be true as well as mostly clean.

"Oh, fun." He gave a little chair dance.

Dawn learned that her date could play piano and had, in fact, been the pianist for a local theatre group in Seattle. Never married, but two or three serious girlfriends. Graduated with honors from University of Washington. Could not remember his degree, but did know Paul was some kind of marketing guru and loved fiddling with computers.

"He's just as curious about you," Pete said. "We're meeting him for dinner. Wanna come and surprise him?"

Dawn shook her head. "Tempting, but no."

"She's not big on surprises," Scott said. "And she likes to get to know people on her own terms. She must really be into your cousin if she's letting you divulge all this information."

Dawn opened her mouth to protest, saw the futility, and shut it again while turning a nice shade of pink.

"Well, well, well," Pete drawled. "In that case, I'll shut up and ask for the check. This one's on us."

"You're doing me the favor." Scott winked at her. "You know how he is. If we got up before noon, we would've done breakfast. I can only restrain him for so long."

The two men shared a look of affection and a quick kiss. While it pleased Dawn, she couldn't help notice the stares from some of the other diners. Scott told her once that it used to bother him, but he'd learned to let it go. You couldn't control other people, only yourself. She supposed that was part of his personal philosophy.

"Ready?" he asked.

She nodded and they walked out together, leaving Pete to pay the bill. When they stepped outside, he held out his arm and she leaned into him.

"You look happy." Scott rested his chin on her head. "I hope this works out for you."

"There's more to life than finding a partner," she said. "I'm fine on my own. You know that."

She felt him nod. "You're one of a kind, Miss Dawn. You deserve to find happiness."

"You make your own happiness, Scotty baby."

"Don't be trying to steal my boyfriend, you hussy." Pete wrapped his arm around her from the other side. "You had your chance. He's mine now."

The three of them laughed at the old joke and said their good-byes. As much as she enjoyed their company, Dawn was glad for the chance to return to the peace and quiet of her world. There was laundry to do and groceries to buy, not to mention preparing for the week ahead. Still, the date with Paul yesterday and lunch with good friends today gave her a sense of contentment.

While running errands and performing household chores, her mind churned. Sometimes it settled on Paul, sometimes it settled on the coming week's schedule of appointments, but mostly it kept coming back to her off-hand remark to Scott outside of Heartland.

You make your own happiness.

Dawn believed in that saying. In fact, she'd go so far as to say she considered it her personal philosophy. Because no matter the external influences, she always controlled what happened on the inside. No matter what happened, at the end of the day she was responsible for her actions and feelings.

Sure, people would say things about her, both positive and negative, but she didn't have to react or internalize any of it. People would also do things to her, both hurtful and helpful, but how she dealt with all that was up to her. You could never begin to control or even prepare for the words and actions of others, but you could most certainly control your response.

Take all of the well-meaning friends and family who hounded her about being single. She could have let that influence her and change her mind so that instead of being happy, she beat herself up for not living up to others' expectations.

Dawn appreciated that people cared for her, but they were not the ones who lived her life every day. Only she could do that, and she planned to do so whether alone or with someone else.

Her phone buzzed. *Survive lunch? Any tips for dinner?*

She considered her response. *Wear a cup.*

Ha! Noted.

Take Paul, now that he'd brought himself to her attention. He seemed like a nice guy, and was both related to and blessed by someone she considered family. She hoped things worked out, even if it was only for a little while. Even though meeting him had been fun, she wasn't pinning her entire future on him. Nor did she plan to spend more time dwelling on the potential, at least once all the debriefings were out of the way.

She was a busy woman...most of the time. Tonight, the plan was to veg out in front of the television. After a productive weekend, she required recuperation time.

At work on Monday, Dr. Goldfarb asked about her weekend. She muttered something about it being okay and having lunch with friends.

"Well, at least you went out," he said. "I worry about you spending so much time by yourself. It's not healthy."

"I know you do." She checked the calendar. "Full day today."

"Week before Memorial Day is always busy, but busy is good." Dr. Goldfarb patted her shoulder. "I better check the rooms to make sure everything is ready."

As if Lucy, their office manager, ever missed anything. Dawn just nodded and reviewed her notes on the patients coming in that day. She thought it added an extra touch if she asked after their kids or remembered the names and ages of their pets.

For the first time, she also found herself wondering about the other parts of their lives. Were they happy? What did each of them believe in terms of having a personal philosophy? It wasn't something you could come right out and ask, since most people would more than likely need to think about their answer.

Whoever the crazy widow lady was, the woman was smart in how she went about asking the question. She could satisfy her curiosity without the stigma of intruding or getting all up in someone else's business. Dawn already planned to take part in the experiment, but now she vowed to complete her essay as soon as possible so the widow would have her response to read. Dawn began to wonder at how many and what type of responses the lady had already received.

Well, she'd likely never know. There was a price to anonymity. Oh, but Dawn would know or be able to guess at some of the other participants since she got to choose five lucky people herself. She'd do her best to make good choices for the widow.

"You've been awful quiet today," Lucy said during the lunch break. "Everything okay?"

Dawn nodded. "I'm fine."

"If you say so. You're not usually so lost in thought. Are you coming down with something?"

"Not allowed." Dr. Goldfarb strode into the tiny breakroom. "We're booked solid this week."

"I'm fine," Dawn insisted. "Let's get back to work."

She tried to be more engaged for the rest of the afternoon, but her thoughts refused to cooperate. When feisty Mrs. Lemon, the final patient for the day, squirmed in the chair, Dawn wanted to ask her what it was like to be a widow. Was it lonely? Had she thought of remarrying? Had she been to Marietta Square this past weekend?

"Are you almost done?" Mrs. Lemon asked. "My youngest daughter is coming home tonight and I want to make her favorite stew."

"You should be all set." Dawn pushed the chair arm up and got out of the way. "You're free to go."

"Thank you."

Dawn cleaned up the room and checked the others to make sure all was in place. Everything looked good.

"Night, Dawn," Lucy called as the hygienist bustled out the door.

Dawn lifted a hand in response, eager to get home and put some of the thoughts that had been swimming around her head all day down on paper. After a quick dinner, she parked herself in front of the computer screen.

When she finally looked up, she found herself caught off guard by how much time had passed. Reading over her words, she approved of the end result. Dawn wasn't planning on switching careers any time soon, but might take up journaling. Although she'd poo-pooed the process in the past, putting her thoughts on paper tonight had been so much fun that it was something she'd be willing to try on a regular basis.

She printed the essay, then had to hunt for an envelope and stamp. On the way back from posting her letter, she retrieved her phone to see what she'd missed. No messages from Scott or Pete, but there was one from Paul.

Wanna chat?

He'd sent it thirty minutes ago, so he could wait a few more. If she hadn't talked to his cousin, Dawn might have thought all the texts—well, sending texts so soon after the first date—seemed a little desperate and potentially clingy. Pete had set her straight, saying Paul was a serial texter and if he decided you were worth his time, he was going to reach out. She'd go with it for now, reserving the right to ask him for space if required down the road.

She grabbed a Coke from the fridge and texted back asking him to call.

Paul: *An actual call? *shaking**

Dawn: *Call or no chat.*

Paul: **sigh* Tough crowd.*

When he did call a minute or so later, the lilt in his voice told her he was amused by her demand.

"I see you survived The Inquisition," she said.

"Yes, ma'am, with the scars to prove it," he responded. "I have to say, I like The Boyfriend."

"Scott."

"He's a good match for Pete," Paul said. "Both of them adore you to no end."

"Natch." Not a word she used often, yet it seemed to fit here.

Paul laughed. "Not a fan of texting, I see. Are you against IM as well?"

"I prefer face-to-face, then phone. I can do IM, especially over texting. Text is more a convenience than a mode of conversation for me."

"Got it," he said. "Speaking of face-to-face, would you like to meet up again this coming weekend? Maybe we could make a day of it rather than a quick coffee and dinner?"

Dawn had wanted to spend at least part of the weekend taking care of her obligation to choose five potential candidates for the experiment. She'd also need a day to run errands and prepare for the next week.

"I can't do a full day," she told Paul.

"Why not?" He wanted to know. "You can't have plans all three days even if it will be Memorial Day weekend."

She couldn't decide if his persistence and logic annoyed or amused her, although she did know it intrigued her enough to want to spend more time in his company.

"How about if I meet you Saturday afternoon and we can take in a movie and then have a leisurely dinner?"

Silence on the other end of the line. Had she offended him or was he thinking things through? This is why she preferred in-person meetings, but at least she'd get tone when he responded to try to figure out what he was feeling.

"Okay, I can do that," he said. "Now, let's compare notes on our respective meetings with cousin and his partner."

"You start."

"Damn, you *are* a tough crowd," he said, amused.

"You brought it up. You have to go first."

"Fair enough."

They spent the next hour comparing notes and continuing to get to know each other. Dawn couldn't speak for Paul, but she thought they were getting along swimmingly. She was almost reluctant to end the call, but had to. With writing her essay and chatting with Paul, she'd spent no time on her usual evening activities and needed to get back to some sort of routine.

Dawn started her Saturday by getting the car washed. She normally washed it herself, but the carwash always seemed to have an eclectic bunch of people hanging out in the waiting room. Most of them would be too bored or distracted to notice someone slipping something into their purse or briefcase.

"Taylor, put that down." A man took a small American flag from a pretty two-year-old girl and placed it back on the table.

"Why don't you play with those blocks in the corner? They look like fun."

The man—mid 20s, medium height, black hair, friendly but with a harried face—gave an apologetic smile to the folks in the room. The two other guys didn't glance up from their phones, and neither did the other woman about Dawn's age. A grandmotherly woman smiled back in sympathy, as did a woman slightly older than Dawn.

Of this group, she leaned toward this last woman, who had short, spiky brown hair with green eyes and a kind face. Her phone captured her attention, but she also took the time to talk to the grandmotherly woman and make faces at little Taylor to get her to giggle.

Dawn slipped the envelope into the side pocket of the woman's purse, the one with what looked like her mail sticking out, and hoped no one noticed. When the attendant called and the woman stood and walked out to pay, Dawn breathed a sigh of relief. One down, four to go.

This was exciting! The project not only had her thinking about her own beliefs, but also about other people. Not to mention going to places she rarely visited in order to choose from a diverse group and hopefully better the odds of selecting people who would respond.

From the carwash, Dawn went to the local grocery store strip mall. She decided to walk around and choose random cars. One envelope went under the windshield wiper of a newer model VW Bug with a purple iris in the flower holder, and another was left on an older dark green Toyota Corolla.

Next stop was the mall since she planned to do some shopping anyway. Time to update the bra and panties portion of her wardrobe. If things continued along the current path with Paul, she wasn't going to let his first sight of her undergarments leave him terrified. Plus, it had been too long since she'd had a fitting and an upgrade, not to mention buying such items tended to improve her overall outlook.

With purchases in hand, Dawn headed to the chaos of the food court. She observed the crowd before deciding on a blonde woman in her early thirties with two young girls. Her first choice hadn't appeared to have kids, and neither car at Publix had a car seat inside. She didn't want to discriminate, so she also chose the tall young man in his mid to late twenties and snuck the envelope into the outside pocket of his laptop bag.

That was it. She had completed all the crazy widow lady's requirements.

To her surprise, Dawn felt a little dejected now that her part in the grand experiment was finished. Even though she'd chosen, she'd never know if or how any of her folks had taken part. Oh well, all part of the greater cause.

Rather than dwelling on it, she took her purchases and headed on home. She had a date to get ready for.

Dawn's Essay

F irst of all, thank you so much for selecting me for this experiment. I can't tell you how thrilled I am to take part. Thinking about something as important as my personal philosophy has been so much fun.

Okay, now that I have that out of the way, on to what you wanted to know. My personal philosophy is that you make your own happiness. No matter what life throws at you, no matter what someone does or says, no one can make you feel unhappy without your consent. And you shouldn't let your happiness rely on what other people think or say or do. Your happiness is your responsibility, so it's more important what you think and say and do.

At the end of the day, you're the one who has to live with yourself. And I'm not talking about living alone or with someone else. I mean that you are the only one who occupies your body, your skin, your mind, your thoughts, and your soul.

Sure, everyone wants to be liked. I want to be liked and I want to be well-thought of by co-workers, family, and friends. But not everyone is going to be like me, and no one is going to like me all of the time.

Even still, I am the one who decides that none of that matters in terms of what makes me happy.

I am responsible for my own happiness.

That does not mean that I have to be a Pollyanna and go around singing and with my head in the clouds. No one can be that way all of the time, not with the junk that life is going to throw at you.

My mom died way before I was ready to say goodbye. I was in my 20s and I still needed her to help guide me through life. Her death hit me hard, and I was depressed for a long time. But slowly I healed, and I realized that she was still helping to guide me whether she was physically here or not. The lessons she taught me were in my head and in my heart and I only needed to stop and take the time to listen to know what she'd say.

Of course, she'd probably be a little disappointed that I'm now nearly 40 and still single, but one of her lessons was that she was happy as long as I was happy. I know she knows I'm okay with my life and that while I may be single, I am not alone and that I truly am pleased with who I am and where I am at the moment.

Getting back to creating your own happiness. I could not control the fact that Mom was taken from me too early, but I can control how I deal with that loss. I'm guessing you understand, since you recently lost your husband. I hope you had a good long life together, and I'm sorry he's no longer with you. I hope this project brings you a sense of peace and that it helps you move back into finding your happiness.

I've given some examples of external influences in terms of other people and outside events, but internal influences can wreck your world as well. People think they're too fat or too skinny, too tall or too short, or a million other reasons to beat themselves up. I think sometimes they also set unrealistic expectations. If I had a new job or a new car or a new house, I'd be content. While having a goal is a good thing, it's not the job or the car or the house that determines how you feel. Only you can do that. Only you can make your own happiness.

Well, I guess I've come full circle in terms of the essay. I hope it's what you're looking for. I wrote from a place of truth, and I'd like to think that feeling comes across. I also hope you enjoyed what I had to say, regardless of whether or not you agree.

But then you didn't ask me to write something you agree with. You asked me to write about my personal philosophy and I think I've accomplished that goal. Best of luck to you with the experiment and in finding happiness in your own life.

Myra

I stared at the envelope in my hand addressed to Crazy Widow Lady. That was me. Could this be real?

Checking the post office box had become an obsession, stopping by every other day, then every day, not quite believing that someone might respond. Yet here was proof. Dare I open it?

Why else had I begun the grand experiment? This person had taken the time and effort to write and send their response, and the whole point of the diversion was to find out what people believed. Of course I would open it.

It was just…the first one. A milestone.

"Everything okay, ma'am?" Someone asked.

I looked up to see a postal employee, a young black woman with her brows knit close together and her head slightly to the side in an expression of concern.

"Yes, I'm fine," I assured her. "Wasn't expecting a letter today."

"Hope it's good news." She smiled.

I smiled back. "I'm sure it is."

"You have a good day now." She nodded and walked away.

How could it not be a great day after receiving this gift? What a wonderous day, and I still hadn't even opened the envelope to read the response.

Once in the car, I decided to prolong the joy and read the response in the comfort of home with Grace by my side. Tonight was book club, but I didn't want to share the moment just yet. I wanted to bask in the news of an actual response, revel in what the person said in their essay, and live with this secret knowledge before sharing it with others.

The few miles home took forever, and I almost broke my resolve at the super long traffic light. Somehow, I made it through the front door and even spent a few minutes greeting the dog before plopping on the couch and slitting open the envelope to read the essay.

A woman had been the first to answer. How wonderful! Hold on...the envelope had no return address and the letter did not give a name. No way to tell if it was from a man or a woman. Not really. But I knew it was from another woman.

Now, who could this be from? Purple Jacket from Marietta Square? The mother from that same outing? Could it be from one of the car windshields? In the end, did it matter? I wouldn't ever know which recipients sent in responses, assuming this essay proved to be the first of many.

"This is too exciting," I used the piece of paper to fan my face for a few moments. "The girls are going to go nuts tonight."

I found myself grinning as I read through the essay again. This woman sounded pleased as punch to have been chosen. And I loved her philosophy since I agreed that you made your own happiness.

Still single at 40, though? Well, all the Women's Movements I'd lived through in my life were all about giving women a choice and if that was what worked for her, then at least she got to choose. And I hoped she had friends to rely on the way I did.

Grace let out a doggy sigh and pulled my attention away from the letter. She needed to be walked and fed, and I needed to get ready for hosting duties. Would we talk about the book at all when they heard the news? Maybe I'd wait until the end to tell them.

Susan arrived first and quickly settled in with her glass of merlot. Mabel and Dolores followed. I must have given off some signal because Mabel kept staring at me as I welcomed everyone and put out snacks.

"Betty won't be here," I told everyone. "Jean got called into work and one of the girls is running a fever."

"Poor little thing," Mabel said. "June still coming?"

I nodded. "You know she's the type to be late to her own funeral."

"Okay, now I know something's up." Mabel jabbed a finger at me. "You get sassy and Southern when you have news."

A grin escaped before I could turn my head away.

"Someone responded!" she guessed.

My blush answered before I could get the words out.

"That's fantastic," Susan gushed. "What did they say? Are you going to share tonight? Where's the letter?"

June chose that moment to arrive, all bossiness and expecting attention. I poured her a glass of wine as she dropped her pocketbook on the floor and flopped onto a chair. She blew a breath upward to knock her hair out of her face and took the glass.

"Why are y'all looking like cats who ate canaries?" she asked. "Were you taking bets on how late I'd be?"

"Better," Dolores said. "Tell her, Myra."

I sipped my ginger ale and slathered some pimento cheese on a Ritz cracker. June glared at me, knowing exactly what I was doing. Sometimes it was simply too easy to get that woman's goat. When I felt she suffered enough…or when Mabel pointedly cleared her throat…I passed along the good news.

"About time," was all she said.

"Come on, Myra, read us the essay," Mabel implored.

"Don't you want to talk about the book?" I asked.

"We don't give two figs about the damn book and you know it," June said. "Let's hear what this person had to say."

"Amen." Susan held her wine glass aloft, and the other women soon followed suit.

"As it so happens." I paused, getting far too much joy from teasing my friends. "I have the response right here. Are you sure you want me to read it now? The book really was good this month."

My friends narrowed their eyes and pursed their lips at me, which told me I'd better start reading or risk some of the crudité being tossed in my direction. With a grin, I pulled the paper from my back pocket and shared the letter.

"She sounds nice," Susan said once I finished.

"And lonely." Dolores took a sip of wine.

June scoffed. "How do you know it's a she? You can't tell that from the essay."

"Please." Dolores scoffed. "No man thinks that deeply or expresses himself so well."

"You got that right." Betty laughed.

"Well, then," June said. "*She* seems independent and level-headed to me. Plus, she's right. You're responsible for your own life."

"How can you get that and Dolores can't get that she's lonely?" Mabel asked.

"Read it again, Myra," June ordered.

I obliged. The thrill of getting a response intensified each time I went over the letter, and I learned something new each time, too. Who knew you could get such a jolt from a short letter? Maybe because the pages were filled with more than words—they were brimming with feelings and personality and her view of life.

"Still sounds lonely," Dolores insisted.

"Just because she doesn't mention friends doesn't mean she's alone." Mabel hunched forward. "The girl's talking about making your own happiness, so why would she mention other people?"

"Everyone needs friends," Dolores said.

"That's right." June waved her glass around. "Where would Myra be without us?"

No way I was reacting to that loaded question. Plus, I was having way too much fun listening to them talk about this person none of them had ever met.

"The poor girl lost her mother," Susan chimed in. "How old was she again?"

I scanned the paper. "In her twenties, it says. And Dawn's almost forty now."

"That's far too young to lose your mama," Mabel said. "She's probably still not over it."

"After nearly twenty years?" June rolled her eyes. "Come on."

"You never get over the death of a parent." Mabel gave a slow shake of her. "I want to hug this woman."

I couldn't help but smile at this conversation. All brought on by slipping a stranger a piece of paper and asking that person to share their personal philosophy. Again, someone we didn't know and would more than likely never even meet. Even if the girl was the only one who responded, my grand experiment was a success.

"Myra, you've been far too quiet," Mabel said. "What do you think of her?"

"She's fabulous." I grabbed my can of ginger ale. "I'm pleased as punch that she took the time to write and send her essay."

"May it be the first of many." Dolores raised her cup of tea.

"Hear, hear." Susan held up her wine glass. We all repeated after her and then sipped our drinks.

"Okay, who needs more?" I asked. "Should I open another bottle? Or would you rather have coffee?"

Consensus was coffee, so I went to the kitchen to grab the pot and cups and take the cheesecake from the fridge. June tagged along, of course, so I made her carry the dessert while I brought the mugs and coffee pot. It was turning out to be quite the evening.

"When do we get to hand out requests again?" June slipped a piece of cheesecake onto her plate. "We don't want to have to wait."

"But you're having such a grand time dissecting the essay," I pointed out.

She made a rude noise. "Not the same."

The other women murmured in agreement. Hmmm... I had promised them they could do their part once three people responded. But more flyers handed out meant more potential responses and even more stimulating nights sharing and talking about what they'd have to share.

"Fine." I sighed through my nose. "Y'all can have a turn now."

"Yeehaw!" June whooped.

"Thanks, Myra." Mabel gave a little clap. "I can't wait to get started."

"Yeah, give us the paper," June insisted.

"I'll go print a stack since I want to check on Grace anyway." I pushed myself out of the chair. "Don't run off now."

Grace whined a greeting at me when I went into my office. For some reason, she'd taken to hiding in there when I had guests over, or sleeping in there if I was busy cleaning the house. If I sat down to read or watch TV, she was right there by my side, but if she felt like she was in the way, this little room had become her sanctuary.

"Hello, girl." She panted while I rubbed her knobby head. "They'll be gone soon."

I booted up the computer, printed the flyers, and resisted the temptation to check the email box that Jean set up for this project. She said it would not be traceable to me, and that the name Crazy Widow Lady would show up if I replied to a message. Jean worked with computers for a living, so I trusted that she knew what she was doing even if I still felt a little uneasy about the whole enterprise.

"We've decided you need a website," June announced when I returned to the living room. "Jean will build it."

"Are you serious?" I gripped the stack of papers in my right hand. "Why in God's name do I need a website? Email is more than enough."

Susan shook her head.

"Not in today's world," Mabel insisted.

My friends had lost their minds. I handed out the flyers, hoping this would be enough to sidetrack them.

"You can put the URL on the letters," June said.

"The what?" I should've known better. "URL?"

"It's a fancy way of saying website address," Susan said. "It'll give people a way to know more about you."

"You could even post the essays online for others to read," Mabel said. "For those who might want examples before writing their own."

"The essays are supposed to be anonymous," I reminded them. "And the letter tells people all they need to know about me and the experiment."

"They can still be *anonymous*." Betty pushed a lock of hair behind her ear. "They don't have to give their names when they post online."

Susan shook her head. "If the person has to provide a user name or email address, someone can track down who they are. Myra's right. We shouldn't have a website."

"Oh, poo, you guys are such spoilsports." Mabel sighed.

"Not the first time you've accused me of that." I lowered myself into the cozy gray chair. "No website."

June rolled her eyes, Mabel sighed again, and Betty groaned. Only Dolores gave me the thumbs up, which caused me to wonder if I'd made the correct decision. She and I didn't come down on the same side on most issues. Still, the woman had a good head on her shoulders and tended to make the logical choice.

"Be happy I'm letting y'all do your part in handing out the letters," I said. "Now, does anyone want more coffee or dessert?"

"Not now," Mabel grumbled.

"Henry's already texted me to ask when I'm coming home." June patted her pocket. "Guess he misses me."

"I should go, too." Susan pushed herself to standing. "Some of us still have to work for a living."

I followed everyone to the foyer and hugged each woman goodbye. After watching them drive off, I took a deep breath and faced the inevitable question: clean up tonight or leave it for the morning?

While my inclination was to do the latter, years of training had me conditioned to do the former. Grace waited for me at the top of the stairs, no doubt looking for a treat, so I went back up to the main level and into the kitchen.

"Sweet puppy." I held out her Milk Bone, which she took ever so gently in her teeth before trotting off to the edge of the dining room to eat.

Within ten minutes, plates, silverware, and cups were in the dishwasher. I took a Lysol cloth and wiped down the counter. Despite Grace's soulful stare, not a crumb was left in my now spotless kitchen.

Do only women enjoy the sight of a clean kitchen? My mother used to say she couldn't sleep if she knew hers was dirty, and I guess she passed that trait on to me.

"Could be worse, huh, pooch?" I stroked Grace's head.

On my final passthrough of the living room, I took the letter from its place on the coffee table. I read through it for the I-don't-know-how-many-th time, then closed my eyes and reveled in my accomplishment.

"Wish you were here for this, Lee," I whispered.

A silly wish, really, on many levels, the main one being that I would not have started this experiment if he were still here. I wanted him here, anyway.

"I'll visit you soon, love," I promised.

I'd been to his grave every day for the first two months. I didn't need my friends to tell me that was unhealthy, so I went once a week after that and then monthly. With Lee, I could feel his presence around me wherever I happened to be, and I felt closer to him in this house than at the cemetery. Still, I wanted to visit the place where his body was buried, even if his spirit was always with me.

Suddenly, I heard trumpets and turned to Grace to see if she heard something, too. She looked at me with her "can I have another treat" face.

"Maybe this widow lady is crazy."

The trumpets blared again and it dawned on me that the sound was the signal for a new email message. I must've left the computer on when I printed the letters earlier. Now who in the world could be messaging me at this hour?

Joe

J oe cursed a blue streak when he saw the flyer tucked under the windshield wiper of his old Dodge. Who did that kind of shit, anyway? As much as everyone hated them, he doubted the companies who advertised this way drummed up much business.

He grabbed the piece of paper, ready to toss it in the garbage. Then he hesitated. Could Pamela have put it there?

They'd only been separated a few months. Three months, nineteen days. But who was counting? He still loved her and hoped to make things right. Maybe she was ready to talk and didn't know another way of getting her message across. Not that writing letters was her style—she could barely sit still long enough to type out a text—but that sister of hers could have helped.

A car horn beeped, reminding Joe he was lingering in the parking lot of the local Publix. He shoved the paper in the plastic bag with the milk, put everything on the passenger seat, and slid behind the wheel.

On the short drive back to the apartment, he thought about calling Pam again. She hadn't picked up the last few times he tried, and he'd opted not to leave messages. They really did need to talk.

And he missed her. He hadn't even seen her in the last month. Her sister or mother were the ones to greet him when he went to pick up or drop off the kids.

Not that he got to spend any real time with Lindsay and Greta. He and Pam had agreed that he could only see them every other Saturday and no overnight stays. He hated it, but stuck to his word.

Joe sighed as he trudged up the steps to his new place. He despised living here. He should be home, but he'd agreed to the separation and he'd agreed to be the one to move out.

He'd done little to make the place comfortable – couch and TV in the living room, mattress and dresser in the bedroom, and not much else. Why put the effort in if he was just going to move anyway? The lease was for six months, the length of the trial separation. Halfway there, and still no idea if there'd be a happy ending.

The flyer reappeared when Joe was putting the groceries away. With a deep breath, he opened the letter. Scanned the page.

The hell? Some crazy lady wanted to know his personal philosophy. Was he on one of those reality shows where they pranked people?

Stuff like this didn't happen in real life. This was so not Pam's style, either. None of his friends would take the time to come up with such an off-the-wall joke and his co-workers could barely even speak English.

Joe plopped onto the couch and flipped on the TV. He'd plunked down a fair piece of cash on the 80" SmartTV with top of the line features, which was the nicest piece of furniture in the apartment.

While ESPN played in the background, he read the letter again, more slowly this time. Sounded real enough. Weird. But still real.

Maybe that's what happened to you when you grew up and your old man up and died on you. When Nana Simmons passed, Pop Pop stopped eating or going outside and started spouting all kinds of nonsense. He didn't ask anyone to write an essay, though.

Losing Nana made him withdraw from the world rather than think about other people.

Would Pamela care if Joe passed? He certainly hoped so, even if they hadn't been married nearly as long. Eight years, and they got hitched because Pam was pregnant with Lindsay. Two of the best days of his life. Marrying Pamela and seeing his first baby girl come into the world.

Joe hadn't wanted a big wedding. Couldn't see the point behind all that fuss. Pam convinced him otherwise. He had to admit, seeing her walk down the aisle in that white dress with a great big smile on her face and her eyes full of love made it all worthwhile. She'd been right to fight for a proper wedding, just like she'd been right so many times over the years.

Not about wanting to separate, though. Not about wanting to end the marriage. She was dead wrong about that.

He thought about the night Lindsay was born. Pamela had a rough time of it, which Joe got to see firsthand. He would've much preferred to be in the waiting room handing out cigars, but Pamela insisted he be with her. And they didn't allow smoking in hospitals these days anyway.

He hated seeing his wife in pain. They finally gave her the numbing shot, and she was better after that. Everyone in the room seemed to have a job to do. The doctor barked orders. The nurses checked the machines or poked at poor Pam. Her mother and sister hovered next to her, patting her hand and glaring at him.

But then the endless waiting turned to a flurry of excitement. The doctor told Joe to stand by him at the end of the bed. Joe watched as Pamela gave birth to a baby girl.

Lindsay announced her presence with a loud cry, and she kept screaming while the doctor checked her out and the nurses cleaned her up. She'd even cried when they put her in her mother's arms. The little thing only stopped when they gave her to Joe.

He gazed down at his tiny daughter, wanting to protect her and feeling helpless in knowing how to keep her safe. She stared back, not blinking even as she gave a huge yawn. Joe was torn between relief and sadness when Pamela's mother took Lindsay and held her for a moment before giving her to Pam once more.

They'd rushed Joe out of the room then, telling him to let everyone waiting know that Lindsay was here and both mother and daughter were fine. He'd been in such a daze he'd followed orders without question. Sometimes it felt like he'd been following their orders ever since.

"What do you think the Dodgers should do here?" one of the ESPN talking heads asked. *"Any way to fix this?"*

Joe didn't hear the response. Thinking about better days, he went to the kitchen for another beer. When he got back to the couch, he sat on the invitation. The crunch of paper made him lean forward to see what caused the noise.

Yeah, he didn't have a personal philosophy and didn't think he'd take part in the widow's experiment. He wasn't much of a writer. He'd do it if it would somehow win Pamela back. If it was anonymous, then he couldn't even tell her. If she was talking to him, that is. He couldn't even try to write something real smart and show it to her. Not if he followed the rules about keeping it anonymous.

Joe balled up the paper and tossed it aside. He was done following rules.

Pamela

Sunday night was the best night of the week if you asked Pam. Yes, the next day was Monday and back to work and school, or day care now that summer break was here. But for her, Sunday was still the best.

By Sunday night, all the craziness of the weekend had settled down. Laundry was done, groceries bought and put away, projects completed, and the meals for the week planned out. The kids were put to bed a little early, so she had some peace and quiet as well as an easy conscience and a calmer mind. Sunday night belonged to her.

Tonight, she decided to clean out her purse while catching up on shows. As the television droned, she set the trashcan next to the tan sofa and dumped the contents of her purse onto the coffee table.

How she ended up with so many receipts, Post-Its and other slips of paper baffled Pam. She couldn't even blame it on being a mother. Her friends had teased her about it long before Lindsay and Greta were born. Of course, in those days, the receipts had been from bars and clubs. Now they were more than likely from McDonalds or Walmart.

Pam picked through the paper, scanning the slips before throwing them out. Many of the Post-It notes were quotes or inspirational thoughts she liked. Pam had a drawer full of them, so she put the latest collection in a pile and set it aside. Someday, she'd type up all those quotes and print them in a little booklet. Maybe on some Sunday night when she truly felt inspired.

The other slips of paper were junk, so those all got tossed. The folded white letter was moved to the seat cushion while she continued the clean-out.

"How did I get so many pens?" she asked the empty room.

They'd been liberated from banks, doctor's offices, cleaners, and even from the hospital where she'd had her mammogram. A couple could go back in the purse, the rest would find a home in the big pen mug on the kitchen counter. The girls could use them for homework or artistic endeavors.

Other odds and ends she found amid the detritus on the table included hair clips, scrunchies, empty snack wrappers, a few batteries, an aux cord to some electronic device, and several lipsticks and other makeup related objects. She also had two almost empty tubes of sunblock and more change than she would have thought possible. No wonder her neck and shoulders ached all the time!

After everything had either been thrown away, dealt with, or returned to the handbag, the invitation was the only item left. It wasn't addressed to Pam, but that didn't faze her. The girls loved to make her notes, the school often handed out memos for the students to bring home, and sometimes her mother or sister Connie would slip her a card with a good saying for her collection or even money if things were really tight that month.

For a split second, she wondered if it could be from Joe. Pam dismissed the idea just as quickly. He didn't have the forethought or the creativity. Besides, even when they were married, he could barely remember to get her a present on special occasions.

Her curiosity now piqued, Pam opened the letter. As she read through the request, her interest grew. Strangely, she also felt a sense of excitement. She wasn't usually chosen for this sort of thing.

Why hadn't whoever left it just come up and asked her to take part? The letter said the essay would be anonymous, but it didn't say the selection process had to be. The longer she thought about the experiment, the more questions she came up with. But how was she going to get them answered?

Oh, the invitation mentioned an email address where you could submit your essay rather than sending it via regular mail. Would the crazy widow lady answer questions or was the email only for submitting the essays? Either way, the woman had to check her In box so Pam decided to write down all her questions and then try to get a response.

First, time to look in on her babies. Not that they were technically babies anymore—Lindsay was eight and Greta six—but to Pamela, they would always be her little ones.

Her girls were the best thing to come out of her marriage. She'd loved Joe, too, especially early on. They'd been happy once upon a time, but over the last couple of years, things had changed. They both had changed. Pam felt like she'd grown up, or at least faced reality, after Greta was born.

"Mom?" Lindsay called when she heard her mother's steps in the hall.

Pam pushed the bedroom door open and stuck her head in the room. Lindsay was sitting up in bed, her long brown hair sticking out and her brown eyes wide. Mr. Bot, the stuffed robot her father had given her for her fifth birthday, kept watch by her side. Pam's heart suffused with love and a little trepidation.

"What is it, hon?" she asked.

"Is Daddy coming home soon? I miss him."

Lindsay asked this question once or twice a week, and Pam still had no answer. Greta stopped asking after the first week, but not Lindsay. She'd been daddy's little girl.

"You'll see him next weekend," Pam said. "He's coming to your soccer game and then you'll spend the rest of the day with him."

"Okay." Lindsay's defeated tone proved she was old enough to know when she was being sidetracked. "Night, Mom."

"Night, sweetie."

Pam pulled the door almost closed and moved to the next room to check on her youngest. Greta had once again kicked the covers off and knocked her pillow to the floor. Pam could not fathom what the girl did in her sleep, but she retrieved the pillow and covered her daughter with the blanket. Greta didn't even move. Pam traced a finger along the girl's cheek and bent down to plant a kiss on the top of her head.

In her own bedroom, she paused next to the stairs to the tiny loft where they kept the computer. As eager as she was to find out more about the crazy widow lady and her experiment, Pam would rather take a shower and get some sleep. Sunday may be the best night of the week, but Monday morning was the worst in terms of getting the girls off to school and herself off to work.

Between work, school, and running the kids around to their various activities, it wasn't until Friday night that Pam had time to think about the invitation again. The girls were with their cousins—Connie's daughter Sophia played on the soccer team with Lindsay, and her son Jacob was a year older than Greta. The cousins were good friends and enjoyed playing with each other.

Pam relished the time alone yet missed her girls. One of the dichotomies of parenthood nobody tells you about.

And some of the other things, like how tough it is being a single parent, you hear but either think it's exaggerated or it's something you believe you won't have to experience yourself. She'd gone into her marriage thinking it'd last forever. Maybe she should've known better, but she honestly believed Joe would have married her even if she hadn't gotten pregnant.

They'd been comfortable until Joe lost his job. The recession hit construction hard, and Pam had to go from working part-time to full-time. She'd excelled at her job as an executive assistant and the company had asked her several times to become a full-time employee. When she agreed, they jumped at the opportunity to promote her.

Last year, she'd been promoted again to manage all the assistants in her department, and found herself amazed at how much she enjoyed the challenge. She'd started to think bigger in some ways, and she got used to being in charge and people coming to her for guidance.

Pam grew in confidence as Joe lost his. He turned to drinking and spending more time with his buddies. He could've taken a job at Home Depot or a garden center. Even if he felt it beneath him, it still would've brought money in and maybe boosted his confidence.

She needed a partner, not another child, and the morning she found him passed out on the front porch for the third time in as many months, she put her foot down and demanded a trial separation.

She missed Joe, and knew the girls missed him, too. But even if he shaped up, Pam wasn't sure she'd take him back. Right now, she wasn't even ready to see him, although he'd be at the game tomorrow.

Okay, enough. Tonight was supposed to be about her, not Joe.

While the computer booted up, Pam glanced through her questions. She'd planned to send them in one message. Would that scare or overwhelm the poor woman? Maybe best to start small and inquire if questions were even allowed.

Hello, she wrote. *I've received your invitation and am considering taking part. However, I have some questions. May I send them to you?*

Not expecting a response right away, Pam concentrated on paying the bills. Even working full time, the money didn't seem to stretch as far these days. With food, clothing, and activities for two young girls, plus the mortgage and regular expenses, there seemed to be little available at the end of the month for treats or adding to college funds.

A ding alerted her to a new message.

"Oh, wow," Pam breathed when checking the sender. With a smile, she opened the email and read the reply.

Crazy Widow Lady: *Hello back. Ask away.*

Pam scanned her list. *Is this for real?*

CrazyWidowLady: *The experiment is quite real and so am I.*

Pamlineta: *Have a lot of people responded?*

CrazyWidowLady: *I've received responses, yes. I'm so thrilled! I can't talk about them, though. This is supposed to be anonymous. Did you read the rules?*

Two can play at this game, Pam thought. She appreciated this woman who stayed true to her rules and the people who responded. If she took part, too, her essay would be in good hands.

Pamlineta: *Yes, ma'am. I read the rules.*

CrazyWidowLady: *So you know I can't say much. What other questions do you have?.*

Pam flipped through the pages with urgency. Okay, better make these count.

Pamlineta: *How long were you and your husband married?*

CrazyWidowLady: *A long time. We were together almost 50 years and married for 45. No children, many pets.*

No children? Pam couldn't imagine life without her girls. Some people got the kids and no marriage, some had a long marriage with no kids. Others had no kids and no marriage, and there were those who had some sort of combo of one or the other. In the end, you had to learn to live with what you got or you'd be a miserable person to be around.

CrazyWidowLady: *Was that it, dear?*

Pamlineta: *No, ma'am. What's your personal philosophy?*

The reply took a long time, long enough for Pam to wonder if she'd overstepped some invisible boundary. Well, no taking it back now.

Several seconds later, the widow responded.

CrazyWidowLady: *I'd like to answer that. It's only fair, since I'm asking the same of you. However, I don't want my answer to influence yours. I hope that makes sense and does not keep you from taking part.*

Pam understood the widow's reasoning even if she was disappointed in not getting the answer.

Pamlineta: *No, I see your point. Can I ask yours after I send in mine?*

CrazyWidowLady: *We'll see. I look forward to reading what you have to say. Goodnight.*

Hmmm…maybe the woman didn't know her philosophy. How ironic. Well, at least Pam had a better sense of the person at the other end of the letter. Now she needed to think about her personal philosophy so she could submit something for the crazy widow lady to read.

The next morning, Pam sweated along with the other parents as they watched their daughters running up and down the soccer field. Even with summer officially a few weeks out, the day was already warm. Lindsay waved to her mother, who nodded and headed to where the rest of the family had stationed themselves. Greta dashed over and hugged her knees.

"Oof," Pam said in surprise.

"Come on, Mom." Greta dragged her the rest of the way.

Connie grinned, her reddish-brown hair a cloud around her head. Blue eyes twinkling, she handed her sister a cup of coffee.

"You look like you need this," Connie said. "Joe's not here yet."

Pam breathed a sigh of relief, even though the respite was temporary. She sipped the coffee.

"We watched *Beauty and the Beast*," Greta announced. "Jake thought it was dumb. I liked it. Belle was pretty and smart. Like you, Mom. She liked to read, too, only she didn't have kids to read to."

"Did Aunt Connie read to you?" Pam shared a look with her sister.

Greta wrinkled her face as she thought about it. "No. Jake is too old for stories. He likes to watch movies and play games. Uncle David played with us."

Her dark brown eyes were serious and her blonde hair bounced as she declared her sentences with emphasis.

"Boys are no fun," Connie said. "Even Uncle David."

"Jake's okay," Greta announced. "Can I have a snack?"

"Get some apple slices out of the bag in the cooler," her aunt suggested.

As the little girl raced off, the sisters shared a hug. Pam leaned into Connie, needing to borrow a little of her strength. After stepping back, she spotted Joe strutting toward them.

"Here we go," she whispered.

The shouts of the coaches and parents, the chatter on the sidelines, and the sound of the wind through the trees disappeared. For Pam, watching her husband walk across the grass was like watching from the other end of the telescope.

At 6'1" and nearly 200 pounds, Joe was a big man. His short dark hair made his face seem more pronounced. Brown eyes like his daughters, broad forehead, pouty lips, all features Pam once looked on with affection and love. Now, he seemed small and far away even as he strode closer. When he called her name, the spell broke. Sound returned, and Joe no longer seemed tiny. Instead, he loomed large and close.

"Daddy!" Greta hurled herself into his arms.

"Hey, pumpkin," he said, his eyes on Pam.

Joe looked tired, Pam thought, and he'd lost weight. She couldn't smell any alcohol, which was a positive sign.

"Hello, Pammy." Joe lowered Greta to the ground.

"Hi," she squeaked.

"Greta, go see if Jake wants a snack, too," Connie ordered.

Connie stepped next to her sister as her niece darted off. Pam nodded her thanks and looked back at Joe.

"Game's about to start," she said. "Lindsay's playing goalie."

"Cool."

"You want coffee?" Connie asked. "Pam, you need more?"

"Sure," Joe said.

"Yes, please." Pam handed her the cup.

When her sister returned it, Pam stood rooted to the spot. She wanted to move, only her legs felt like two tree trunks encased in concrete. Where was that telescope feeling from a few minutes ago?

"It's good to see you again." Joe placed a hesitant hand on Pam's arm. "I miss you, babe."

The touch freed her limbs and she twitched away from him.

"Don't be like that." He pushed out his lower lip. "I do miss you. And the girls. I'll bet Lindsay's excited to be goalie again."

Pam nodded, not sure she could speak. She'd missed him, too, although she couldn't let him know that. He remembered how much his daughter loved playing keeper, and he didn't reek of alcohol. She'd take the positive where she could.

"Daddy, are you staying for the whole game?" Greta asked.

Joe hunkered down to her level. "Sure am, babe," he said. "Then you gals are spending the rest of the day with me."

"Mom, too?" Greta's eyes grew wide.

"If she wants to." Joe smiled at his girls.

Despite the naked plea in Greta's big brown eyes, and the hopeful look on Joe's face, Pam knew the trouble ahead if she gave in to either one.

"Not this time," she said, finding her voice. "It's just you and Lindsay and your dad this afternoon."

"Hey guys, the game's starting," Connie prodded. "Grab a seat if you want it."

Pam threw her a grateful look. Connie squeezed her shoulder and turned her attention to the field. Sophia liked an audience, and would sneak peeks at her parents to make sure they were watching. Lindsay was too busy defending her territory to pay attention to anything else, although she would rush to the sidelines at halftime.

Connie's husband didn't attend often, mainly because Saturday was a busy day at the store. He managed a Lowes and felt he needed to be there to support his staff and to be on hand in case of any questions or issues.

Joe did his best to be at the games, and Pam knew Lindsay appreciated it. Greta liked having her father around, so Pam was the odd woman out in that regard. Joe had been—still was—a good father even if he hadn't done so well as a husband.

"Watch the game, sis," Connie whispered. "Or cop a squat and keep an eye on the little ones."

Pam opted for the latter, figuring Joe would be more likely to leave her alone that way. She eased herself into the stadium chair and half-watched, half-listened as Jake and Greta played some game on the iPad. At their age, she would've been reading or playing Barbies with her sister.

Somehow, she must've dozed off because it was halftime sooner than expected. The kids were still on the iPad, but the temperature was definitely warmer.

"Looking good out there," Joe called to Lindsay as she jogged by. "You made some really nice saves."

"Thanks, Dad." Lindsay blushed. "Hey, Mom."

Pam waved to her, then Sophie as she loped by.

"I'm going to get a hot dog," Joe said. "Y'all want anything?"

"Can I come?" Greta begged.

"Me, too?" Jake piped up.

"Ladies?" Joe asked.

Connie nodded and Pam followed suit. The snack bar, two tables run by some of the parents, was close by and easy to see if anything happened. Not that it would, but it made the moms feel more at ease.

"How you holding up?" Connie asked when Joe and the kids were out of earshot.

Pam let out her breath. "It's hard," she said. "I'm a little surprised he's left me alone so far, though."

"I think he's too afraid of what you'll say."

"That makes two of us," Pam said.

"You're not ready to let him come back, are you?" Connie's face grew stormy.

Pam shook her head. "I'm taking the full six months."

"Good." Her sister's face relaxed.

"I do need to talk to him." Pam levered herself out of the chair. "That's much easier to get into than out of."

"The chair?" Connie asked with an arched eyebrow.

"Yes, the chair." Pam nudged her sister. "Silly girl."

When the food crew returned, Connie led the little ones off to play on the swings. Pam knew that was her cue to start the conversation with Joe.

"Hey, Joe," she called.

He turned to look at her, his mouth full of hotdog and his eyes mixed with fear and hope. She didn't know what to say next. They used to be able to have a conversation. Even after they got married and the girls were born, they'd spend half the night talking. Not only about the bills and the house and the kids, but about shows and the news and what each of them thought about what was going on in the world.

"I got a job." Joe crumbled the hot dog wrapper in his hand. "Platt-Roberts won the bid for the new housing development."

"Are you back working in the office?" Pam shaded her eyes from the sun to see his face.

"No, Gary O'Sullivan is the PM for this job," Joe said, his eyes downcast. "Bob said he'd put me on as front-end superintendent or even general superintendent next time."

"That's good."

The conversation faltered, and the former couple looked at each other, then away as they thought about what to say next. Joe wanted to tell her again how much he loved her and missed her, how much of a thrill he got standing next to her, but he'd tried before and been ignored. Pam wished she could say everything that she'd been feeling, that although she still loved him, she didn't think their future was together, but she couldn't bring herself to hurt him or to put the final nail in the coffin of their relationship.

"How's the new place?" she asked. "The girls said last time you hadn't decorated yet."

Joe shrugged. "What's the point if it's temporary?"

He went to throw out his trash. Pam watched her husband walk toward her again and tried to deal with her conflicting emotions. Whoever said there was a thin line between love and hate must not have questioned his or her relationship.

One thing Pam decided was that she'd be better off not seeing Joe for the time being. As difficult as it would be, she needed the space to think and to continue being on her own.

"How's the Corolla?" she asked when he stood beside her again.

"Good."

Connie and the kids reappeared. Greta looked at her parents, then hugged her dad around the leg. Joe placed a hand on the top of her head and gave her a loving look.

"Are you still riding horses?" he asked.

"No." She pouted. "Mom says it's getting too hot. I hope I get to do it again soon."

"You will, honey," Pam said. "Stay with your dad. I'm going to stretch my legs."

Pam gave a slight shake to her head when Connie tried to follow. Sophia would have a fit if her mother didn't appear to be watching. Besides, Pam wanted to be alone. If only it was Sunday night and she could relax and not think for a few hours.

No one warned her that "happily ever after" sometimes comes with an expiration date. She'd stood in front of the pastor and promised to be with her husband for better or worse. No one told her how amazing the better could be, nor did anyone inform her that worse could mean the nasty accusations hurled at her by a drunk or losing the love of her life to something beyond her control.

No one in her family was a big drinker. Although she'd experimented with alcohol and weed in school, Pam didn't enjoy the feeling of being drunk or high. Joe would have the occasional beer or two at parties and sporting events, but nothing had prepared her for what would happen when he was no longer the bread winner.

Cheers drew her attention back to the field. Based on the high fives, Lindsay's team must have scored a goal. That would put the girls in a good mood.

Needing to take her mind off Joe, Pam kept walking until she reached the parking lot. Seeing her old green Toyota, she was tempted to use it to drive far away from this mess. Instead, she banged her fist against the hood a couple times and trudged back to join her family in watching the soccer match. For the remainder of the second half, she made small talk and played with Greta and Jake while doing her best to empty her mind.

"Daddy, did you see my last save?" Lindsay shouted as the teams jogged off the field after the final whistle.

"I did indeed." Joe swept his daughter up in a hug. "You get better every time."

"Mom, did you see?"

Pam grinned. "You did great, hon."

"I'll see you later, Linds," her cousin Sophie said. "We've got to take Jake the Flake to karate class."

"I'm not a flake." Jake smacked his sister on the arm.

"Stop it," Connie warned. She waved to the others and told Pam she'd check in later.

Alone with Joe and the girls, Pam fought off the memories of better times. Making sure Lindsay and Greta had all their stuff proved a worthwhile distraction.

"What time should I have them back?" Joe swung an athletic bag over his shoulder.

"Back?' Lindsay wailed. "We're not staying over?"

Joe appealed to Pam with a raised eyebrow, but she shook her head.

"Sorry, sweetie, maybe next time."

"That's what you say every time. Why can't Daddy come home?"

Pam sighed. She was not fighting this battle today. "Have them home by eight," she told Joe. "Make sure they eat something healthy for dinner."

"Like pizza?" Greta piped up.

"Only if you have salad and broccoli, too."

Greta considered this. "Can we put broccoli on the pizza?"

"Up to your dad." Pam bent down to hug her youngest. "You be good. You too, Lindsay."

"Yes, ma'am." The girl hugged her mother.

With a final wave, Joe led the girls away. Pam watched them go, her heart a little sore at seeing their father hold Greta's hand while he placed an arm around Lindsay's shoulders. The three of them made a nice picture.

After a few minutes, Pam followed in their footsteps and drove her minivan to Publix, then home. She put the groceries away and started a load of laundry. In looking at the fine layer of dust on the entertainment center, she decided to give the house a good cleaning while the girls were away.

Cleaning would keep her mind on something other than Joe and the girls. The exercise might also wear her down enough to sleep tonight, and she could use the time to think about her assignment.

As many slips of paper and Post-It notes as she'd gathered and stored over the years, Pam felt she should know her personal philosophy. But then again, maybe by reading so many motivational phrases and sayings, she'd absorbed the knowledge from all of them rather than just one.

The smell of citrus filled the house as she sprayed, scrubbed, and vacuumed. Her mother believed that a clean house meant a free mind. Pam would have to disagree with her on that one, although not to her face.

Pam loved a clean house, but with two growing girls that ideal proved too difficult to maintain. Her house wasn't dirty—she kept it as tidy as possible. You'd still find dust and toys and books lying around, and Pam was okay with that. Life was more important than housekeeping.

Was that her personal philosophy? No, just something she believed. She believed many different things, including kindness and doing what she thought was right and that her children came first, but those were not her mantra. Her personal philosophy was an overarching belief about herself and the world, and she was completely clueless as to what that might be.

No, that wasn't quite true, she argued with herself while transferring clothes from the washer to the dryer. She had an entire library of quotes and just needed to see which ones resonated enough to consider them as her core belief.

She scanned through some of the slips of paper.

In order to succeed, we must first believe that we can. Nikos Kanaztzakis

You are never too old to set another goal or to dream a new dream. CS Lewis

Life is really simple, but we insist on making it complicated. Confucius

Start by doing what's necessary; then do what's possible; and suddenly you're doing the impossible. Francis of Assisi

Okay, this wasn't getting her anywhere. While nice quotes to hang on a wall, they weren't what Pam considered a philosophy. A philosophy went deeper than "be good to yourself" or "don't ever give up". She wished the crazy widow lady would share her belief or at least provide examples on the invitation.

Then again, people would just choose one of the examples for their essay. People were forever taking the easy way out, a habit she tried to keep her daughters from developing. They needed to make their own way in this world, with all the positives and negatives that went along with it.

Was "you need to make your own way in this world" her personal philosophy? Perhaps, so Pam jotted that one down and put it in a special pile before returning to the other notes.

The secret of change is to focus all your energy not on fighting the old, but on building the new. Socrates

Women are like teabags. We don't know our true strength until we are in hot water. Eleanor Roosevelt

One's philosophy is not best expressed in words; it is expressed in the choices one makes…and the choices we make are ultimately our responsibility. Eleanor Roosevelt

The last quote brought goosebumps. Even someone like Eleanor Roosevelt once thought about her personal philosophy. The concept might be new to Pam, but it was not new to history and the world at large.

On a whim, Pam shoved the notes back in the drawer and went upstairs to the computer. She entered "personal philosophy" in the search engine and gasped at all the entries. Quotes from Aristotle, Confucius, Steve Jobs, Albert Einstein, and so many others popped up. No wonder she couldn't settle on her own motto—there were too many choices.

"These are from other people," Pam muttered. "I need my own."

She thought about the Eleanor Roosevelt quote while folding towels. Pam's actions expressed her belief better than words. She believed that and tried to teach her daughters through both her words and her deeds. She remembered all the lessons her mother taught her growing up, and Pam felt like she continued to learn every day. Not just from her mother, but also her sister, co-workers, and even the girls.

Pam used all sorts of opportunities to broaden her knowledge. She listened to NPR while alone in the car, went to seminars and conferences at work when she had the chance, and she and the girls watched PBS more than mindless television shows. They watched some of those, too—you needed dessert along with the meal. On their trips to the library, she encouraged them to read biographies as well as fiction. She wanted them to enjoy learning the way she did so it would become a habit for them for the rest of their lives.

Never stop learning.

There it was. Her personal philosophy. A belief that she embodied through actions, lived every day, and yet never even knew was there until someone asked. How awesome was that?

When Joe brought the girls home, Pam sent them upstairs to get ready for bed and stepped out onto the porch with her husband. He looked at her, eyes wide and body stiff, as if readying himself for a blow.

"What did you learn today?" she asked.

"I...ummm..." he stammered. "What do you mean?"

Pam chided herself for lobbing the question out there. "Sorry, I was watching a documentary about the Roosevelts and I found out all these things I didn't know. So I wondered what you might have learned today."

Joe's face crinkled in confusion. "That I miss you?"

Okay, so we were back on this carousel. Pam thanked him for bringing the girls home on time and headed inside to check on them. Greta was in the bathroom brushing her teeth, and Lindsay was getting into her nightgown.

"What did you learn today?" Pam asked her.

"That you won't let us spend the night with Dad," Lindsay replied.

Pam cleared her throat.

"That broccoli on pizza tastes pretty good."

"Better," Pam said. "Did you wash your face and brush your teeth?"

Lindsay nodded.

"Me, too!" Greta cried as she came into the room.

"Good job. Lindsay, you can read for a little while if you want," Pam said. "Or come watch TV with me and help fold the laundry."

"What about me?" Greta climbed onto the bed.

"Hey, you have your own room," Lindsay cried.

"Come on, Greta." Pam held out her hand. "I'll read to you."

"Okay!" Greta jumped off the bed and, grabbing her mom's hand, towed her from one bedroom to the other. "Can we read *The One Hundred and One Dalmatians?*"

"I don't see why not." The book had been one of Pam's favorites as a child as well. "First, tell me something you learned today."

Greta scrunched up her face. "Jake said Hannah gets to do horseback riding this session. She better not get to ride Cinnamon!"

"You'll ride again in the fall," Pam promised. "Let's read. Do you remember where we left off?"

"Pongo and Missus ran away to get the puppies."

Pam found her place and continued the story until Greta's eyes grew heavy. She covered her daughter with the blanket, gave her a light kiss, and slipped out the door. Lindsay's light was on, but Pam decided not to peek in and possibly start any new battles. Instead, she went downstairs to finish folding the laundry.

She resolved to ask each of her daughters every day, and to have them ask her, what they learned that day. Today, Pam learned she had a personal philosophy. And Sunday night, her favorite night, she planned to write an entire essay on the topic.

Pam's Essay

Before I received the invitation to participate in this experiment, I didn't give my personal philosophy much thought. I'd been collecting inspirational quotes for several years because I liked reading them. I also found looking at them again helped my mood and my outlook when things got tough. I didn't consider any of them to be my motto, and in the end I did not find my personal philosophy in the pile of notes. Instead, I found it within myself. That makes sense, I guess, since my personal philosophy is never stop learning.

I'm writing this essay on a Sunday night after my girls have gone to bed. Sunday night is me time, and I'm thrilled to spend this one typing up my essay. I hope to instill a love of learning in my girls, and I've actually already started.

Well, I guess I've been teaching them to love learning from day one. I read to both of them while they were in the womb, when they were babies, and I still read to them even though now both of them are well able to read on their own. I've read biographies, fiction, money guides, newspapers, and poems to them over the years, and I hope this has given them a nice diversity and understanding of the options available to them in terms of how to get information and what to read.

Last night, I decided to start asking each of them every day what they learned today and I want them to ask me the same thing. That should spark some interesting dinner conversations as they get older! I'm also hoping it gets them thinking now so they start planning what they want to say every night.

The thing they learn every day does not have to be some grand knowledge of life or the universe. Last night, my oldest said she learned that broccoli on pizza tastes good. I liked that, because it meant not only did she find out something about food, but she was willing to take a chance and was happy with the result. Maybe this spirit will allow her to go outside her comfort zone another time and learn something else about food or about herself.

Learning is everywhere if we open our minds to the opportunities. And I think it goes beyond books and school. There's only so much you can learn sitting at a desk listening to a teacher drone on. There's also only so much you can learn from a book. Reading a cookbook is fun, but I don't consider it learning until you start making the recipes.

Even if you fail, at least you tried. How many times did Edison fail before inventing the light bulb? How many times did Elizabeth Blackwell hear "no" before becoming the first female doctor?

I've read so many stories about people who never went to college or even who dropped out of high school and ended up being successful. I only went to college a few years before becoming pregnant, dropping out and getting married. But even though I was no longer in school, I continued to learn. I read books, attended classes, took advantage of free seminars at work or the local library. The opportunities to learn are everywhere, people just need to see them. And be willing to take advantage of them.

I can't imagine what it's like not to want to learn. We should learn something new every day, even if it's as simple as broccoli tasting good on pizza.

My girls are smart and funny and curious about the world and I can only begin to imagine what other facts they'll bring home over the years. I'd like to think they got these traits from me, so I look forward to the facts that I'll share with them over the years, too.

I don't expect my own dinner table experiment to mean that my girls will become doctors or teachers or anything like that. I just want them to develop a true love of learning because I think having this ability helps to make your world better and helps you to deal with the adversity the world is going to throw at you. I would never have learned that I can install a new faucet if the one in our kitchen hadn't broken. We couldn't afford to pay a plumber so I gave it a shot and, amazingly enough, was able to fix it. Knowing I can do something like that is an amazing confidence booster, and that confidence is also what I want to pass along to my girls.

As you probably guess from the questions, I emailed to you the other day, I'm a curious person. Curiosity is key to learning, and I'm guessing that you're curious as well or you wouldn't have started this experiment.

Myra

O
h, lordy. The email was from someone who'd received an invitation. Her online name was Pamlineta, and she wanted to know if she could ask some questions. I'd set up an email account to accept essays, not answer questions.

Now, now, another side of me said, the whole reason behind the experiment is to find out more about people. With that reasoning, I should be glad that someone wanted to pose questions. After all, hadn't I kicked this off by asking about their personal philosophy?

With a fair amount of trepidation, I replied in the affirmative, and waited for the next blast of trumpets, which came quickly.

Is this for real? Pamlineta asked. I suppressed a chuckle. With one essay received and another person asking questions, it was actually getting to be almost a little too real. And who knew it would be so scary and thrilling and life-affirming all at the same time?

Once again, I told her yes and the response zinged back.

"She must be young," I muttered to Grace, who'd taken up residence by my feet. "Smart, too, and cautious, asking questions before sending in an essay."

For that reason alone, I liked this woman. If it was a woman. Pamlineta certainly sounded like a female name.

Now she wanted to know if I'd received many responses. What would she think if I shared that I'd only gotten one back? I didn't want to lie, but I felt the truth might frighten her and I found myself really wanting to read her essay. So, I fudged a little and tried to redirect focus by asking if she'd read the rules.

That did the trick, but then she asked how long Lee and I had been married. *We're still together, hon. Death doesn't end the marriage, it merely separates you from the one you love.* I couldn't send that response, even if it captured my feelings. No, best to keep it simple.

When I didn't get a response right away, I worried that even my generic answer gave something away. Well, there was no rule that said I couldn't reach out, so I sent a new message asking if those were all her questions. When she came back asking about my personal philosophy, my heart skipped a beat.

While it was a fair question, I wasn't ready to disclose it. Mainly because I didn't know my personal philosophy. For Pamlineta, I told her I didn't want my response to influence hers and was not surprised when she pushed back.

If she sent in an essay and remembered to ask after submitting hers, then I would answer her question. That bought me some time to think of my personal philosophy...in case someone else asked the same question.

I said good night and goodbye to Pamlineta and shut off the computer before someone else sent me a message.

"Come on, Gracie Grits," I said to the dog. "Time for bed."

She yawned, then stood and stretched before following me to the master bedroom. As I got ready for bed, my thoughts remained on the conversation with Pamlineta. Had I said the right things? Should I have responded at all?

"Of course you should have responded," June said. "You might even get more people emailing with the same type of questions."

That thought caused me to stop in my tracks. I'd invited June over after dinner for a nice, long walk around the neighborhood. After a day of cleaning out the garage, or starting to, I needed to get away from the house.

"Face it, Myra, you're going viral." June grinned.

Grace whined and tugged on her leash, so we continued our walk. "I don't want to go viral." I shook my head. "You can't be both viral and anonymous, can you?"

"Hmmm." June pushed out her lips. "Probably not. But it's too late now."

"What do you mean?"

"You've handed out the essay to several people, and you're letting your friends hand them out. Plus the people who write the essays are supposed to slip them to people, too."

"Oh, my."

What in the world had I started? Sometimes the feeling terrified me, and other times, like now, it thrilled me. Would Lee be proud of what I'd managed to do?

"Then again," June said. "You've only received one essay. The experiment might end up being a dud."

Nothing like a best friend to bring you down to Earth.

"I think you'll get more, but you never know." She paused to stretch her right calf muscle. "On a different note, did you find any more treasures today?"

"More like junk."

She chuckled. "Are you sure? You thought the sports crap was junk, too, until Roy looked over it."

"True."

At least the sports stuff had other people who might be interested since the player or the team generally had more than one fan. The garage stuff was the accumulation of life, of marriage, of items where the only other person who might derive the same pleasure from them was no longer around.

Programs from plays, ticket stubs from the days when paper tickets were still common, old photos of cars and people and pets and various trips, knickknacks that weren't good enough to display yet were too special to get rid of. In short, all sorts of souvenirs that once held value and then faded away as new souvenirs took their place.

I took a deep breath, exhaled through my nose, and gazed out at the neighborhood as we ambled along. Like me, the subdivision had been young once. Also like me, most of the houses still held up despite their age.

The Murphys painted their house every five years, changing the color each time. They chose yellow last round, which gave the place a Caribbean look. The Robeys next door asked the HOA to paint their red brick white, but were voted down. Painting siding was allowed, but not brick, since according to the board, painting the brick changed the integrity of the house. Instead, Charles and Mary planted white flowers along the cement steps beside their driveway and next to their front stoop.

So many of the other original families sold off their homes to younger families, or to fund the transition to senior or assisted living. Lee made me promise not to follow that path, and we made sure through life insurance and retirement funds that I wouldn't have to. My own retirement fund and the strength of our investment portfolio also saw to it that I could remain in the old homestead.

"You're all of a sudden quiet." June nudged me with her elbow.

"Just thinking," I said.

"About how you're going to spend the money Roy's getting from Tony's?"

"I don't have it yet. Roy's coming by in the morning to pick everything up. And Salvation Army's due later this week. Gonna be weird having all that space."

"What are you going to do with it?" June asked. "Ten thousand's nothing to sneeze at."

"I suppose not." I watched Grace sniff at the base of a mailbox and wondered what coded messages she could read there. "Might give it to the shelter."

June stopped and grabbed my upper arm. Her dark brown eyes grew wide and her mouth dropped open. Good thing she couldn't see herself or she might've gotten even more upset at how crazy she looked.

"Myra, you…you can't," she stuttered. "What the hell's a shelter going to do with all the money?"

"Make sure dogs like Gracie here go to good homes, or to take care of them when they don't," I said as if it were obvious. "Cats, too. Maybe even rabbits."

She made a rude noise and flung her hands in the air. "People could use that money, too, you know."

Maybe I shouldn't have shared my plans with her. June never had been an animal person, nor was she one to give money away. Then again, she and Henry weren't shy about spending, on themselves or their girls, either.

"Lee may have provided for you, but that money won't last forever," she pointed out. "You may need the funds someday."

"I'll be fine," I assured her. Besides, I finished silently, ten thousand doesn't really go that far these days. "I'm not worried about me."

"Well, I am."

"Well, stop," I said, and let Grace pull us forward so we continued walking. "I'm going to be just fine. I've got all these essays to read and share now, don't I?"

"You'd be better off giving one of those people the money," she muttered.

I chuckled. "So along with slipping them the letter, I should slip in a cool Ben Franklin to convince them to send in an essay?"

June relented and laughed a little, too. That's when I knew that although I may not have won, the subject would be dropped for the time being.

When we finished our circuit, we shared a hug, then she drove home while Grace and I went into the house. I gave her a treat and decided I deserved one, too, so I made some tea and cut a piece of pound cake.

"Should we read or watch TV?" I asked the dog. She yawned and drank some of her water. "Up to me, I see."

I tried the TV, but even with however many channels I received, none of them were playing anything of interest. I perused the bookshelf, but nothing there jumped out at me, either. What should I do now? The garage beckoned, as did all the papers to pore through in the study. Time enough for all that tomorrow. I'd done enough of living in the past for one day.

"When does it get easier, Lee?" I asked aloud.

And how long after someone was gone was it no longer weird to talk to them? In my case, I hoped the answer was never. Like I told Pamlineta the other night, I still considered myself a married woman. Call me a widow. Give it whatever fancy name you wanted. I was and always would be Mrs. Liam (Lee) O'Malley, and not even death could strip me of that title.

Needing to switch my thoughts and my mood, I turned the TV back on and asked the remote to find me a romantic comedy.

"You sure you don't want any of this?" Roy asked as he loaded the first box into his black Ford Explorer. "None of us'll mind."

"Thank you, but I'm good." I gave him a brave smile. "I have plenty to remember Lee by. Better someone else get some use out of these things, someone who can appreciate them."

Roy ducked his blond head and went back inside for the next box. I remained outside, breathing in the early summer air and enjoying the warm sun on my face. Grace whined and head-butted my leg, so I gave her a few pats.

"Mabel said to tell you she'll call you tonight." Roy added the next box to the backseat. "She's worried you'll be sad."

"I'll be fine."

Roy nodded. "Still miss talking to him myself," he said. "Lee was a good friend. No one could talk baseball quite like him. He remembered details from games decades ago that I don't even think the players could recall. Watching sports ain't the same without him."

"Appreciate hearing that, Roy." I sniffed and directed my attention on Grace. "I know he enjoyed going to games with you, too."

"Best go get the rest of the boxes." Roy turned his craggy face from mine and shuffled back into the house where I wouldn't see him tear up.

It was good to know that other people missed Lee, to be reminded that even though it might feel like it, I was not alone in my grief. Lee had been loved by many, and I'd tell him that this afternoon when I went to visit his grave.

"Do you want some help?" I asked Roy before his next trip.

He shook his head. "No need for you to hurt yourself lifting these heavy boxes. Besides, I've only got the one left."

After that last box was loaded, I hugged Roy tight before sending him on his way. He just nodded again and climbed into the SUV. He gave a little wave and backed out of the driveway. Grace and I watched him go. I really did hope whoever was next to receive Lee's treasures found the same joy in them that my husband had.

I should've stayed outside enjoying the sunshine, but I felt the need to check out the downstairs study now that some of the items were gone. I could see more of the worn brown carpet, and it made me rethink that particular choice.

"Guess I could redecorate, huh, Gracie Grits?" I asked.

The tears came quickly, and I sank to the floor with my back against the wall. Why did grief have to come in waves? Wouldn't it be better to get it all over with at once?

No, I answered myself. If I had to deal with the pain of losing Lee all at once, the sorrow might well have killed me, too. The waves were getting smaller. I needed to take comfort in that fact. Pain was good. Healthy. And helped make moving forward a blessing. I could allow myself to love Lee, miss Lee, and still manage to live my life without him by my side.

The holes in the room matched the ones inside my soul, although the spaces in the house would only grow as I gave away more and more of Lee's things. The space in my heart would, however, remain the same size as my love for my husband.

"And that," I told the dog even though she couldn't hear my thoughts, "is why I'm the thinkingest woman he's ever known."

Grace followed me up the steps and I rewarded her with food. I snacked on red grapes and cheddar cheese while planning the rest of the day. The hours tended to stretch out for me, even with the prospect of new essays. Those I had to wait for, and I could only handle so much of deciding what to keep and what to give away of Lee's books, clothing, and other items. Guess what I needed was yet another hobby.

My thoughts drifted back to my conversation with June the day before, when I'd foolishly told her my plans to donate the money from the sports memorabilia to the shelter. I still planned to do that, but maybe I could also donate my time.

As much as I wanted to pick up the phone and call them, I knew the more prudent course of action would be to research them online. Then I'd at least know what services they needed assistance with and which ones I could reasonably offer to help with.

I pulled up the animal shelter's website and read through their volunteer page. I met the main criteria of being over 18 and loving animals, although I had no marketing experience and could not be expected to assist with their social media efforts. I was happy just getting my computer to work.

Medicine crew I could do, even cleaning crew. No fostering, though, at least not yet. Grace and I were still getting to know each other. No need to bring another animal into the mix at the moment.

Working with the Shy Crew. I could handle that. And it must be so joyful to see a terrified dog or cat become an outgoing, loving creature.

"Hmmm….volunteer orientation is twice a month," I read aloud. "Oh, look, the next one is this Monday."

That knowledge inspired me to pick up the phone and leave a message. I also sent them an email with my contact info and potential areas of interest. That ought to be enough to get me started. I considered checking out their Facebook page, but didn't want to have to dig up my password.

No, it was time to get out of the house and go visit Lee.

Even though the entrance to the cemetery was right off a main road, the grounds were peaceful and well-cared for. You could almost pretend you were strolling around a pretty park. If you ignored the intermittent headstones and the solemn people you encountered.

Lee's family had been residents of the area for more than a century, which garnered him (and me, one day) a place near the back of the acreage. A gorgeous old southern oak guarded the O'Malley corner, and the groundskeeper had planted a row of tiny pink flowers along the edge of the walkway.

"You'd hate it," I told Lee.

He'd wanted to be cremated, and I'd honored that request, as well as the request of his mother to make sure he was buried in the family plot. As a woman, I found myself charged with keeping the peace even after the parties in question were long gone.

"But I like it because I get to talk to you and Mama Kate won't haunt me. Guess that's what happens when you're the last one standing."

The branches of the oak tree swayed in the breeze, which I suppose was the only answer I was going to get. Although I would've welcomed the visitation, there'd been no flickering of lights or TVs going on and off in the house after Lee passed, only endless silence. At least until I'd brought Gracie home.

"Oh, but I miss you, Lee." I knelt next to the ground. "Life's getting easier, I suppose, or maybe I'm focusing on living more these days. You know the girls see to that."

I found myself telling him about the experiment almost as if he could impart his wisdom on the undertaking. He loved chatting with people, even knew the name of every employee at our local Ingles, and most of those at Walmart and Belk, when I could drag him along to go shopping with me.

Lee wasn't much of a reader, but he would've gotten a kick out of the essays. If he'd still been alive, we probably would've extended the team to all the husbands. Then again, if he were here, I wouldn't have started the experiment.

"Funny thing, life, huh, Lee?" I asked.

The wind continued to cause the leaves and branches to sway, and part of me fancied that this show was Lee's way of agreeing with me, or at least letting me feel his presence.

"We never did get to say goodbye, did we?"

All the weeks. Days. Hours I'd spent by his side as he slowly faded away. I stayed with him through the pain, wiping his fevered brow with the cool green washcloth I'd brought from home. I stayed with him through the long nights, my butt in the hard plastic chair and my head gently laying on his once-strong chest.

He'd run out of water that day and asked me to fill the pitcher. No, he couldn't wait for the nurse. So I'd gone, just a quick trip down the hall to the little kitchen where I'd refilled the ugly brown pitcher.

When I returned, he was gone.

Lee knew what he was doing. He always did. And I knew he wanted to spare me the pain of watching him go.

I couldn't yell at him. Not only because he'd passed beyond hearing me, but because of the look of utter peace on his beautiful face. I'd almost grown used to the twisted face of pain. Oh, but I could forgive him leaving on his own with that gift of seeing him at peace.

The tears slid down my cheeks, and I did not wipe them away. Instead, I bowed my head and let them flow freely.

"We may not have said goodbye, but you bet your ass we're going to say hello again someday. You're not done with me yet, you crazy old coot."

My purse buzzed, and after a few seconds I realized my mobile phone was ringing. I dug it out and said hello as I pushed myself to standing.

"Is this Myra O'Malley?" A man asked.

I answered in the affirmative.

"Excellent. I'm Steve with the local animal shelter. Are you still interested in volunteering?'

Carol

That familiar feeling of being overwhelmed washed over Carol as soon as she stepped into her home office. The room consisted of a desk, chair, reading chair, bookshelf, and filing cabinet. At the moment, only the sliding desk chair and some of the beige Berber carpet could be seen. The rest of the furniture and floor was covered in paper, architectural rolls, and sample books.

"So much for saving trees," she muttered as she ventured into the mess. "Why did I agree to this?"

Five years ago, after turning 40, Carol and her best friend Marla decided to quit their day jobs and open a pottery painting place. Ceramics, wooden letters, wine glasses as well as other items could be decorated. Or groups could opt for instructor-led painting. Both women loved art and teaching, and their previous careers as executive assistants gave them some insight into business. Not as much as they needed, but they learned along the way.

Kiln Me Now opened in the Perimeter Square shopping center just over four years ago. The business was thriving so they decided to open a second store, *Kiln Me Again*, in the new Elysium shopping center in trendy Alpharetta.

Since Carol lived only a few miles away, it made sense for her to manage the new store. They'd been planning for months, and still had longer to go before the proposed grand opening in early September. Carol should've been more excited. Instead, she felt a sense of dread.

Why she felt this way, she couldn't say. After all, this wasn't like before. When they'd opened *Kiln Me Now*, Carol and Marla had no idea if the store would be a success. They'd taken the shot, followed the dream, and made a real go of it.

Kiln Me Again, on the other hand, was almost guaranteed to succeed. Customers had been asking for an Alpharetta branch and were super-excited for the place to open. They already had bookings for the first several weeks, right through Halloween and into the holiday season.

That should make her happy. Instead, it made Carol nervous. Maybe it was all the planning and other items left to do that made her uneasy.

"You okay, babe?" Her husband Jim placed a hand on her shoulder. "You've been standing there for five minutes. You going in or not?"

She twisted toward him and snaked her arms around his back, burying her face in his chest. He hugged her back and kissed the top of her head as she did her best not to dissolve into tears.

"What in the world?" he whispered.

"I'm sorry." She let go and dabbed at her eyes.

"For what?" His brow wrinkled in concern. "Talk to me."

"It's the new location," she said. "I...I don't know."

Jim ran a hand over his short dark hair. His brown eyes were soft above his dark blue polo. He looked so solid and there and safe. Carol could see the confusion and worry on his scraggly face, which made her want to hug him again.

"I thought you were excited," he said. "Has something changed?"

Carol shook her head, afraid to speak. How could she explain all her anxiety and fear about the coming expansion? Yes, she should be thrilled at the chance to grow her business. She had been at the start. Now that the construction phase was almost complete, and the inside of the store was beginning to come together, reality had set in.

"I don't think I can do this." She wiped at her eyes again.

"How is it different than the other store?" He guided her to the desk chair and, after removing stacks of paper, sat in the reading chair. "Aren't you doing the same thing?"

"Yes and no," she said.

Jim settled into the chair, knowing that with his wife the "yes and no" or "it depends" response was usually followed by a detailed explanation of why she could not put her answer in a specific category. He had also learned, despite his nature, that he should listen, ask questions if clarification was needed, but not offer any suggestions on how to fix the situation unless specifically requested to do so.

"Okay," Jim said. "Hit me."

"I'm worried." Carol swiveled in the chair.

"Figured out that much on my own." He smiled. "As your accountant, I can tell you that I think you'll do great."

While Carol appreciated his support, she wasn't ready to articulate her thoughts. Talking them out with Jim usually proved helpful, sometimes even more than discussing them with Marla, only now Carol wasn't sure how to begin.

"Why don't you go on to bed," she suggested.

"So you don't need me?" He cocked his head. "You're scaring me a bit."

She pulled him from the chair. "I'll be fine. Would you make sure Jordan finished his homework? He has a math test tomorrow."

"O-kaaay." Jim scratched at his chin.

"I'll be fine," she promised. She started to push him from the room.

"Are you calling Marla?" He stopped in the doorway. "Because I don't mind lending an ear."

"I know, and I love you for it." She gave him a peck on the cheek. "I'm a bundle of nerves at the moment. I'm going to make a cup of tea and then just sit here and go over things."

Jim gave her a searching look. She knew where to find him if she changed her mind. He turned and headed down the hallway to check on their fifteen-year-old son. From there, he'd read and wait for his wife to come to bed, hopefully in a calmer state of mind.

Carol brewed her tea and returned to her home office. She took the mound of papers her husband had moved and placed them on the black reading chair. If she managed to straighten in here, she thought, she'd probably never find anything again. The rest of her home might be spic and span, but her working space was always a disaster. The downside of being an artist, she supposed, although she and Marla did try to keep the store in some semblance of order. Luckily, a little mess with an art studio was to be expected.

Of course, patrons also expected to be taken care of, and the staff did their best to make sure everyone had fun. Some groups were better than others. Although each class was unique in its own way, after a few years in business, Carol could recognize and deal with certain personality types.

By far, her favorites were the Meetup groups. Although the promised numbers might not show up every time, at least everyone wanted to be there. These classes could also be the toughest in making everyone feel comfortable, since sometimes people were meeting each other for the first time. Given the opportunity to relax and chat before starting the class helped, and the folks who attended a Meetup session generally loved the end result.

Even though most Meetup organizers opted for decorating pottery or wine glasses, the ones who did the painting on canvas were the most serious. A couple of times, Carol and Marla had heard complaints about the paintings being too easy. The point was to have fun, not to become the next Picasso.

The corporate outings were the most competitive. Participants spent far more time comparing their work to their neighbors. She made sure to repeat the instructions and provide more hands-on guidance for those sessions.

Carol also had to cajole and tease some people more during corporate events, since not all of those the folks wanted to be there. She'd disliked the whole team building experience back in her executive assistant days, although God knows she'd both planned and attended enough of them. Besides, she felt art was more fun than bowling or cooking or yet another happy hour.

Whether they did the same picture on canvas, a special piece of pottery, or wine glasses, at least each member of the team had a unique souvenir at the end of the night along with good stories to share with friends, family, and co-workers.

Given all the offices in the Perimeter area, *Kiln Me Now* held corporate events several times per month. Alpharetta should be more of the same. Carol would have to check on the Meetup groups, but Alpharetta tended to be a fairly social area. The restaurants were always packed on weekends, especially the ones featuring live music.

Carol would take company team building and social groups any day over the bridal showers Marla loved to host.

"Hey, it's getting late," Jim said from the doorway. "I thought you were coming to bed."

"One sec," she said.

"One," Jim counted. "Okay, let's go."

He opened his eyes wide and nodded convulsively. God, she loved this man and all of his crazy ways.

"Yes, sir." Carol stood and followed him out to the hall.

Jim grabbed her, tossed her over his shoulder, and made tracks to their bedroom, where he dumped her on the bed.

"Now that's where you belong." He waggled his eyebrows and twirled an imaginary mustache. "And if you don't stay, I'll tie you to the bedpost."

"We don't have a bedpost."

"Hmm....then I'll just have to get creative." He leaned down and gave her a big, sloppy kiss.

She giggled. "Please, sir, can I have some more?"

"Get ready for bed and put on that pink and black number and I'll think about it," he growled.

"You've been that good a boy?" She laced her arms around his neck.

He nodded, his brown eyes big and serious, but his lips twitching as he held back a grin.

"I'll think about it."

"Think hard," he mouthed.

"You do the same." She kissed him, then slid from the bed.

"Already on it," he called while she sashayed to the master bath.

She gave him a little wave, then shut the door. Did she even still have the pink and black negligee?

Carol woke refreshed and relaxed. She had a sneaky suspicion that had been her husband's goal, but she didn't care. The sex had been that good. She only wished he could've stayed to have breakfast with her. He got Jordan up and out the door on time, which was about as much of a stress reliever as the night of love-making.

If only she could relax a little longer, but duty called. She needed to take a shower and meet Marla at the store.

When she stepped downstairs, Carla found a Post-It note from Jim on the fridge. *Have a great day! Love you!!* He could've sent a text, but the little note meant more. What had gotten her so worked up last night anyway?

Five minutes into the meeting with Marla, Carol remembered.

"We need to decide if we offer everything at once or stagger the topics. How many classes per week can you handle? What's already on the books? Should we hire extra staff or wait and see if we'll need them?" As Marla fired off the questions, she paced the tiny office. "When's the last time you talked to the builder? Should we…"

Carol let the questions drift over her head like smoke. Her partner, a petite woman in height and weight, made up for her lack of stature with fierce energy. Even in their corporate days, Marla had been the one to get things done and to make the work as much fun as possible. She was the instigator, the idea generator, and Carol the steady plodder who turned the dreams into reality.

Kiln Me Now had been one of Marla's brainstorms, and Carol had somehow found a way to turn it into a brick and mortar reality. She'd forgotten how much stress was involved in the planning and overseeing of details that tended to overwhelm them both.

"Are you even listening?" Marla's auburn curls bounced in irritation. "Do you know how much we have to do? Whose idea was it to open a second store? What were we thinking?"

"Yes. Yes. You. And I don't know," Carol said from her safe spot perched on her desk. "I meet with Bruce this afternoon, and it's all going to work out."

Marla paused. "How can you be so sure?"

"I can't," Carol admitted. "I'm more nervous and scared than you are. *Kiln Me Again* is on my shoulders."

"No." Marla shook her head. "We're partners. Oh, Carol, what were we thinking? And why did you listen to me?"

"Because you're right," Carol said, realizing as she said it that the comment was true. "Our business manager, your dear husband, approved the idea and our accountant, my darling hubby, also gave it the green light. And our customers are ecstatic and ready to start bringing us business. So you and I might be scared shitless, but everyone else believes in us."

Marla leaned onto her desk and put her head in her hands. Carol decided her next career would definitely not be as a motivational speaker. She considered giving her partner a hug, but changed her mind and waited for Marla to make the next move.

"Let's concentrate on the current store for now," her partner said after a minute. "We need to come up with our event schedule for the next few months and try to plan staffing, too."

"Works for me." Carol jumped down from her desk and went behind it to sit properly in the chair. "Let's get to it."

The two women worked for the next few hours, feeling quite productive once they finished. They'd decided to take a break for lunch and were getting ready to head out when Carol's phone buzzed. She considered ignoring it, but changed her mind when their builder's name flashed on the screen.

"You need to get over here now," Bruce barked.

"Okay, but what—"

"Just get over here."

He hung up, leaving Carol to stare at her phone in confusion. The contractor was generally a calm man, patient and easy to get along with. What in the world could have caused him to be so abrupt?

"Who was that?" Marla asked.

"Bruce," Carol said. "He ordered me to meet him at the new store. Like right now."

"Did he say why?"

Carol shook her head. "No. Just to come now."

"Odd."

"I know, and he's got me all worried again. Bruce doesn't strike me as the type to panic, but he sounded kind of gruff."

Marla handed Carol her keys. "Should I go, too?"

"Too much to do here. I'll call you as soon as I find out what's going on."

"I hope it's not serious."

"Agreed."

Carol grabbed her purse and dashed out the door. The drive only took twenty minutes. Plenty of time for several terrible scenarios to run through her mind, each worse than the one before. She and Marla had worked too hard and had too much riding on this store for something to go wrong now.

The parking lot at the Elysium Center was more crowded than she'd expected. She parked as close as she could and hurried to the store. Bruce met her at the entrance. The moment she spotted him, her anxiety intensified.

Normally the builder tended to be neat in his dress and appearance, but today his deep green company polo was untucked and he wore jeans instead of khakis. His blond hair looked mussed and he paced as his gaze went back and forth between the storefront and the parking lot.

"Bruce, what's going on?" she asked, nearly breathless.

"That fancy pet food place that's going in next door had a leak." He stopped to face her. "The sprinkler head blew over the storage racks in the back and the place flooded."

"Our store?" Her heart filled with dread.

"Yeah, the new floor is ruined. And there's some damage up high, but not to us." Bruce blew out his breath. "They're going to have to replace the drywall along the dividing partition. It's a firewall so it'll have to be reinspected."

"Is that it?" Better to have all the bad news out of the way.

Bruce nodded. "I'll talk to the county, but I don't think they'll give us a Certificate of Occupancy until the pet place is done on their side."

"Okay."

"We're removing the flooring to dry out the concrete," he said. "That'll take a few days."

She groaned. They were already on a tight schedule and could ill afford a major delay. She'd call and let Marla know what would need to happen as soon as she understood the full scope of the problem.

"How soon can you guys choose new flooring?" Bruce tucked in his polo "If you go to the warehouse and choose something already in stock, it'll go that much faster. I'll have my guys work over the weekend if they need to."

Carol nodded. "We'll pick something out tomorrow. Can I see the damage, please?"

"Yeah, sure," Bruce said. "Follow me."

The front of the store was dry and looked fine, but the back portion was soaked. Carol could see the remains of the water, which Bruce and his team had swept out the back door. Two men were squeegeeing the floor while another set up several industrial fans. The whole scene made her want to cry.

"Don't be scared." Bruce placed a hand on her upper arm. "Water damage always looks worse than it is."

She certainly hoped that turned out to be true.

"In a few days, it'll dry out like I said," he continued. "After that, we'll put down the new flooring. Grand opening's not for another couple months, right?"

Carol nodded, her hand over her mouth.

"We'll take care of you," he promised.

"Thank you, Bruce. I'll be in touch."

"Yes, ma'am." He guided her around the equipment to the front of the store and back outside.

Carol stood in the sunshine while he returned to his team. She debated calling Marla, not ready to face the stream of questions. Instead, she took a deep breath and headed to her car. A plain white envelope lurked beneath the windshield wiper of the Chevy Cruze. She grabbed it and tore it open. If there was more bad news, she wanted to know right away.

The letter inside wasn't from the developer or the owner of the pet food store like she suspected. No, it was an invitation to take part in some crazy widow lady's experiment on what people believed.

She looked around, wondering if she was on one of those new reality practical joke shows. Would Howie Mandel or Betty White suddenly appear trailed by a camera crew?

When nothing happened, Carol read the letter again. The last twenty-four hours had been strange, and the invitation added to the sense of the surreal. She needed time to digest everything, but she also needed to get home and check on Jordan and think about dinner. Taking care of her son and putting a meal together were things she could understand. The rest of it would have to wait.

Jordan was playing video games and once the meatloaf was simmering in the oven, Carol slipped into her garage studio. Shaping clay was also something she could both understand and control.

She began by softening the clay with her hands, waiting for inspiration to strike. To set her mind and fingers free, she concentrated on the good parts of the day. The simple joy of waking up pleasured and refreshed. The planning session with Marla. Then Carol recalled the the request to share her personal philosophy.

Was the woman for real? Carol wondered again if it might be a hoax. Even if it was, she could still think about her personal philosophy. She didn't have to write the essay if she didn't want to go that far.

The clay warmed beneath her hands and her fingers started to work it into something useful.

Carol wasn't sure what she believed. She hoped that she was a good mother to Jordan, that he would go to college and get a good job and live a happy life. But didn't every mother want that for her children? That was how things should be, not a philosophy.

Philosophy. Greek for love of wisdom.

But what did the Greeks consider wisdom? For Carol, it went beyond being smart or knowledgeable. Someone could memorize all the facts he or she wanted to and still be a complete idiot.

Wisdom was searching for the truth. Wise went beyond intelligence. To be wise, to have wisdom, was sharing your truth with the world. Carol had no idea what her ultimate truth might be. Most days, she was happy simply knowing she'd survived to fight another day.

Her fingers broke the clay into smaller pieces to roll them flat and shape them into oblong curls.

Marla kept a plaque by her desk that read: *I am strong, I am invincible, I am woman.* Would that be her partner's personal philosophy? Carol would try to remember to ask, maybe even tonight if she needed to distract her partner from the minor setback with the new shop.

When things got really tough, Carol would try to buck herself up by saying that this too shall pass. She believed that no matter how bad things seemed, things would be better on the other side. She didn't know how long it would take to reach that other side, but there was always light at the end of the tunnel if you just kept going.

"Hey, Mom, the oven's making noise."

Carol dropped the clay piece and looked up to see her teenage son leaning on the open door and hanging over the garage step.

"What?" she asked.

"I think dinner's ready," he said.

"Okay, be there in a sec," she said. "Take the meatloaf out, please."

She glanced down at her work. All those flattened oblongs. What was she trying to make with these?

A daisy! She was trying to make a daisy. Her mother's favorite flower. She hadn't made one of those in ages, although she wasn't surprised her body had gone there. Daisies always made her feel better. Such happy little flowers, as her mom used to say.

"Moooom," Jordan cried.

"Coming!"

Carol placed the piece in Tupperware, washed her hands, and went back in the house. While Jordan had followed instructions to take the meatloaf from the oven, he had not turned off the timer or the oven itself. Torn between exasperation and amusement, she mashed the buttons and the high-pitched beeping stopped.

"Finally," Jordan said.

"You know you're allowed to do that, too." Carol grabbed a potholder and transferred the pan to the back of the stovetop. "It doesn't take some kind of magical Mom power."

"Whatever." He shifted from one foot to the other. "When are going to eat?"

"Ten minutes," she said. "Fifteen, tops."

"'Kay." He slumped out of the kitchen.

Carol decided to call Marla while she put the salad together since dinner could be an excuse to get her off the line. She hadn't even glanced at her phone since getting home, and the number of texts and missed calls took her by surprise.

"Can't these people wait for anything?" she muttered as she scanned through them all. "Guess no one taught them patience is a virtue."

Marla sent the most messages, the last one ten minutes before, so she must have worked herself into a real panic. Her husband Gary had also called but hadn't left a message. Well, as their business manager, he needed to know what was going on. Best to call them back and try to ease their fears.

"Oh my God, where have you been?" Marla exploded the moment she picked up. "Gary said there was water damage. What if we get mold? How are we going to choose new flooring in a few days? Who's paying for this? Have you called the insurance company?"

"I didn't think about the insurance," Carol admitted.

"Gary said if it's not our fault, we're not paying."

"Of course not. Bruce says it looks worse than it is," Carol said. "Why don't you and Gary meet us at the store tomorrow and we'll sort it all out?"

Letting Marla continue her rant, Carol went to the fridge to get the lettuce and fixings for the salad. She didn't have time for potatoes, which she usually served with meatloaf, so salad it was. Well, she did have instant potatoes. The boys weren't crazy about them, and neither was she, but they'd do for tonight. The ding of the microwave would lend credence to her excuse of needing to go to put dinner on the table.

"I can't believe this is happening," Marla wailed. "Are we ruined? How bad is this going to delay us?"

"Bruce says we can still open on time," Carol said. "He says his guys can work weekends if they have to."

"And how much is that going to cost?'

Jim chose that moment to walk in, all smiles when he caught sight of his wife. The smile faded as he noticed her distress combined with the disarray in the kitchen. She tried to smile back and nod hello while putting a casserole dish of hot water in the microwave.

"Give me that," he ordered. "How long?"

"Three and a half minutes," she said to him, then somehow managed to get off the phone with Marla.

"Gary filled me in and so did Bruce," Jim told her. "Let's eat and then we can talk business. I need a break."

"Me, too." She kissed him. "You're on potato duty while I finish the salad."

"Got it."

By the time Jordan sauntered downstairs several minutes later, dinner was on the table. For the next thirty minutes, they talked about their upcoming trip to Seattle and everything they wanted to do there. Jim's sister lived outside the city and had been begging them to visit for years, which they agreed to do over winter break.

After the table was cleared and the kitchen cleaned, Jordan disappeared while Jim and Carol retired to the living room.

Jim had stopped by the new store on his way home and talked to Bruce. He agreed the water damage was minor. They should still call the insurance agent in the morning, just to be on the safe side, but Jim felt any claims would also be minor and covered by the other contractor's insurance company.

"I told Marla she and Gary should meet us there in the morning," Carol said. "Then Marla and I will go pick out new flooring."

"That's my smart girl." Jim gave her a squeeze. "Anything else interesting happen today?"

For a second, she wondered if the invitation might have come from him. For another second, she hesitated while she decided if she should share it with him. No, she preferred to keep it a secret. The invitation had been given to her, not both of them. And she rather liked the idea of having something all her own.

"Hon?" he prompted.

"The new store keeps things interesting enough," she said. "How about you?"

Jim spent the next bit regaling her with stories from the office. She'd always thought a bunch of accountants would make for boring material, but Jim made the ones in his firm sound like a riot. They never seemed quite so funny in person, though in their defense she tended to see them at fancy corporate events and not in their natural habitat.

Carol laid her head on her husband's shoulder. A bunch of accountants. Was that the proper term? There was a pride of lions, a clowder of cats, a tower of giraffes, and a gaggle of geese. So bunch was too boring. A sum of accountants? She liked that and shared it with her husband.

"Where do you come up with this stuff?" he asked with affection. "A sum of accountants. I'm going to start using that."

"You do that." She patted his knee. "I'm going back to the studio to finish the piece I started before dinner. Don't let me work too late. Lots to do tomorrow."

He smiled at her. "I won't go to bed without you."

"Thanks." She patted his knee again before pushing herself off the couch.

Back in the studio, she returned to her daisies and pondered the crazy widow lady's experiment. By opting not to share it with Jim, she realized she'd decided to take part. Now she needed to come up with a personal philosophy.

That was going to be tough. Finding five random people to slip a blank envelope to would be easy. She didn't even really have to think about it, just choose a likely person from one of the classes she taught on a weekly basis.

She rolled out the stem for the first daisy, enjoying the feel of the vibration and the muscle memory of having done the same thing thousands of times before.

"What do I believe?' she muttered. "What do I believe?"

Her mind returned to what it had started when Jordan interrupted her. No matter how bad things got, you had to keep going and believe there was light at the end of the tunnel. You couldn't get to that light, couldn't reach the other side, unless you kept going. To stop, to give in to despair or to simply stop believing, was to die.

When she and Marla quit their jobs and opened *Kiln Me Now*, they'd been scared and had all sorts of obstacles in their way. But they were determined to succeed, and they weathered the storms together and kept their eye on the prize and all sorts of other clichés and managed to build such a successful business that they were actually opening a second store within five years of opening their first.

When her mother passed away a few years before, Carol had been inconsolable. Sharon had been more than a mother to Carol.

She'd been best friend, teacher, mentor, and the rock on which her foundation had been built. No one ever believed in her or provided as much faith as Sharon. To have her taken suddenly, killed by a drunk driver in a senseless accident, had been more than Carol could bear. Not even Jim could get through to her, and she'd spent the first week after the funeral in bed, not wanting to ever get up again. She could easily understand the widow's grief and need to do something to take her mind off her loss.

Sharon would have loved the experiment. She was curious about others, too, and chatted up strangers no matter where she happened to be.

Carol had not really gotten over the death of her mother. She'd gotten through it by knowing there were other people to love and who loved her that were still alive. And she knew from having lost her father years before, and a best friend in college, that the pain eventually would fade.

You found your way through the pain to the other side. Whether it was loss or illness or relationship issues or anything else with the potential to suck you under, you had to fight your way past it. No matter what, just keep going.

Take the current situation with *Kiln Me Again*. Yes, it sucked, but they'd survive. Maybe…okay, for sure there was more pressure this time since they already had a loyal clientele. But that was one of the positives. Those customers would understand should there be any rescheduling or delays.

They'd work through any battles with the insurance company and the pet food store owners. She and Marla would find new flooring and Bruce would get it installed and everything would be on track again. Things might be tough now, but they'd be rough again once the shop was up and running.

Challenges and obstacles were part of life, which is why you just had to keep going. Carol wondered if that was the same as never giving up, and decided they were related yet not quite the same. For her, not giving up referred to a goal, not to life overall. Just keep going was for everything, not just something you wanted.

She stepped back from the clay to take stock of her work. She'd made a bouquet of daisies, which needed a flowerpot or backdrop in order to complete the project. Carol would take care of that over the next few days.

"I'm going to send that to the widow," she decided in a burst of inspiration. "I'll send it along with my essay."

The essay that she still needed to write, although she knew what she wanted to say. All that remained now was how to say it, and finding the time to put her thoughts on paper.

Carol's Essay

My mother loved daisies. Her name was Sharon, and she passed away a few years ago. I think I'm sharing that with you since you're dealing with your own loss right now. Mom would've enjoyed the way you're working through it, with the experiment and wanting to know people's personal philosophies. She also liked learning more about people and would always talk to the person in line next to her at the bank or to the cashier at the grocery store.

Mom also taught me pottery. Daisies were the first things I learned me how to make. When I got the invitation and started thinking about my personal philosophy, I also started working on the daisy bouquet plaque I included. I'm guessing I'm the only one who sent a gift, but since you were the inspiration, I wanted you to have it. I hope it brings a smile to your face and eases your mind for a moment or two.

Okay, enough rambling. You didn't ask for my history, you asked for my personal philosophy, which is "just keep going". Or I guess you could say "just keep swimming," like in Finding Nemo. I know that may sound simple, but sometimes it's the hardest thing you feel like you'll ever have to do. But you have to do it, or at least I believe you do, or what's the point of taking the next breath?

When I say to just keep going, I mean in the face of loss or stress or all the challenges life throws at you. I don't think it's possible to be alive and not have thought about giving up at least once.

I've dealt with several losses in my life, including both parents (at different times, thankfully) and also my best friend to brain cancer when we were still in college. Those were dark days, especially losing Mom. There were days I didn't get out of bed, even though I had a husband and a son to take care of.

But I just kept going. And every day the pain got a little less, and I remembered a little more that I had a husband and a son who were still alive and who needed me. I needed them, too.

So you just keep going through loss, which is one of the big things that can knock you down. Little things knock you down, too, and sometimes it's several little things chipping away that eventually wear you down. But you keep going.

My friend and I own a business. I'm not going to say the name or what we do since the point is to be anonymous. So, we own a business, and I'm sure you can imagine the challenges that go along with it.

We weren't businesswomen when we opened the store. We were career women, I guess, lifelong executive assistants, so at least we were used to dealing with difficult personalities. And we're both strong women, so all of that helped us learn what to do and how to run a business. It wasn't easy, though, and as I'm writing this I realize that we need to take our knowledge and help other women who want to start their own businesses.

I'm getting off track again, so I'm glad you're not grading these essays. Writing was never my strong suit, although my husband would probably tell you that nonlinear thinking is. Anyway, my friend and I worked through all of the challenges of getting the store opened and we worked through all the stress of making it successful.

We hadn't hired staff before. We had customer service experience, but it's different when your butt is on the line and not a corporation. We really had no idea what we were getting into, but we knew what *we wanted and we just kept going through all the obstacles and now we're successful enough to be opening a second store.*

A florist friend of mine told me that in the language of flowers, daisies mean innocence. He told me that one year when I was buying a bouquet of them for Mother's Day. I like that, because I think you need innocence in this world if you're going to make it through.

Yes, you have to just keep going, but by doing so you also have to believe that you'll get to that other side. And sometimes belief and innocence are intertwined. So the plaque represents not only a thank you for inspiring me, but a reminder of my personal philosophy. I hope that you enjoy the gift.

Brad

A fter the four-dog sled races, Brad discovered that Harley, Ethan, Juliet, and Buck made the best team. They were four for five and finished in the top three each time they raced.

Brad enjoyed watching the dogs run, the gray and black of their coats a sharp contrast to the white snow. Harley barked when happy with his performance, and Buck was tireless—as long as he received a steady stream of treats.

"How's it coming?" Joel leaned over the cubicle wall. "Status meeting in thirty."

"I know." Brad nodded. "It'll be good."

"Demoing?"

"Not until next week."

Joel's computer beeped, announcing an incoming call. Brad closed his eyes, pinched the bridge of his nose, and exhaled. He opened his eyes and moved his hand back to the mouse to continue his task.

Mush! Mush! was his brainchild and the first game he'd pitched to receive the green light from the decision panel. For now, Brad was the sole designer of the game, but if the beta group liked his demo, he'd get a team of people to assist with the next phase. If his luck held, Thought Bubble Games would actually release the game to the public.

That dream remained a long, distant reality. Even though it was a massive thrill to get to phase one, the continued progress allowed his hopes to remain alive.

Brad kept the pitch and the concept simple. You were a musher with three dogs to start off. The dogs would have different skill sets – wheel, middle, or lead – along with good traits and bad habits. You trained the dogs to increase their abilities and raced them to improve skills and earn money. The tracks and routes of the races varied. Some were simple snow-covered paths, others contained jumps or hills, and some had frozen rivers to cross or villagers to save.

The race winnings could then be used to enter more competitions, acquire additional dogs, or purchase items such as dog food, better sleds, and other odds and ends both necessary and fun. The funds could also be used to pay monthly dues, which were based on the league you qualified for.

"Hey man, time to go," Joel said.

With a groan, Brad saved his progress before locking his computer and trudging after his co-worker. Although a necessary evil, Brad dreaded the bi-weekly status meetings. Two hours of listening to co-workers talk about their projects and pretending to pay attention. Did anyone ever remember what was said?

Since no phones were allowed in the meeting, Brad tended to think about his own projects or plan ahead for the weekend. *Mush! Mush!* was coming along better than expected, although he still had to research dog trials and bad habits. Gamers preferred a sense of reality in their games, and they loved to post comments when something did not live up to their stringent expectations.

Pondering the game was much more fun than thinking about the weekend. Maddy wouldn't be back from Pennsylvania, or PA as she called it, for another week and both Drew and Mark were out of town.

On the positive side, having nothing else to do would force him to work on his project with almost no interruptions other than his chocolate Lab, Rocky, needing attention. Maybe he could get some "study" time in as well by playing Xbox or Steam. Always good to keep an eye on the competition.

Brad heard Joel start to talk and knew he'd be next. When Steve, his manager, called on him, he was ready.

"Game's progressing well," Brad said. "On track for the demo next Friday."

"Have you decided on a platform?" Steve asked.

"Not yet. Looking to release as arcade or app, but need to do some research to gauge interest for in-game purchases."

"Excellent," Steve said. "Noah?"

Only getting a single follow-up question was a good sign, although Brad knew everyone was saving themselves for the demo. Demos could be brutal, and he planned to do what he could to avoid a negative outcome if at all possible.

"You coming to happy hour?" Joel asked on their way back to Cubeland.

Brad shrugged. "Think I'll head out."

"Suit yourself."

Brad grabbed his laptop and keys and slipped out before anyone else could corner him. He enjoyed happy hour most of the time, but tonight he wanted to be home.

Rocky stood at the window waiting for him, tail going full throttle. With Drew and Mark both out, having the dog there to greet him felt better. There was nothing worse than coming home to an empty, silent house.

"Hey, pal." He rubbed the top of Rocky's head. "How you doing? Didja miss me?"

Rocky barked his answer. When Brad stopped petting him long enough to put his stuff on the table, the retriever whined and butted his leg.

"Okay, let's go."

Sometimes Brad took the easy way out and let the dog in the backyard, but today he felt like a long walk. Rocky liked the idea as well, wagging his tail and pulling on the leash.

"Easy, boy." Brad gave a gentle tug to bring the dog to heel.

When Rocky continued to pull, Brad gave in and started to jog. At least for a few minutes, then he had to slow to a walk, but this time the retriever slowed, too. Brad let him sniff so he could take care of business.

Back at the house, Rocky went to rest in his bed in the living room while Brad made a sandwich and settled in front of the television. With the drone of the TV in the background, he checked email, caught up on the news, and played around a little. His phone buzzed at a key point, but since it was Maddy calling, he chose to respond.

"Hey, babe."

"Hi. Miss me?" she asked in her breathy voice.

"Always. What's up?"

"Nothing. Wishing I was there with you." She sighed. "Mom's still trying to get me to move back to Harrisburg."

Brad grunted.

"I know. I don't want to, either. But Uncle Bob has that air conditioning business and I could work for him as a receptionist or something. I guess it's better than working at Starbucks, and he is family."

"What about becoming a nurse?" Brad asked.

"Yeah, I might do that, too," she said. "I guess I don't know what I want to do."

Brad made a conciliatory noise.

"Well, I miss you."

"You'll be back in another week, right?"

"Brad, do you miss me?" Maddy demanded.

"Of course," he said, although he wondered if he was telling the truth.

"Good. Dad's yelling again so I better go. I'll text you later."

"Sounds good."

"Um…bye, I guess."

"Bye," Brad said, then threw in an automatic "love you."

"Love you, too."

Brad ended the call. Rocky cocked his head and whined.

"Don't give me that look," Brad said. "I do love Maddy. Or I did. I dunno."

And he didn't know for sure. They'd been together for three years, although lately it felt like much longer.

She was gorgeous, with big boobs, blonde hair, and blue eyes. Still, the girl loved to talk and sometimes he wanted to sit quietly and watch TV. Maddy needed a lot of reassurance and called or texted him several times throughout the day.

It was cool at first, but now he wanted some space. His job took more and more of his time, and he was getting really good at coming up with concepts and designing games.

Rocky barked and Brad patted him on the head.

"Weird having the house to ourselves," Brad said to the dog. "Should we see who's online?"

Without waiting for a response, he grabbed a controller and turned on the XBox. He scrolled through the list of friends to see if anyone was already using multiplayer. Two friends were playing *Call of Duty*, but it looked like they were on a campaign and he didn't want to join mid-battle.

Brad scrolled through his games and paused at *Red Dead Redemption*. It had been a while, so why not? If he started, someone would ask to join and they'd see what kind of virtual trouble they could get themselves into.

Friday morning found him yawning, but back in the office hard at work on the dog sled game.

He spent the morning studying film of past Iditarods and other sledding races. Man, those dogs worked hard, but they also looked like they were having fun. Their fluffy tails were high in the air, swishing back and forth, and their pink tongues hung out of their mouths while puffs of air escaped into the sky.

"Bet that guy is freezing his balls off," Joel said.

"He's wearing tons of layers," Brad responded. "And he's used to it."

"Still cold and he's not moving. Dogs are doing all the work. Dude just has to stand there."

From what Brad had read, the musher did way more than just stand there, but he didn't argue. Instead, he grunted and continued watching the footage. He needed the game to look as realistic as possible.

"You think people will want to play that?" Tanner, another co-worker, asked.

Brad shrugged. "We'll see."

He certainly hoped they would. People liked dogs and they liked racing. These animals were different from horses, which usually only appealed to tween girls. There was money in appealing to that demographic, sure, but Brad preferred to create something he'd enjoy, too.

Besides, he really wanted to have a game popular enough so he could tell people he created it. A modest success where enough people played or had heard of the game would do. Maybe something he could show off a little. Something to prove to himself, his family, and all the kids from high school that Brad McKenzie became a success before the age of thirty.

He was cutting it a bit close, but he still had a few years to go. He'd have other chances, but this was the game he considered his real shot. If it didn't get past the demo stage, or it tanked after release, he'd be relegated to designer status and might not get another chance.

"Hey, man. We're going out for lunch. Wanna come?"

Brad shook his head. "Think I'll take the laptop home and work from there the rest of the day."

"That's two days in a row, man," Tanner leaned on the cube wall.

"You know how it is at this stage." Brad shrugged. "One little mistake and everything turns to shit."

"Yeah, we know," Joel said. "Going to be a long weekend, too, huh?"

"Pretty much."

Next week's demo weighed heavily on his mind. He could try to claim he wasn't nervous, but these guys knew the truth. Most of them had either been through it or planned to get there, so he hoped they were on his side.

"Have a good one, man." Joel nodded. "Catch you next week."

"Yeah, see ya." Brad gave a half-hearted wave in response.

Back at home, he spent the rest of the day and into the evening with his head in the game. He decided on two races for the demo, one with four dogs and the other with five. In real dog sled racing, a musher used an average of 16 dogs, but that wouldn't work in the gaming world. The screen size and ability of one person to keep an eye on all those dogs would frustrate rather than entertain or annoy the player.

Brad opted to create six dogs. The real game would have more, but six would give the testers a chance to pick and choose their initial stable and switch them out for the different races.

He still had several challenges, like building the terrain and trying to find that delicate balance between pleasing the true gamers while still appealing to the masses. One of the first questions the testers would ask was about the intended audience, and saying "everyone" was not an option. He needed to be able to tell them both men and women between the ages of 15 and 35, casual and serious gamers.

If, universe willing, he got the go-ahead and the game passed all the other hurdles, the marketing team would help refine the audience and get the word out. But he still had to have a good product, and a good demo session, or the game would be dead in the water.

Rocky whined and rested his head on his owner's knee.

"You want to go out. Okay. I guess I can take a break."

The dog danced in a circle and panted while Brad snapped on the leash. He grabbed his Braves cap and slipped it on before stepping outside. The evenings were definitely getting more humid.

Rocky towed him along, unfazed by the temperature. The dog didn't seem too bothered by the weather until the temperature dipped below freezing. Then it was Brad forcing Rocky outside for a walk.

When the duo returned, a black Ford F-150 sat in the driveway. Drew's truck, but he was supposed to be on a weekend camping getaway with his girlfriend.

"Oh, shit," Brad muttered.

He liked Tiffany. She was low maintenance and got along with Maddy. Still, he had work to do and didn't want other people around.

"Might as well bite the bullet." He opened the door and stepped inside.

Drew sat slumped at the kitchen table, an open beer in front of him. His camping gear was piled next to him, and he appeared to be alone.

"Thought you were spending the weekend in the mountains." Brad walked into the kitchen. "Too many bugs?"

"Nah, man." Drew shook his head. "She dumped me."

Crap. A breakup meant a mopey housemate, which was way worse than having a horny couple around.

"Sorry, buddy."

What were his chances of getting back to his game? He wanted to be a good friend. He did. If he went back to the computer now, it would be rude. If he stayed, he'd have to listen to the whole sad saga. Quick, he told himself, find a happy medium.

"You want to go to Jerseys?" Brad asked. "Grab a bite and hang for a bit?"

Drew looked up and pushed a clump of hair out of his eyes. A big guy at 6'3" and about 250 lbs, at the moment he resembled a kid whose favorite team had just lost the Super Bowl.

"Why not?" he asked. "Gotta eat, right?"

"Right," Brad agreed. "I'll drive."

"Cool."

Although he'd still have to listen to the "she done me wrong" song, he'd at least get to eat and be a good friend. And he could work on the game after they got back. He'd made excellent progress today and he had all day Saturday and Sunday to add the finishing touches. Plus, Drew was right. Had to eat.

They rode in silence on the short drive to the restaurant. Once they sat down, Brad steeled himself for the story.

"She friggin' dumped me, man," Drew began as soon as their drinks arrived. "How could she do that?"

"Did she say why?" Brad took a sip of his soda.

"Apparently she didn't see the relationship going anywhere." Drew traced a drop of condensation down the beer bottle with his fingertip. "It was fun, she said. She just couldn't see a future with me and she wants to get married and start a family."

"You don't?"

"Fuck. Hell no, man," Drew said. "We're too young to settle down."

"I guess." Brad perused the menu.

"You wanna marry Maddy?" Drew asked.

"Not really. She's too flighty for me."

"Great bod, though."

Brad had to agree with him on that one. About getting married, he wasn't so sure. It wasn't like he hadn't thought of it, but more as something that would happen down the road.

"What can I get you boys?" the waitress asked. "Y'all here for trivia?"

Brad ordered a burger, then asked, "Trivia?"

"Yeah. We're doing trivia on Friday nights now." She leaned in. "Those three girls behind you are here to play."

The boys turned around to check them out. The girls—one blonde, two brunette—were about their age and were staring back at them. The blonde grinned, and the brunette with the big blue eyes waved. The other one giggled.

"You look safe enough," the blonde said. "If you're any good, you can play with us."

Drew blinked. "Good at trivia?"

"Sure, that too." She waved them over. "Annie won't mind. That's the waitress. I'm Emma. This is Rachel and Dakota."

Rachel was the one with blue eyes and Dakota was the giggler. Brad looked at Drew, who shrugged. Maybe it was a little soon, but they were only going to play trivia. Where was the harm?

"So?" Emma challenged.

"Tell us how to play." Brad took his drink and moved to their table. "We're trivia virgins."

"Oh, we know how to take care of virgins." Dakota winked, then explained the rules, which seemed simple enough. Basically, you answered questions and assigned point values based on how confident you were in your answer. Not much different than the bar trivia from college except here everyone got the chance to answer.

"Do you play a lot?" Brad asked.

"Not really," Rachel said. "It's fun to do once in a while. We usually play at Dantannas, but thought we'd try here tonight."

"We like to win," Emma said. "You get a discount on dinner if you win."

"Cool," Drew said.

They chatted for a few more minutes before the game started. Rachel kept the score sheet and Emma kept the little pad of paper where you wrote your answers. That meant the girls played often enough to have developed a system, which told Brad he needed to be on his toes.

"First question is usually a gimme," Emma said. "They get harder every round."

"Ah." Brad drank some of his Coke.

"You'll get the hang of it." Rachel smiled at him. "Shh, it's starting."

Brad refrained from pointing out that she had been the one talking and listened to the announcer.

"What river is Washington crossing in the famous portrait?"

Emma rolled her eyes. "Duh. Potomac."

"Umm...duh. Delaware." Rachel corrected her friend before Brad had the chance.

"Are you sure?" Emma demanded.

"She's right." Brad spoke up. "You're thinking the river next to Mount Vernon. That's the Potomac."

"Oh yeah." Emma tried to sound as if she truly had made that mistake.

"Nice going," Rachel whispered to him when she took up the answer.

Drew stared moodily into his beer, making Brad wonder if they should've stayed at their own table. Then again, his roommate would've been sullen regardless, and this way he might end up having some fun.

As the game continued, everyone got to know each other better. Emma specialized in pop culture questions, Dakota knew her history and geography, and Rachel handled almost all other categories, but sports were her strong suit.

"I have an older brother," she said when Drew asked how she knew the Dolphins were the only undefeated NFL team. "And a father."

"Do you watch?" Brad asked.

She nodded. "We go to games, too. Dad has season tickets to the big three. Braves, Hawks, Falcons. Oh, and the new soccer team."

"That takes some serious coin," Drew said.

"He's a lawyer." Rachel sighed. "So what do you guys do?"

Drew worked in a customer service center for a large technology firm and Brad explained his job as a video game designer.

"That's either really fun or really hard," Rachel said.

"Both." Brad chuckled. "What do you girls do?"

Rachel worked as an office manager, Emma was a barista while earning her business degree, and Dakota worked as a paralegal.

"Why don't you play trivia with your boyfriends?" Drew flagged the waitress for another beer.

"Ethan plays poker with his buddies every other Friday," Emma said. "Rachel's single and Dakota broke up with her boyfriend last week."

"Mine dumped me tonight." Drew gave the girls his puppy dog eyes.

Dakota fell for it, offering her sympathy. Emma went outside to smoke, leaving Brad and Rachel to answer the next question. Luckily, it was about video games and he had no trouble providing the answer.

"So do you have a girlfriend?" Rachel asked.

"For now," Brad said. Realizing how that might sound, he tried to explain. "She's visiting family in Pennsylvania for a few weeks and might move back. We're kinda growing apart anyway. It's not like it sounds. I want—"

"Relax." She placed a hand on his upper arm as she stood to take up the answer. "I totally get it."

Great. At least one of them did. He hadn't expected to meet a girl tonight, not one who liked sports and played video games. Rachel was pretty, too, with killer blue eyes. He liked talking to a girl who could keep up with him. It was a nice change from Maddy and he found himself listening more because he wasn't worried about being misunderstood.

His girlfriend wasn't stupid. She just wasn't into all the same things he was and didn't always get his references. Even just hanging out with someone like Rachel showed him how much he and Maddy had grown apart.

Brad glanced over at Drew, who was deep in conversation with Dakota. Well, it hadn't taken them long to get over their breakups.

"That was fast." Rachel nodded toward the couple as she returned to her seat.

"Heh," Brad said. "How many more rounds?"

She glanced at her sheet. "Three more questions before the final. We're doing really well. You'll have to join us again sometime."

Was that the singular or plural "you"? Did it matter? He already had a girlfriend. Not to mention a very important project to get back to and concentrate on for the rest of the weekend.

Emma breezed back in, taking her place at the table and the conversation as if she hadn't been gone.

"Ethan's winning," she informed everyone. "That'll keep him happy. Ethan's my boyfriend, in case you forgot."

"Is he coming over after?" Dakota asked.

Emma made a face. "He didn't say. Probably."

The team was in second place going into the final question. Rachel explained they had 20 points to use if they wanted to. When they heard the question, she beamed.

"Oh, we're betting it all," Emma leaned back with her hands flat on the table.

"You know the name of the first Kentucky Derby winner?" Brad asked, incredulous.

"Aristedes," she whispered and wrote the name on the slip of paper. "I was one of those horse crazy girls growing up. Only time I use the knowledge is when it comes up in trivia."

"Wow."

"You go, girl." Dakota held up her hand and Rachel slapped it for a high five.

Winning the game should've capped off the evening on a high note, but they were sad to be parting.

"Can I have your number?" Brad found the courage to ask Rachel. "In case we want to play again or something, I can let you know."

She narrowed her eyes, then sighed. "Yeah, okay. Give me yours, too."

Drew and Dakota also exchanged numbers. Emma rolled her eyes and hid a smile as she went up to retrieve their winnings. They paid for their meals and walked together to the parking lot.

"Well, good night," Rachel said. "Nice meeting you. Hope to see you again."

"Yeah. Night." Brad gave a half-hearted wave.

He felt a little down watching her walk away with her friends. He had her number, he reminded himself, and his friend had the number of one of her friends. The evening wasn't a total loss.

"You doin' okay, man?" He asked Drew on the drive home.

Drew nodded. "Good to get out. Thanks, man."

"No prob."

"Hey, what's on the windshield?"

Brad looked where Drew was pointing. An envelope was shoved under the windshield wipers on the passenger side. If it didn't blow off before they got home, he'd toss it once they were there. He hated when people stuck flyers on cars.

When they got to the house, he grabbed it and balled it up.

"Dude, aren't you gonna read it?"

Brad shrugged. He could hear Rocky barking, so he went inside and greeted the dog.

"I want to know what it says."

Knowing better than to try to argue or distract someone who'd been drinking, Brad gave in and handed the flyer to Drew before returning his attention to Rocky.

"I don't get it," Drew said a few minutes later.

"What are they selling?"

"Nothing." Drew handed him the paper.

Brad read through the letter, which wasn't an advertisement after all. It was an invitation to take part in an experiment some old broad thought up. She wanted to know your personal philosophy. She was crazy all right!

"I don't get it," Drew repeated.

"Some old lady wants you to write an essay."

"No friggin' way!" Drew said. "I barely even wrote for school."

Brad chuckled. "I'm going to do some work. You okay?"

"Yeah. Tonight was fun. Those girls were hot. Forget Tiffany. I'm over that bitch."

"Getting out was good." Brad figured that was the safest response. "Back to the grind for me."

Drew trudged up the stairs. After giving Rocky a treat and a rub on the head, Brad returned to his office. He'd expected to get more work done on the game, but instead he found himself thinking about the letter. He even retrieved it from the kitchen and brought it to his office for another read.

The idea sounded just as insane as the first time. Did this lady really expect people to respond when there was nothing in it for them? No reward, no publishing the essays. Nothing.

"Ridiculous."

What would Rachel think, he wondered. She seemed like a smart girl. Hey…maybe she left the envelope on his car.

Nah, someone else must have done it. She'd only left the table to take up the answer and go to the bathroom, and he didn't think she'd been gone long enough to also dash to the parking lot and back. Emma had gone out to smoke, but even knowing her a few hours, Brad could tell this was not her style.

Rachel seemed like the type who might send in an essay, though. Maybe if he sent one in and then chose her as one of his victims, they'd have something else to talk about. The whole thing was supposed to be anonymous, but that didn't mean he had to obey the rules. He could follow the spirit rather than the letter of the law.

Brad warmed to this idea, forgetting for the moment that he had a girlfriend, not to mention a game he was meant to be focusing on.

Brad's Essay

Not sure I can make it to 500 words, but I'll give it a shot. That concept goes along with my personal philosophy anyway, which is "don't be afraid to take risks."

I've seen it happen too many times, to family and friends. They stay in a job they hate or a relationship past its prime or even in a house or a town where they feel safe. They may believe it's the right thing to do, but really they're miserable.

I don't want to be miserable. I want to be happy. And happy doesn't come easily. Happy takes work. That's another thing I've learned, but I wouldn't consider it my philosophy.

Do you need examples of how I came to choose my personal philosophy? I might as well. It'll bring me closer to the word count. I'm not used to working with a word count. Other reqs, sure, but no one cares about word count in game design. At least not the types of games I design.

My cousin Jamie wanted to be a writer. She was a good one, too. Still is. I always got a kick out of reading her stories growing up. But when she tried to publish them, she got a couple of rejections and gave up.

After three or four magazines told her they weren't interested, I told her there were hundreds of other magazines, not to mention online mags that she could try. She could even self-publish like every other writer seems to be doing these days. Jamie wouldn't go for it. Someone she didn't know and hadn't ever seen didn't like her work so she was done. I think if she'd continued to take the risk of putting her stuff out there, someone would have been smart enough to see her talent and publish her work.

I'm not going to have the same thing happen to me. Nope. I'm going to have the guts to take the risk.

That applies to work and personal life. It doesn't mean jumping out of airplanes or doing something really stupid—it means not being afraid to take a chance to make something better or make yourself a better person. If you don't take risks, how will you ever know what you're really capable of?

I'm under the word count, but I've said what I needed to say. I shared my personal philosophy and how I came to adopt it, so there's really not much else to share. Your letter said we could go slightly under, so I hope this gives you what you were looking for.

Myra

"What are we up to now?" Mabel perched on the edge of her chair, so eager to hear the answer I thought she might tumble off.

"How many new ones?" Dolores asked. "Have you read them yet?"

"Who do you think gave them the letter?" June asked from the armchair.

"Myra handed them out," Betty said.

"We *all* handed them out," Mabel insisted.

I did my best to take in all their questions and comments. Once we received the second essay, we'd started getting together every other week rather than once a month for book club. Not that anyone thought about books, except maybe me and Susan. Books or essays, we were all still caught up in the lives of people we didn't know.

"Come on, Myra." Mabel practically bounced in her seat. "Do you have more or not?"

"We're up to eight now." I leaned back into the chair and crossed my legs. "No way of knowing whose batch each one is from."

Personally, I liked it that way. The idea was to get responses. Did it matter who snuck them the letter, whether it was me or one of my friends or even one of the respondent's victims? In the end, finding out what made someone tick was what I was after.

"How many are new? You didn't say." Susan sipped her vodka tonic.

"Only two, and I'm pretty sure one of them is from a guy. Younger man from the sound of what he had to say."

That had surprised me, although I couldn't say for sure why. I'd slipped the invitation to both men and women, and women weren't the only ones who could put words on paper. Still, it caught me off guard to hear from what I assumed was a guy.

"Read that one first," June insisted. "Wait, is there more coffee?"

I nodded. "And kiwi lime pie, if anyone is interested."

"Forget the dessert, we want to hear what the boy said." Dolores thumped her empty glass on the coffee table.

"Two seconds." June jumped up and dashed off to the kitchen.

When she returned with a full mug, all four women stared at me as I took the sheet of paper from the purple folder on my lap and shared the contents of the first essay.

"He does sound young," Betty agreed.

"These millennials do love their gadgets and games." Susan chuckled. "I'll bet it's kinda fun, though."

"Do you think we'll know if it ever gets published?" Mabel asked. "Is that what they call it?"

"Doesn't matter." I waved away the question. "Do you want to hear the next one?"

Everyone bobbed their heads, reminding me of a group of children at story time. Which proves the theory that humans need stories, but also need each other to survive. As difficult as it was getting by without Lee, the path forward would've been oh so much more difficult without friends to walk it with me.

"Earth to Myra." June cleared her throat rather pointedly. "Do you copy?"

I gave her a dirty look while I picked up the next document. "Yes, Major Tom. Sending data now."

Was that even the right way to say that? Science fiction hadn't ever been my favorite genre, although that may well be beside the point.

"Here we go."

After I read the submission, everyone clamored to see the artwork that the author mentioned. I picked up the daisies, marveling at their beauty and simplicity. The white of the flower contrasted with the green leaves and the bright red pottery. Such delicate work. The woman who created this piece was a true artist.

"Wow." Susan traced her hand over the petals. "This is really pretty."

"You could hang it on a wall," Mabel said.

"In the kitchen," Betty offered. "Right along the side wall, or maybe over the sink. Yes, over the sink. It would look amazing there."

The other women murmured in agreement. Even though I hadn't given much thought of where to place the art, I liked Betty's suggestion. However, it inspired me to decide on the perfect place.

"I'm going to put the daisies in the bedroom right above my nightstand."

"Don't hide it away," June said. "We want to see it when we come over."

Betty picked up the artwork and held it against the wall between the two side chairs. Okay, *that* was indeed the perfect spot.

"Myra, get a hammer and nail," June ordered.

Sexist and out-of-fashion as it may be, Lee had always been the one to fix toilets or even to hang pictures. He did keep his tools in the garage, and he kept them orderly, so I should be able to find something as simple as a hammer and nail. Right?

"Back in a flash," I said.

Grace padded behind me as I trekked out to the garage. Although we ostensibly had space for two cars, we rarely parked them in here. My Civic got the driveway and Lee preferred to keep his truck at the front of the house. "Easier for a quick getaway," he used to joke. The only time our cars saw the inside of the garage was during an ice storm.

The rest of the time, we treated the garage as an extra room for tools, holiday decoration storage, and the repository for unwanted items. I'd made attempts to start decluttering the garage, but usually found something else to focus on.

"Guess I'll keep chipping away at it." I sighed. "Well, at least cleaning things out helps fill the days."

I'd retired when Lee was first diagnosed, and I had no desire to go back to work now. No need, either. The days could seem long and lonely, even with friends stopping by, essays to read, and volunteering at the shelter. Cleaning helped, too.

"Okay, better grab the goods before the girls send out a search party."

Grace woofed her agreement and returned to her detailed inspection. The entre garage smelled of sawdust and grease. The tools were stored along the left wall, the larger items on the wall and the standard items on the countertop Lee built for them.

The hammer was easy to find. The nails should've been, but it took a moment for me to realize that of course they would be in one of the drawers. And who knew nails came in so many different sizes? How did you know which one was the right one for hanging a simple pot of daisies?

I grabbed a few different options and returned to the living room, Grace once again trailing behind. Susan held out her hand and I gave everything to her.

"You know how to do this?" I asked.

"Sal barely changes a light bulb around our place." She put the hammer on the chair and the nails on the table. "He's also too cheap to pay someone so I learned how to do basic household repairs."

How had I not known that? I guess I never asked. Interesting that this experiment helped me learn not only about other people, but also my close friends. Did that mean even Lee had secrets he took to the grave with him?

"Is it straight?" Susan asked around the nail in her mouth.

"Yes," I said.

"No," June said. "Left side needs to come down a smidgen."

Susan obliged June. I didn't see the difference, but in the end it didn't matter. The daisies had found their home.

Mabel clapped as Susan backed out of the chair. She handed me the tools, and I set them by the top of the stairs. I'd get them back to their place sometime tomorrow. No need to journey back to the garage again tonight.

"What a nice gift," Betty said from her spot on the couch. "Shows the kind of woman she is even more than the essay."

Dolores nodded. "Are you keeping a record of what people say, Myra?"

"Record?"

"Of the different philosophies," Dolores said. "That way you don't have to reread the essays to remember and you'll be able to look at the philosophies all together."

My friends were full of brilliant ideas tonight! I'd considered keeping the essays in a book, but not to have the actual messages laid out as well. If I did that, I could see how similar some might be, not to mention a quick way to see how various people interpreted their different worlds. Sheer genius!

"I will now," I told Dolores. "What else did we think of this woman? Carol."

"How do you know that's her name?" June demanded. "The essays are supposed to be anonymous. We've been guessing man or woman."

"Her name was on the envelope with the gift. Return address, too." I explained. "Pam's name I took from her email. Pamlineta. The young man I don't know. His email name made no sense to me. The others either didn't have a return address or I couldn't tell from their email name."

That answer seemed to satisfy June. Even though the respondents were meant to be anonymous, I preferred knowing the names. Made the people seem more real, which was the point, after all.

"Anyone else send you questions?" Mabel wanted to know.

I shook my head and looked away, but my friends somehow picked up on the fact that something was wrong.

"What?" Susan asked.

"It's nothing," I assured them.

"Your shoulders are up to your ears," June said.

Betty came over and sat on the floor next to my chair, her hand warm against my knee. I reached down and squeezed her hand with mine.

"Tell us, Myra," Betty said in a quiet tone.

"No new questions, but someone did send a nastygram," I admitted. "They were pretty harsh."

"Internet trolls," Susan muttered.

"People can be assholes sometimes." This from June.

I took a deep breath and let out a shaky sigh. "Yes, they can." I took another deep breath and continued. "This person wrote that I should butt out of other people's business and that what I was doing was just modern-day snooping. They said this anonymous business was total b.s. and I was only trying to find a way to steal someone's identity."

"That's an over-reaction to a simple invite if I ever heard one," Mabel said. "I hope you deleted the message."

"I did indeed."

The other women murmured their sympathies. I took comfort from their support, but the email had shocked me.

"Do you think one of us gave him the letter?" June asked.

Where this person had gotten the flyer hadn't even occurred to me. By now, with all of us handing out letters and the respondents doing their piece, there were several ways the author could've gotten his or her hands on a copy.

"Anyone could have given him the invite," Susan spoke my thoughts, which told me I wasn't the only one who'd had them. "All he had to do was not respond. No need to be nasty about it."

"We don't know it's a he," Dolores pointed out.

"Of for Pete's sake, no woman would be that mean," June said. "At least not to a stranger. Southerners know better."

"Just because the person lives in Georgia doesn't make them a Southerner," Betty insisted.

"He or she may not live here, either," I weighed in. "They could've been visiting family or just passing through. It's not like I asked for someone's life history before slipping them a sheet of paper."

That comment silenced the group for the moment, so I took the opportunity to sneak into the kitchen to check on the coffee and get the dessert ready. I'd been too busy to bake, but you can't go wrong with kiwi lime pie from Publix.

By the time I returned to the living room, the noise level was close to normal again. June took the coffee pot and topped off everyone's cups. Betty relieved me of the pie. She sliced it up and handed it out while I sat back down in my spot. I smiled when Betty gave me my slice, and she winked in return.

"We were talking," Dolores said once everyone was settled again. "Should we share where we handed out the letters?"

"Why? We're not going to find the person who sent the email." I balanced my plate on my knees. "I shouldn't have brought it up."

"Yes, you should have," Mabel jabbed a finger in my direction. "You've shared all the essays that have been sent in. This may not be the same thing, but we still need to know. We're in this together, Myra."

The other women all nodded.

"Thank you," I told them from the heart. "If you want to tell where you handed out the invitation, you may."

"Maybe it'll give you ideas for next time," Susan said around a mouthful of dessert.

"Next time?" I leaned forward. "We're not giving anyone else the invitation. Any new ones'll come from the people who decide to respond."

Everyone looked at me as if I'd kicked a puppy. The tartness of the kiwi lime pie suddenly seemed overpowering and it took me a few tries to swallow it. I hesitated, not sure how to respond to the angry glares.

"No more essays?" Mabel whined.

"I didn't say that," I insisted. "I just meant we wouldn't be sneaking the invitation to anyone else."

"For this time." Susan placed her plate and fork on the table. "What about for round two?"

"What do you mean?" I scratched my forehead. "The experiment is to ask people to write essays about their personal philosophy and that's what they're doing."

The room grew warm as my friends continued to stare at me. Grace, feeling the tension, bumped her large head against my knee. I stroked her, which calmed both of us and kept her from growling.

"But there are more questions to be asked," Mabel explained. "What they believe about God and the universe, are they happy, did they become what they wanted when they grew up."

"When they grew up?" June snorted. "No one becomes what they wanted and no one ever really grows up."

"That's the truth," Dolores proclaimed. "My body might be in its seventies, but my mind feels like I'm still in my forties."

"Hold on." I held up my hands to stop the chatter. "I wasn't planning on doing more rounds of this experiment. It's meant to be one and done."

Hurt looks all around.

"I'm sorry, ladies."

"Promise us you'll think about it," Mabel said.

Lord, this was just like them trying to get me started on a hobby. And now that I had one, they wanted more. This had really snowballed!

"Okay, I'll think about it."

I woke up the next day with no formal plan. Grace needed to be walked, and this afternoon was my turn on the cleaning crew for the shelter. Beyond that, the hours stretched out long and lonely.

When I was working and then taking care of Lee, I pretty much knew what each hour would entail. Even after he passed, I knew each day would be filled with finding ways of dealing with the fact that he was no longer around. Now that I seemed to be through the first several stages of grief, I had hours and hours with no set tasks, no set schedule. After all these years, I wasn't equipped to deal with free play.

"Come on, Gracie Grits," I called as I pushed myself out of bed. "Let's go for your morning walk so you can do your business."

She panted a smile and wagged her tail, whining and dancing by the front door. Such a sweet thing, and I enjoyed taking care of her. Or having someone to share my life with, since most of that life had been spent with Lee. Maybe not having kids wasn't the blessing I'd always considered it to be. If Cassie'd lived, or if we'd tried for another, I'd have someone other than myself to focus my energy on.

I let Gracie tug me outside. The cool morning breeze played with my fine, dirty hair, reminding me that I needed to take a shower. It also reminded me of the fact that I was still here, still alive.

"I suppose that's a good thing," I said to Gracie, who looked up from sniffing after a cookie and cocked her head at me.

No, I knew it was. What was it that first respondent, said? You make your own happiness. I agreed with that philosophy when I read her essay, and it seemed even more true at the moment.

I'd read many books on the theory of happiness, especially lately. Seems like everyone wants to know what it takes to be at peace with yourself, or what someone else considers to be the basis for being happy. Someone else meaning people from other countries, different classes of society, and those who'd lived a long life.

They even had a center for happiness in California...no, Washington state. Not to mention tests online that would reveal to you how content, or not, you were.

"Poppycock," I informed the back of the dog's head.

How had we arrived at a time and place where you didn't know how you felt until you took a test that provided the answer? Society relied too much on data, and analyzing that data, rather than on experiencing life in the moment.

That girl had the right of it, which only proved she was further along than the rest of the world. Or was the pursuit of happiness a uniquely American ideal? Somehow I doubted that, although I did wonder what part intelligence, education, and age played in how someone viewed happiness and how they determined whether or not they experienced pleasure in their daily lives.

I'm sure there was an experiment out there that had already asked that question, but I still couldn't help but wonder. Most of those scientific trials asked the questions for you, and often gave you the choice of answer, too.

What if, instead, a crazy widow lady slipped you a letter asking you to define your own happiness in an essay?

"Oh, good God, those damn women have gotten to me."

They had me thinking of the next essay topic and here we weren't even finished with the first. Enough of all that, time to burn some physical energy by doing some power walking rather than strolling along with Grace.

"Keep up, girl," I said as I strode forward. "I'll show you what a real walk is all about."

Liz

"Mom, I need my pink shirt!" Brenda commanded from the kitchen archway. "Mr. Bradley said to wear pink today."

"Can I have another scrambled egg?" Cameron asked without looking up from his iPad.

"Me, too," Bethany whined and craned her neck to look at the screen in her brother's hands. "With cheese."

Liz stood at the sink and gazed out her kitchen window at the front lawn, which remained green and lush even in the dog days of August.

"Girls, give your mother a moment." Charlie leaned in to give her a peck on the cheek. "Don't forget dinner at Almanzo's tonight. We're celebrating the new merger. Wear that sexy black number."

"Mom, my shirt," Brenda wailed.

"Try your dresser or closet." She turned to respond to her husband.

"UGH!" Brenda trounced up the stairs with as much noise and drama as possible.

"I want another egg," Cameron whined.

"Me, too," Bethany said.

"Bye, hon." Charlie squeezed her shoulder. "See you tonight."

"Have a good day," she said automatically.

Liz watched from her window as he strolled down the sidewalk and into the detached garage. What she wouldn't give to be going to work, too.

"Egg. Egg." Cameron chanted, soon echoed by Bethany.

"Enough!" She thumped her hands against the porcelain sink. "You've had your breakfast. Go get ready for school. There'll be hell to pay if Brenda has to take you again."

Bethany squealed and darted from the room. Liz slipped the iPad out of Cam's hands as he followed. They passed Brenda on her way down, but she ignored her younger siblings. The teenager had found her shirt and wanted to grab a breakfast bar and be on her way to pick up her friends.

"Why don't you sit down and have a real breakfast?" Liz asked her daughter.

"I ate with Dad," she said. "And I need to get to school early for pictures."

"Fine, go." Liz waved her out the door. "I'll wait for carpool."

While Brenda ran away, Liz went upstairs to hurry the other two along. Anita Mayhew, this week's carpool mom, was a pain and Liz wanted to avoid speaking with the woman this time. She liked her daughter Rebekah, who was in Cam's class. Heck, she preferred all the carpool kids to their mothers.

As the kid-packed SUV pulled away, Liz exhaled in relief. She welcomed the peace and quiet of not having her beloved children—ages 17, 9, and 6—constantly needing something from her. Or her husband talking about the bills, the house, or some corporate event the wives were expected to attend.

When they weren't here, she could almost relax. But, with them gone, she only had herself for company. Most of the neighborhood wives worked. Those that didn't championed causes and met for lunch as often as possible. Liz was on the board for the local library, volunteered for pediatric cancer, and attended some of the lunches. However, ever since Bethany started school full-time last year, Liz found herself dreaming of her days as a receptionist for a large insurance company, back before she'd met Charlie or had the kids.

Charlie's dream family consisted of a wife who stayed home. His father left when he was three and his mother worked several jobs and long hours to keep them afloat. Charlie had studied and worked hard to put himself through college and law school, wanting to be able to provide for his mother and his future family. He wanted to make it possible for his mother and his wife not to have to work. He would take care of everyone.

Liz had admired this desire and wanted to make him happy so she'd agreed to be a stay-at-home mom. She'd wanted it, too, and she loved the time spent with her little ones. Not so little anymore.

Liz's dream had been to not become like everyone else in their set of friends. The men earned the money and were catered to because of it. The women married well, moved to Buckhead, and became the Atlanta version on the Stepford wives.

"Buckhead Betty," Liz muttered.

After Cameron started kindergarten, Liz volunteered half days at the library. She did that for three years and then Bethany came along. She and Charlie discussed her keeping the position, but they'd both agreed to her being a stay-at-home mom and he wanted to stay with that arrangement.

At least before the younger ones started school, she filled her days with play dates, trips to the park, and sports to interact with other adults. Liz didn't care if she chatted with a nanny, an au pair, or an actual parent. She liked getting to know people outside her circle.

In Buckhead, however, you were supposed to stay within your own neighborhood, community and class of people. The rules were ridiculous, and after all these years Liz still didn't have all of them down.

Perhaps because they came from blue-collar backgrounds, she and Charlie had trouble fitting into the Buckhead mold. No matter how hard she tried, Liz did not enjoy tennis even if Charlie liked her in the little white tennis dresses. Charlie confessed that he hated golf and only played when he couldn't get out of it.

Liz rather liked that neither of them played the required sports. That meant they could spend their weekends together, even if "together" meant carting the kids off to karate, soccer, horseback riding, or ballet and cheering them on from the sidelines or wings.

"Enough fussing and farting around." She pushed her coffee cup away and stood. "I have errands to run."

She needed to sign Cam up for karate, see if a spot had opened up in advanced beginner ballet for Bethany, and stop by the library.

Her friend Corinne was volunteering, which gave a lift to the day. Corinne loved to share job openings she'd heard about, mostly receptionist or officer manager type openings, but Charlie never thought it was a good idea when Liz mentioned them. He did so out of love, pointing out how tired she seemed to be from running the kids around to their various activities. Still, there had to be a way to make both of them happy.

"Liz, how are you?" Corinne smiled. "Did you like the Brit lit? I hope some of the terms weren't too bad."

"They do have funny ways to say the same things, don't they?" Liz handed her the books. "It took me a few times to figure out that 'knock you up' just meant to pick up at a certain time."

Corinne chuckled. "Using petrol instead of gas used to get me. Did you like the story?"

Liz nodded.

"Excellent." Corinne came around the counter. "Let's see what we can find interesting for you today."

The two women found several books, which went into the canvas bag Liz purchased as a way to support the library. As a board member, she helped raise awareness and funds. As a reader, she did her part as well.

"My real estate agent mentioned his assistant is retiring in a few months." Corinne nudged Liz. "I can help you update your resume."

"What resume?" Liz asked. "It's been six years since I worked here with you."

"Um, you have board member experience," Corinne said. "You've organized fund drives, donation events, plus you know how to type and use a computer. I've seen those complicated spreadsheets you put together."

"I'll think about it." Liz repositioned her bag to a more comfortable spot on her shoulder. "And I'll need to talk to Charlie."

Corinne harrumphed. "I'm sure he'll be fine with it. Charlie seems like a reasonable man."

Her husband *was* reasonable...plus she had been thinking about her old job at an insurance company this morning. Liz would love to do something like that again. The agent might be more understanding if one of the kids got sick at school and she needed to pick them up. That was another one of Charlie's points—her needing to be there on the rare chance something happened.

"Oh, fine," Corinne said. "The woman's not retiring for a few months. Plenty of time to decide."

Liz hugged her friend goodbye and headed out to the next errand. Her mind stayed on Corinne's proposal, however. She'd have to find the right time to tell her husband. The problem was that he was always working, even at home, or he was at some corporate event or travelling. Breakfast seemed like the only time she saw him during the week, and she knew better than to try to have a discussion with the kids around.

After enrolling Bethany in ballet, Liz swung by the dry cleaners and couldn't help but overhear the conversation of the two women standing in front of her.

"Girl, who cares what he thinks?" The redhead in the green jacket asked. "Do it anyway."

The petite blonde in the pink shook her head. "I couldn't," she whispered. "He'll be angry if he finds out."

"He ain't gonna find out unless you tell him," Green Jacket insisted. "Besides, he ain't the boss of you."

"He's my husband."

"So? That don't make him the boss. Marriage is a partnership, girl. Ain't no boss in a partnership. You go on and do what you wanna do. T'hell with what your man thinks."

Liz paid for her dry cleaning and headed home. She made it before carpool drop off, so she grabbed the mail and went inside. After putting the bag with Charlie's shirts on the coat rack in the foyer, she flipped through the mail while waiting for the kettle to boil.

A plain white envelope hid among the flyers, bills, and magazines. Liz turned it over and held it up to the light. No distinguishing marks as far as she could tell.

She tore open the envelope and read the letter inside. The microwave shut off with a loud beep. "This has to be a joke," she thought as the first sip of coffee touched her lips.

Who left it in the mailbox? Liz couldn't imagine any of her neighbors taking part in such an unusual experiment and certainly not an anonymous one.

But someone put the letter in the box and she doubted anyone would drive through a Buckhead subdivision and randomly place invitations in people's mailboxes. Which led her back to the idea that one of her neighbors had done it.

Maybe the invitation was meant for Charlie, not her. Should she share the letter with him?

No, she decided as she pulled the piece of paper closer to her chest without being aware of it. She'd gotten the mail, like she did every day, sometimes chatting with Gloria, the mail lady. It was hers.

But did she want to take part in the experiment, assuming it was real after all?

"I don't know," she muttered.

Liz hadn't given much thought to a personal philosophy and the last essay she'd written had been in her college days. Plus, no one wanted to hear what she had to say. She was sure the other people's essays were better and more interesting than hers would be.

"Did you make cookies?" Cam demanded. "Where's my iPad?"

Where had he come from? She hadn't heard the van outside, or the front door open.

"No screens until after dinner," she said. "Have an apple or some grapes if you want a snack."

"Mom, Adeline's dog just had puppies. Can we have one?" Bethany asked.

Liz looked up to see Cam leaning on the still open front door, his backpack slung on the floor. Bethany had shed her bookbag as well as she came over to hang on the back of her mother's chair.

"Guys!" Liz snapped. "Cam, shut the door. Pick up your bag and hang it on the hook. Were you raised in a barn?"

"That would be cool if we were," Cam said.

"Yeah," his little sister agreed. "I could have a pet cow."

"Bethany, go hang up your belongings." Liz did her best to give them "the look," which worked, at least long enough for them to follow her instructions.

"Tell me one good thing and one bad thing that happened today."

"Mrs. Collins was out today and we had a sub," Cameron said. "Jason Coyle got hit by a softball in gym and got to go home early."

Liz thought she knew which was a positive and which was a negative, but with Cam she wasn't always sure. She turned to Bethany, who gave the matter grave consideration.

"Michael Gaffney chased me on the playground and tried to kiss me. That was bad." She grinned, showing her missing tooth.

"Then I socked him in the tummy and that felt good. No one saw and I didn't get in trouble and that was good, too."

"You're in trouble now," Cameron said. "Right, Mom?"

Liz knew she should at least scold her daughter, but she couldn't bring herself to do it. Standing up for yourself was a positive.

"Go watch TV or read." She waved them off. "I have to get ready to meet your dad. Brenda's in charge tonight."

They groaned, but their demeanor changed as they pushed at each other and headed into the den. Liz needed time to get ready for the fancy dinner and she'd also need to leave early enough to beat the Atlanta traffic. Brenda should be home from band practice before she left.

As she took a shower, Liz's thoughts returned to the way her youngest had stood up for herself. Bethany was lucky not to get caught, and lucky the boy didn't tell. She was right to fight back, though, and Liz hoped she continued to do so.

Maybe she could learn a thing or two from her daughter. Not that Liz wanted to or felt the need to punch Charlie in the stomach. Like the girl in the dry cleaners had said, marriage was a partnership, and a partnership meant she got to do what she wanted to do, too.

As she finished her shower and dressed for dinner, Liz found her inner strength growing. Tonight was not the best time to talk to Charlie. No sense mentioning this during a big event. Better to have it out when she had his full attention.

"Hey, Mom, I'm home," Brenda called. "Dad already texted and wants to know if you've left yet."

"Text him back and tell him I'm on my way."

"But you're not."

"He doesn't know that and he'll be happier if he thinks I am." Liz checked herself in the mirror. "So send it."

"Will do."

Liz put the finishing touches on her makeup and stepped back, pleased with her appearance. The last step was to go back downstairs and have Brenda zip her up.

"Who's the letter on the table from?" her daughter asked. "The one about the philosophy experiment."

"No idea," Liz said. "Feel free to respond if you want."

Brenda wrinkled her nose. "No thanks. I just wanted to make sure it wasn't a school assignment or something. Are you going to do it? Is that why you left the letter out?"

While she liked the concept, Liz wasn't sure she even had a personal philosophy. Right now, all her concentration and energy needed to be going toward finding the right words and direction with Charlie. She didn't have time for crazy experiments.

"I don't think so," she told Brenda. "Do what you want with it. Okay, I better go. There's money on the counter for pizza."

"Got it," Brenda said. "It's not my first rodeo."

Liz smiled to herself at hearing her husband's favorite saying come out of her daughter's mouth.

"You better hurry. I texted Dad you were on your way like five minutes ago."

"Traffic was bad." Liz gave her daughter a quick hug.

Brenda rolled her eyes.

Traffic was rough, but Liz made it to the event on time. She left her car with the valet and waltzed into the restaurant lobby.

"I expected you earlier." Charlie gave her a peck on the cheek. "You look nice, though. What happened to the sexy black number?"

"Not the right event," she said.

Had he asked her to wear the black dress? If so, she'd forgotten.

"The green's nice, too," he said. "You're always gorgeous."

Maureen

Where had the years gone? How had that little orange bundle of fur become the old, decrepit cat she missed so much? If he was here, Diego would be curled up on her chest or by her feet, purring up a storm. But Diego wasn't here, and his absence left a hole in her heart and in her life.

Nineteen years. A good long life for a cat. The equivalent of early nineties in human years. She'd be happy to live that long and should be happy to have had so long with her darling boy.

Yes, she appreciated the time, but she also missed him. They'd been together, just the two of them, for all of those nineteen years. Every once in a while, boyfriends would intrude, but rarely for very long.

Maureen's friends were concerned about her. She knew because their texts, calls, emails, and Facebook posts or messages asked her how she was holding up. Several also mentioned getting together, but those she put off. For now.

Her growling stomach reminded her that life went on and that sustenance was required. At some point. With a sigh, she turned on her side and willed herself to sleep.

The shrieking of the phone woke her an hour later, and she made the mistake of answering it without thinking.

"Maureen Tanner, where the hell are you?" her friend Judith snapped. "You said you'd come to the coffee Meetup today!"

When had she said that?

"I'm having a lie in," Maureen said. "I'll go next time."

"A lie in? What's that?" Judith asked. "Whatever it is, stop doing it and rejoin the world. We need you."

"I'm not ready." She placed an arm across her face. "Okay?"

"No, it is not okay," Judith barked, then softened her tone. "Look, hon, I know you're upset about Diego. He was a great cat. He lived a long time. But he's gone and you're still here."

Maureen sighed. "I know. I'm going back to work on Monday, and I'll be back to doing Meetups soon, too."

"When?" Judith demanded.

"Next Saturday. The pottery class. Okay?"

"Perfect! See you there."

Maureen turned off the phone and hid it under the pillow. With a huge effort of will, she threw back the covers and propelled herself out of bed. A wave of dizziness washed over her, proving how much she'd needed to get moving. She ignored the blankets, brushes, and toys strewn about the room and headed straight for the master bath.

The hot water felt good, as did washing her hair. Even if all she did was blow dry her hair and put on clean sweats and a clean T-shirt, at least she'd done something today. When her stomach continued to growl, Maureen went downstairs in search of food.

The nearly empty fridge and pantry had enough to scrape by for the next few meals, but a trip to Publix was definitely in her future. Perhaps that could be the test of a return to the real world, since that didn't require having to dress up, but she would have to interact with other people somewhat.

And speaking of others, it was time to return all those messages before everyone really started to get concerned. As long as she seemed to be okay, the masses should be satisfied. The last thing she wanted was a horde of well-meaning friends knocking on her front door.

Stop wasting time and get to the store. This from her inner voice, and she automatically followed orders. The bright sunshine coupled with the brisk fall air blew away some of the mental cobwebs. Maureen took a deep breath for the first time in a few days.

"Life marches on," she said to herself while unlocking the car.

The entire shopping experience seemed a bit like a dream, and once all the groceries were put away, Maureen found herself wondering what she'd purchased. She'd gotten eggs and cheese at least, so she made herself a quick meal of scrambled eggs. To her surprise, everything tasted good.

Okay, time to head back upstairs to get on the computer and respond to all the sympathy messages. In the study, her eyes immediately went to the fleece blanket where Diego used to sleep while she worked, read, or played. The fact that her old boy was not there to greet her brought fresh tears.

"Oh, Diego." Maureen bent down and stroked the blanket. "I miss you so much."

Some people might think her crazy for being so worked up over the loss of a pet, but those people could go fuck themselves. Diego had been a living, breathing, thinking being who shared his life with her. He brought her joy, entertained her, and also infuriated her on occasion, just like all her human relationships.

Other than the first ten weeks of his life, Diego had been with Maureen. For nineteen years, she'd fed him. Loved on him. Brushed him and played with him. Took him to the vet and cared for him through all his old-age maladies of kidney disease, high blood pressure, pancreatitis, and everything else until his quality of life reached the point where she allowed him his right to a good death.

Maybe if she had a husband or child or other animals, it might not be so bad. She doubted it. One of her good friends from way back in elementary school days was married, expecting her first child, and they owned a dog as well as a cat that passed away a few months back. Both Felicia and her husband had been torn up by the loss of their pet.

"Ah, hell." Maureen took a long drink of water and wiped the tears from her eyes. "Best get to it."

The next hour was spent responding to all the messages, writing *"thanks for your support. I miss my Diego, but I'm hanging in there"* so often she almost started to believe it.

When she finally finished, what struck her was the sheer number of people who'd expressed their sympathy. A few years ago, only family, co-workers, and a few close friends would've even been aware of her loss. Maureen tended to be a loner, preferring her own company or Diego's to that of most people. She'd had her tight circle of friends, which worked well until things fell apart.

Amy got married and moved back to Florida, Darlene found a girlfriend and drifted away, and Thomas, while still on the fringes, started hanging out with the guys more often. Which was fine, and what brought Maureen to Meetup and a whole slew of new friends.

"You made it!" Judith wrapped Maureen in a bear hug. "I'm so proud of you!"

"All I did was leave the house and come to art night," Maureen said as if it was no big deal. "I didn't think I had a choice."

"You didn't," Judith confirmed. "Come meet everyone. Lots of new folks tonight."

Maureen trailed behind her friend, who led her to a group of five other women. Men rarely attended the painting events, although they were equally welcome. Secretly, Maureen felt that men should attend. What better chance to be alone with so many women?

"Okay, we have Stephanie, Rhonda, Melissa, Jane, and Helen." Judith pointed to each one in turn. "Ladies, this is Maureen."

As everyone nodded and shook hands, Maureen did her best to find some detail to help her put face to name. Stephanie wore a blue scarf that matched her eyes. Rhonda was tall, dark-skinned and big-framed. Melissa was a tiny waif with a patch of thin blonde hair. Jane wore bright pink lipstick. Helen had gray hair and appeared reserved. Judith with her authoritative air and streamlined appearance she already knew.

How did she seem to these women? Maureen had put on makeup and styled her wispy brown hair, plus she wore a nice kelly green sweater with her jeans. No one would guess part of her was still in mourning.

"Welcome, everyone." A short, dark-haired lady in a painting smock greeted them. "Are we all here?"

Judith nodded. "We are."

"Excellent." The woman clapped her hands together. "Follow me and we'll get you all set up."

"Are you the instructor?" Judith asked.

"Yes, I'm Carol." She gave a nervous laugh. "Sorry. I should've said that up front. Okay, let's go."

While the rest of the group tagged along, Maureen hung back a few paces. Art had never really been something she excelled at. She could appreciate what others had done and liked going to the different art festivals around Atlanta when she had the funds and the opportunity.

"Quit dragging your feet and come on." Judith pulled at Maureen.

"I'm soaking in my surroundings." Maureen yanked her arm back. "Give me a minute."

Judith rolled her eyes, but left her alone.

The foyer where the group met up betrayed none of the controlled chaos that existed beyond the frosted glass door. Maureen supposed this was by design, although the contrast between the metal and wood entryway and the concrete, paint-speckled back area proved disconcerting at first.

The back room buzzed with activity yet remained welcoming. Sample paintings hung on the right side above finished pieces of ceramics. The variety of objects that could be decorated and then fired in the kiln were arranged along the left wall. Several long tables filled the center of the room, with two of them already full of patrons conversing or working on their selected pieces.

Further into the shop were rooms for private parties. In the one Carol led them to, blank canvases were already waiting on the table along with a cup of water and another cup with different sized paintbrushes.

"We have smocks for you to wear so please put one on." Carol smiled. "They're along the back wall."

Maureen followed directions, nodding at the other women in her group. Helen had brought a bottle of wine and was passing it out in tiny plastic cups. Judith, as usual, brought homemade cupcakes and placed the box on the side table for everyone to enjoy.

"I thought we were painting pottery," Maureen whispered.

"Change of plans," Judith said. "Grab a spot."

Knowing the futility of trying to argue, Maureen shrugged and found a place between Judith and Rhonda. She gulped the wine, doubting it was enough to have any effect.

"Ready to get started?" Carol asked.

They all nodded.

"Great. So tonight we're all going to be working on the same painting, but you'll be able to add your own flair."

"What if we haven't painted before?" Stephanie hunched in on herself.

"Not to worry," Carol said. "I'll walk you through every step. Now, the painting we'll be doing tonight is called Orange Cat."

"What the fuck?!" Maureen shoved her stool back and glared at Judith. "I can't believe you sometimes."

Maureen stormed out of the room and found her way outside. How could Judith have done such a thing? Of all her crazy stunts, this one took the cake. Tricking her here by saying they were working with pottery and not creating a painting of an orange cat.

An orange cat! Diego had been gone one week and Maureen still missed his warm, purring presence every single day. She could barely stand to look at all her pictures of him and now Judith wanted her to paint him? Was the woman out of her freaking mind?

I can't believe she would do this!

Maureen walked up and down the strip mall sidewalk. Any thought of leaving was trumped by the fact that her purse remained inside the shop. She could just walk across the parking lot to Starbucks and wait until everyone left, but that wouldn't be very mature of her.

The door to the studio opened and Maureen turned to see Judith stepping out, followed by the instructor.

"I'm so sorry," Judith said. "I didn't mean to upset you."

"Well, you did." Maureen crossed her arms.

"Look, I thought you'd like it. I swear." Judith held up her hands. "I thought the painting would be a way to honor Diego."

"We can choose another painting," the instructor said. "We don't have to do this one if it's going to be a problem."

Maureen looked at Judith. Her slumped body language and sorrowful expression proved that her intention had not been to piss off her friend. *She's telling the truth.*

"We can do something else like Carol said. Come on, Maureen," Judith pleaded. "I really am sorry."

"Okay." Maureen exhaled. "Okay."

"Yes!" Judith bumped her friend with her shoulder. "Let's go back in before the others think we're nuts."

"Better they find out up front," Maureen quipped.

"How about a new painting?" Carol held the door as they went back inside. "Maybe Winter Tree or Ocean Sunset?"

Judith raised her eyebrows at Maureen. So it was to be her decision, eh? As much as it would hurt, maybe creating a picture of an orange cat would be a good way to remember her boy.

"Let's stay with the first choice," she said. "I'll explain to everyone why I was upset."

"I'm sure they'll understand," Judith said.

Maureen wasn't so sure, but once again Judith proved to be right. She explained to the other women that she'd lost a beloved pet after nineteen years, and he happened to be an orange cat. As they listened, everyone grew silent and their eyes filled with both sympathy and empathy.

"I lost my kitty George to cancer two years ago." Helen dabbed at her eyes. "He was thirteen."

"My beagle Kelly was ten," Rhonda said. "I still miss her happy bark and how excited she got when I came home for the night."

"Thank you." Maureen blinked back tears, then took her spot in front of an easel.

"Let's get started." Carol clapped her hands. "Now, how many of you have painted before?"

With the drama behind them, the group got down to business. Only Helen had painted before, leaving the rest of them on a level playing field.

"To start, choose your colors for the background," Carol said. "You'll need three complementary colors. I'm going to do indigo, maroon, and forest green. Stay away from orange. We'll be using that later on."

Those were good colors. Maureen opted to follow suit and so did a few of the other women. Judith, ever the rebel, went with purple, red, and yellow.

"Also add some white and black on your palette," Carol instructed. "We'll use that to lighten or darken the shades to your liking."

Helen refilled everyone's wine cup after getting her paint. The women chatted as they put paint onto their palettes. Even Maureen started to relax and enjoy the evening.

"Does everyone have their colors?" Carol asked.

"Yes," Judith said as the other women nodded.

"Excellent." Carol held up a medium sized paintbrush. "Does everyone have one of these at their station?"

There was much giggling and clinking as they each searched their supplies. Even though the instructor had not said to, they all held up their brushes as if to show they could follow directions.

"Wonderful," Carol said. "Now we're going to do a two-color background with the third color as darts or triangles in the corners. Go ahead and decide which color you'd like to go where. I'm going to use the maroon and forest green as background with indigo at the corners. Let me know when you're ready to move on."

Maureen chose to do indigo and maroon as her backdrop with forest green corners. The women shared their choices with each other, talking them through to compare and get feedback. When they quieted down and looked to the front of the room, Carol described the next step.

"Now you can mix the colors to your satisfaction. Once you have that part done, test your brush and start filling in the background." She demonstrated the technique. "If you have questions, let me know."

"What if we mess up?' Melissa asked.

"Don't think of it as messing up," Carol said. "Art is like life. There is no right or wrong way. You experiment a little and it all works out in the end. At least in painting class, we give you directions and I'll help everyone along the way."

Even if all she was doing was mixing colors and filling in the background, Maureen found the process soothing and she also enjoyed seeing her blank canvas bloom with color.

Carol delivered on her promise, visiting each of the women in turn and responding to questions or guiding them along the way. Once everyone had completed their backgrounds, they stood and walked around the table to see the results. Maureen thought the different color combinations were unique and quite lovely, even without the focal point being added yet.

"Alright, ladies." Carol drew their attention to the front of the room. "We'll let those dry for about twenty minutes. Go ahead and have a drink or some food before we begin phase two."

After everyone washed their hands, Helen refilled the wine glasses and Judith handed out butterscotch cream cupcakes. Maureen's favorite. She tried to express her thanks, but Judith waved her off.

The eating, drinking, and chatting made the twenty minutes pass quickly. They also used the time to find out more about each other. Most were single or newly single or newly divorced, depending on how you wanted to look at it. Only Jane was still married.

That ratio was pretty much par for the course for a Meetup group, and as far as Maureen could tell, none of the women were on the hunt for a new man. She saw that quite often in the larger over 40 groups and felt relieved at not having to deal with any of that crap this evening.

"Check your canvases to make sure they're dry. We're using acrylics so they should be." Carol said. "Let me know if they're not."

All were dry.

"Excellent. On to phase two."

Maureen steeled herself, knowing that they were moving on to creating the orange cat. Carol took them through each step with patience. An excellent instructor, she managed to get the class to pay attention, follow directions, and complete each step correctly.

As the cats began to take their shapes on the different canvases, Maureen marveled at how alike and different they all were. Some were a darker or lighter orange, some had a fatter or thinner face, some had green eyes and others more yellow-gold, but at the core they were all the same essential painting.

Her own cat had darker orange fur and green-yellow eyes like Diego. While seeing his likeness displayed on canvas caused some emotional pain, overall the exercise was quite therapeutic.

"Well done, ladies!" Carol exclaimed. "You should all be proud of your work."

"This was fun." Stephanie grinned.

"A total blast," Helen agreed.

"Wonderful," Carol said. "Go ahead and wash your hands, clean up, and we'll give the paintings a few more minutes to dry."

The women lined up to use the sink in the back. They talked about how much they enjoyed the event and Judith promised to schedule another one soon. One of the women suggested meeting at a nearby restaurant for drinks.

"We'll schedule post-painting drinks next time," Judith said. "Or maybe we can do dinner beforehand."

"That would work," Rhonda said.

While the others chatted, Helen pulled Maureen aside and handed her a business card.

"You're going to think I'm off my rocker," she said, "but I'm going to suggest it anyway. I volunteer with The Pet House. Have you heard of them?"

Maureen nodded. "That's where I adopted Diego as a kitten."

"I started working with them after my George crossed the rainbow bridge and it helped immensely." Helen paused. "I think it might help you with your Diego, too."

"You want me to be around other cats after I just lost one I had for nineteen years?" Maureen asked, eyes wide.

"I told you that you'd think I was nuts." Helen chuckled. "It may sound that way, but when you see all those sweet kittens and frightened older cats who just want a little love, you'll change your mind."

"Oh, I don't think so." Maureen tried to return the card. "Thank you."

"Keep it," Helen insisted. "Think about it."

Not wanting to be rude, Maureen put the card in her purse. While she couldn't bear the thought of being around other cats at the moment, someday that might change.

"Please check your paintings," Carol called out to bring every-one's focus back to their project. "When you're ready, we'll take a group picture."

"Use my phone," Judith suggested. "I'll send it to everyone and put it on Meetup."

"Good idea," Melissa said. "I can't believe I actually painted this."

"Now you'll have the painting and the photo as proof," Jane said.

After enduring the photo session, Maureen was free to leave. She took her painting, said her goodbyes, and escaped outside. While she'd had fun, she was more than ready to return to her retreat.

It was too quiet, she realized after stepping inside and no kitty came to say hello and complain about her absence. When would she get used to Diego no longer being around? Longer than a week, obviously. And Helen wanted her to be around cats again? *Crazy, crazy woman.*

Maureen dug in her purse to find Helen's card to throw it out. Instead, she found a sealed, plain white envelope. No name, no postmark, just a regular envelope.

"This better not be a bill," she grumbled. "I paid online and I can print my receipt."

But it wasn't a bill. It was an invitation from a crazy widow lady wanting Maureen to take part in a stupid experiment about personal philosophies.

The idea was indeed crazy, and it made her wonder if the invite came from Helen. She'd only met the woman tonight and already resented the intrusion into her life. One insane idea was enough, thank you.

Wait. Helen was divorced, not widowed.

However, the rules of the experiment did state that if you took part, you had to select others and pass along the invitation. Helen did seem like the type who might enjoy sharing her personal phi-losophy, although in truth any one of their group could've slipped the envelope into her purse. Maybe everyone who went tonight received the same invitation.

She sent a text to Judith, asking if she'd found a plain white envelope in her purse tonight.

No, came the reply. *Was I supposed to?*

Maureen considered before responding, not wanting to get Judith's curiosity up and then get bombarded with questions.

No. Probably came from somewhere else. Sorry.

When Judith didn't respond after a few minutes, Maureen knew she was safe. She didn't have contact info for the others, except Helen, so Maureen would go on the assumption that no one else had been invited to take part in the experiment.

Which led to the next logical question: did *she* want to take part? Maureen hadn't even considered her personal philosophy, much less what it might be. The whole idea seemed more than a little kooky.

As she got ready for bed, and even after starting to drift off, the letter and its contents stayed on her mind.

Points to this crazy widow lady for not only coming up with the idea, but for being able to follow through and carry it out. The experiment must already be somewhat successful. Maureen had determined that the widow had not chosen her, which meant that someone who'd already taken part had selected her.

Although curious, Maureen had no idea how many people had opted to take part or what phase the experiment was in. She could be in round two or round thirty-two.

Considering all the potential responders brought her back to a thought she'd had many times before. While she wouldn't consider it her personal philosophy, Maureen did marvel at all the different people in the United States (and the world, really) with all their various passions and interests.

You wouldn't know it to look at her, but Maureen was an avid soccer fan and attended every Atlanta United home game. She cheered for the U.S. Men's Team during the World Cup, joining several other fans at local bars to watch the matches and commiserate when the team was eliminated.

She sometimes watched football, but had to be dragged to baseball, basketball, or hockey games. Yet other people loved basketball and despised soccer. Somehow, they all had their supporters and managed to endure.

That's what intrigued Maureen – that somehow there were enough people watching the games, either on television or in person, to keep all of the different games viable.

And it wasn't just sports. With all of the different television channels these days, somehow most of them managed to stick around. And not everyone watched the same things. You had tons of murder mystery shows, although Maureen couldn't see the appeal there. You also had vampire shows, history-based shows, movies, and some stations played reruns of shows that had long since been off the air.

Even if you rarely watched television and preferred to read, there were books for almost every taste. Literary fiction, popular fiction, science fiction/fantasy, memoir, biography, and so many others. Some readers probably dabbled in several categories, while others remained true to one or two.

The sheer volume of available options for filling time never ceased to amaze Maureen, and it boggled her mind to think of all the different people and their various interests, most of which never crossed.

The reader might be curled up with a book while the basketball fan was watching the game and screaming at the TV. Both the book and the game affected the individual's mood, but neither knew of the other. The reader couldn't care less if the Hawks won their fifteenth straight, and the basketball fan couldn't be paid to read the latest James Patterson novel.

That dichotomy intrigued Maureen, but also helped her when she got lonely or was going through a rough patch. While her world might be torn apart by having lost Diego, somewhere someone was adopting a kitten or puppy that would be their companion for the next fifteen to twenty years.

With all of the different people in the world, and all their unique interests and issues, why would the crazy widow lady focus on wanting to know someone's personal philosophy? Weren't there more interesting things to discuss?

Maybe the woman should start a discussion Meetup group where the participants shared their interests. On second thought, maybe not. The beauty of Meetup was that a group existed for almost every interest imaginable. People joined ones that matched those interests, so starting one to find out what other people were into probably would not work.

Maureen tabled the question of whether or not to participate in the crazy widow lady's experiment, although she was more heavily on the side of no.

A week later, she reversed her decision about participating in the widow's experiment and about reaching out to Helen to work with The Pet House. Maureen phoned Helen and agreed to meet her at the shelter.

When Maureen arrived, the older woman at the front desk went to get Helen. Even in the lobby, she could hear the cats. *Is it too late to turn around?*

"I'm so glad you came." Helen came into the lobby and gave her a quick hug. "I know it wasn't an easy decision to make. What changed your mind?"

"I was lucky to have had Diego such a long time." Maureen hesitated before continuing. "If I hadn't adopted him, who knows what his life would've been like. I want to help someone else find the same happiness with a kitty they adopt, but the ones who have to wait to get adopted deserve to be loved and cared for in the meantime."

Maureen wiped at her eyes, surprising herself at the depth of emotion her speech engendered.

"Well said!" Helen patted her on the back. "Ready to go in?"

A nod was the best Maureen could manage.

Helen held the glass door open and, after a moment's hesitation, Maureen stepped inside. A large office desk took up the left corner, and an elderly strawberry-blonde volunteer smiled at them. The lobby showcased displays of cat-related products, from jewelry to figurines. Bins for donations of cell phones, soda points, and other items lined the right side of the lobby. A set of doors beckoned from that side, and Maureen guessed the animals were housed behind them.

"Please sign in,' the desk volunteer said. "Make sure to use the hand sanitizer before going into the shelter area."

After they completed both requests, Helen led the way into the main area.

The first thing that struck Maureen was the row of glass windows overlooking a nice wooded area. The cats must love that, she thought, and indeed most were perched where they could look outside.

A petite calico bumped against her leg and Maureen bent down to pet her. She stroked the cat, who turned her head to indicate she wanted her ears scratched. Diego hated having his ears scratched. In fact, he did not like being touched around his head at all.

"Doing okay?" Helen knelt next to Maureen and stroked a tuxedo cat. "Misty loves people."

"I see that." Maureen gave the calico a final pat and stood.

The sheer number of cats in the room overwhelmed her. The room was quite large, and it would take several strides to reach the other end, but there still had to be twenty cats in there, of all sizes and colors. Maureen spotted Siamese, gray tabby, calico, gray and white, all white, and a couple orange tabbies.

"These are the main residents," Helen said, anticipating the question. "The kittens are kept together until they're six months old. We also have the med kitties and new residents in the back."

"Med kitties?"

"Cats who are sick or need to be separate from the main population," Helen explained. "Our new residents are quarantined for ten days before we start to introduce them to the main area. On top of that, we have still more cats and kittens in foster care. It's a huge operation."

Maureen tried to respond, but one of the orange tabbies was approaching. Oh, how he reminded her of Diego. That feeling of sensory overload returned.

"Let's go see the babies and get you some kitten therapy." Helen guided her to the back of the shelter.

They were greeted by three volunteers. Susan, a husky brunette, was on med duty. Janet, a short girl with long black hair, was working on a tablet computer and Beth, a willowy brunette, was spending time with the new residents.

"We have all kinds of volunteer opportunities," Janet said. "What are you interested in?"

"Um...." Maureen responded.

"Not sure yet," Helen said. Turning to the others, she explained, "her kitty just crossed the rainbow bridge a few weeks ago so I thought coming here might help."

"Definitely," Beth agreed. "When Delilah crossed, it helped me."

"After Merlin crossed, I took in fosters," Susan said. "Mostly moms with babies so I could help but not have to keep one. It worked wonders until I was ready to give one of them a forever home."

"Thanks," Maureen said.

As if sensing her unease, Helen also thanked the other volunteers and motioned Maureen into the kitten area.

The room held seven or eight kittens, a couple sleeping but most playing and jumping around. She'd forgotten the sheer rambunctiousness. A solid gray one stopped playing to investigate the visitor. When Maureen lowered herself to say hello, a white one with a few black spots jumped on her back.

"I'll get her." Helen laughed and pulled the offender off. "That's Gloria."

"No worries." Maureen grinned. "They're little bundles of energy."

She spotted a tiny orange kitten who reminded her of Diego at that age. This baby had his whole life in front of him. She hoped he lived as long and had a life as good as her cat. After several minutes of playing with and stroking the little ones, Maureen was ready to move on.

"You want to see the rest?" Helen asked.

Maureen shook her head. "I'm done."

"Too much?"

"I think so."

"I'm sorry." Helen touched her arm. "I thought this might help. I guess it was too soon."

"Oh, no." Maureen followed her out the door. "It was good to be around other cats. But I think I need to take it in small doses."

"Understood."

When they were back in the office area, they could hear Janet on the phone, sounding upset and telling someone not to worry. She hung up and cradled her head in her hands. Helen went over and asked what was wrong in a gentle voice.

"That was Melanie." Janet fought back tears. "Someone told her about an elderly neighbor who had to go into senior care. Her kids are threatening to have her cat put down."

"Oh, no." Helen placed a splayed hand on her chest. "Can't we take her?"

"We're full, even in foster." Janet took a tissue from the box on her desk. "Cat's only two or three years old. Mel said she's really shy. Pretty little gray and white cat with a patch over one eye. Here, look."

Janet turned her iPad so they could see. The cat in question was curled up on the old lady's lap. The cat's face looked directly at the picture taker, and something about it sparked a response in Maureen.

Take this one home. She's meant to be yours.

"I'll take her," she found herself saying.

"Don't put yourself through that," Helen said. "It's too soon."

"We'll figure something out," Janet said. "She's in Fulton and the animal shelter there's not bad. We'll call other rescues, see if we can find a place somewhere else."

Maureen appreciated their responses, but she'd already decided the moment she saw that face. She'd lost her elderly cat, and this cat had lost her elderly human. They could help each other heal, which is exactly what she told the volunteers.

"Maybe I'm the crazy one this time, but I'm not letting that creature suffer," Maureen insisted. "Call the lady back. Give me the details and I'll go pick up my cat."

Janet looked at Helen. "Are we allowed to do that?"

"Get Mel on the line and ask her," Helen said. "I'll vouch for Maureen."

Maureen wrung her hands as Janet, then Helen, talked to Melanie. She could tell from the words and body language that all was not going well, so she steadied herself for what they had to say when they finally hung up the phone.

"Good news is you can have her," Helen said.

Maureen let out her breath. "And the bad news?"

"We have to have the cat checked out at the vet before we can release her. It's our policy and Mel won't budge."

"What vet?" Maureen asked. "I'll pay the bill."

Helen smiled and patted her friend's shoulder. "Thank you. We'll take you up on that. For now, you'll have to fill out the adoption paperwork so that when she's ready, you can take her home. You can do that now, or when she's ready to be released."

"Give me the forms." Maureen held out her hand.

"I'll print them out," Janet said.

"What's her name?" Maureen asked.

"Mittens."

"Mittens," Maureen repeated. "I might shorten that to Mitty."

"Up to you," Helen said. "You're a brave woman."

"Brave. Crazy." Maureen shrugged. "Six of one."

"Here you go." Janet handed her several pages of forms. "Just so you know, it's okay to change your mind. We would understand."

Maureen smiled and took the forms. She would not change her mind. Hopefully the old woman would rest easy knowing her little one was being cared for. While she might not go so far as to say that fate played a role in her decision, Maureen knew Mitty belonged with her now.

Maureen's Essay

When I first got the invite, I didn't think I'd be participating. I hadn't given my personal philosophy much thought, but then I knew exactly what it was. My father used to tell me all the time while I was growing up: "Listen to your inner voice—it's never wrong."

I thought he meant trust your gut. He said that was important too, but not what he meant. He said everyone had a voice inside telling them when something was right and when something was wrong. All you had to do was listen.

Honestly, I thought Dad was crazy at first, but as I got older I learned what he meant. Your gut might be sending the signal that something is wrong with the guy you're dating. Your inner voice will tell you to break up with him. It might come as a whisper or a scream, but it will tell you what to do.

I experienced that guidance a few weeks ago. My cat, Diego, passed away at age nineteen and I was inconsolable for a while. I know that's not quite the same as losing your husband, but loss is loss and I was hurting. Not wanting to leave the house or spend time with friends or....well, you know.

Finally, though, I had to face reality again. At a Meetup, I met a woman named Helen who volunteered at a local shelter. The same shelter where I adopted my Diego all those years ago.

Somehow, Helen convinced me to visit the shelter. At first, I was overwhelmed, but still loved spending time with kitties again. Then, as I was about to leave, a call came in about a young cat whose owner could no longer take care of it, and the kids were threatening to have the cat put down.

Was I ready for a new pet? I didn't think so, but my inner voice urged me to take her. I surprised myself as much as Helen when I offered to take the cat home. They didn't think I was ready, either, but I insisted and Mittens is now curled up in her cat bed beside the desk as I type this essay.

Mitty, as I like to call her, is different than Diego, of course. She's a dainty eater, for one, while he was a huge slob. He had to sleep on the pillow next to mine, and so far this one hasn't curled up with me once. That may change, though, once we get to know each other better.

Are you a pet person? For some reason, I like to think you are, which means you understand what I'm saying in terms of loving animals.

Listening to my inner voice brought me Mitty, but it's been right about other things, too. Like my house, when I didn't think I'd ever be a home owner. But my apartment kept charging for every little thing and when they started charging for water, too, I decided if I was going to be paying for all this stuff, I might as well be doing it for my own home.

Even with all that righteous anger, I was still terrified when I began looking at houses. None of them were right. Some had weird layouts or needed too much work. Others I liked the upstairs and not the downstairs or vice versa. I was ready to throw in the towel and just keep renting when my inner voice rather strongly suggested that I look in the area just north of my target zone. I checked out some of the listings online, found one I really liked and when my agent and I walked in, I knew it was the one.

I took a chance with my job, too, based on the guidance of my inner voice. The company was just starting out and there was no way to know if it would be successful, but it turned out to be a huge success and my bank account has most definitely benefitted. Beyond that, I love the people and the work, too.

It was one of my co-workers who led me to Meetup. I hadn't heard of it before and when she told me she met her current boyfriend through the site, I was skeptical. There were enough dating apps out there, thank you.

But she insisted it wasn't like that, and my inner voice chimed in and said it was worth checking out. Right again. I've met some really good friends through Meetup, although I had to try different groups and different activities until I found the ones that fit.

You have to be brave and willing to take risks or nothing good or fun will happen in your life, but your inner voice will direct you on which risks to take and which to pass on. That's what I believe, anyway. It may have taken adopting Mitty for me to realize that I did indeed have a personal philosophy, but it had been a huge part of my life all along.

Rose

Rose sat at a gray wrought-iron table outside of her favorite coffee shop, sipping a green tea frappe and watching the activity at the busy shopping center. What luck to have such an exciting place so close. And Sunday afternoon was always a good time to observe people, plus it had the added benefit of getting her out of the house for a few hours.

As she watched, Rose noticed how common courtesy and the awareness folks had for other human beings seemed to be waning. No one checked before backing out of a parking space, yet somehow they managed to avoid smacking into each other.

Other people took the idea of pedestrians having the right of way a little too far. They'd walk three or four abreast down the middle of the parking row. Some parents even let their children run and play, and then would not move when a car came along. Again, no one ever seemed to get hurt, which was a good thing, although still a miracle.

In her day, Rose had been taught to be aware of cars, that they were bigger and stronger and it was her job to move. She had raised her children the same way.

Nowadays, people bent their heads and tapped on screens, hardly saying a word to their companions. You couldn't tap out all your thoughts on those tiny screens. Besides, the only way to truly know what someone was thinking and feeling was to listen to their tone, pay attention to body language, and…well, ask them!

Rose felt glad that she was closer to the end of her life. She didn't want to become a robot and lose the human touch. What would these kids have when they were her age, assuming the world hadn't ended before then?

"The internet doesn't forget," her grandson Danny told her.

"Neither do I," she said.

He laughed, but she had not been joking. She knew how to rely on her own mind for directions, for how the sky looked on her wedding day, for what happened on family vacations. Would Danny's generation be able to say the same thing?

Rose sipped her tea. This new age did have its advantages, and the array of beverages and pastries available at the local coffee shop was certainly one of them. She enjoyed her drink as she continued watching all the goings-on at the shopping center.

A harried woman clutched her shopping bag while herding two teenage children to the car. A portly man crossed the road to the gym. Another, thinner man entered the sandwich shop. No one seemed to be happy, but then maybe they would've preferred being home rather than out running errands. Rose could hardly fault them for that.

"Dude, what happened?" someone asked.

Rose turned to see a young man in his twenties greet another man of roughly the same age, only this one wore a cast on his left leg.

"You won't believe it." Broken Leg grinned.

The two men went inside, depriving Rose of the story behind the injury. Just as well. It probably featured a sport or activity she wasn't familiar with. She had more tea, shut her eyes, and let the different conversations float around her.

"If he liked you, he'd text you back," a female voice said. "I say let him go and move on to the next one."

"Well, maybe."

"Trust me. Don't waste your time on someone who doesn't want you."

Excellent advice. Rose almost wanted to jump in and second the girl, but didn't want them to know she'd been eavesdropping. Having raised three kids and spent time around her seven grandkids and three great-grandchildren, she knew it was best to let them find their own path.

She'd done a good job, too, because all three of her children still kept in touch, plus she saw the grands who'd stayed in the area. Her oldest boy, Chad, moved to Denver after college, so she didn't know his girls as well as she would've liked, but all of Kenya's and Egypt's brood knew Grammy Rose.

Yes, her husband Carl named the kids after countries in Africa. Rose hadn't been crazy about the idea, but at least there was a reason behind it, not like the crazy names they came up with in today's world.

Egypt's oldest girl, Rebecca, named her baby Nevaeh. Heaven spelled backwards, of all things. Why not just name the poor child Heaven and be done with it? Becca just shook her head and said she liked the name.

That was her right, Rose supposed. At least Becca's girl had a proper father. And both parents had decent jobs and had gotten hitched before bringing another life into this world.

Not that being a single mom was always wrong. Kenya's girl Keisha had her boy Kaleb on her own, and she took excellent care of that child. He had just turned four and was as cute as a bug. One look at him and you knew he was loved and cared for.

Rose wished she saw them more often. The once weekly family dinners had become monthly and now were held even less often. Kenya and Egypt claimed they were too much work, and Rose supposed they had a point. It seemed harder to get everyone together these days. Another downside to getting old, or maybe yet another sign of the times. Rose couldn't make up her mind on that one.

"Have you found a job?" A woman in a pink coat asked the dark-haired man sitting across from her.

"Still looking," he said in a tone that meant not to push.

Maybe if he trimmed his facial hair, sat up straight, and tried to look more confident, the young man would have better luck. Rose shushed herself, even though the poor mite couldn't hear her thoughts.

"Have you called Ben?" Pink Coat asked.

Bearded Man nodded. "Meeting him Tuesday."

Okay, so maybe the boy didn't like being interrogated, but he was too polite to say so. She'd let him be, then. Pink Coat also got the hint.

"I don't know why I have to learn this shit," another male voice said.

Rose leaned back and tilted her head to see a male college student sitting with an older man, presumably his father.

"Who cares about Plato these days?" the son asked.

"Learning how the great minds of history thought will teach you how to think as well," the older man said. "Like algebra teaches you to think critically and solve problems with creativity."

The student snorted.

"Yeah," the father said. "I didn't believe them when they tried to sell me on that crap, either."

But that changes when you get older, Rose finished for him. She didn't have the benefit of a college education. Daughters weren't sent to college in her day. Even some of the men didn't go. It was more important to get out there and start earning money to help support the family. Fortunately, that had changed and she and Carl sent their three, including both girls, to good universities.

All seven grandkids were college graduates or beyond. Danny had a Masters degree, not to mention there was a lawyer and two doctors in there, too. Rose and Carl had lived long enough to see the rewards of all their hard work, but his heart gave out the year before Egypt graduated from Emory.

This talk of ancient philosophers and losing husbands reminded her of the letter someone had slipped her the other day. Rose wasn't sure where it came from or when she'd received it, but she did know she would not be taking part in the crazy experiment.

Rose understood all too well the pain of losing a loved one. She didn't know how they survived after Carl passed, but somehow they made it through Christmas and Egypt's graduation, plus all the weddings and babies that came along after. Sometimes, even now, she didn't know how they'd done it, just that they had.

The loneliness ate away at her. No matter how many friends and family members she surrounded herself with, no matter how many activities she lined up to keep busy, she still missed her Carl.

"Mama, why don't you remarry?" Kenya had asked after her own wedding. "There's lots of older single men at church."

Kenya spoke the truth on that score.

"Mr. Emerson is a good catch," her daughter said.

"Kyle Emerson is a horny old toad," Rose said, which made Kenya laugh.

Rose had thought about taking up with a man again, and there were times when she'd been so hungry for a man she nearly gave in to temptation. But a quick roll in the hay wasn't what she wanted. Nor was another marriage. She loved Carl, still thought of him as her husband, her one and only, to this day. No other man could replace him, in her heart or in her life.

She did just fine on her own, thank you. The silence might get to her at times, but she was not afraid to be alone.

That was a skill these youngsters could not seem to master. Always with the phones or rectangles—tablets, Danny said they were called—or watching TV. Always with a screen. And always going somewhere or doing something and not taking the time to sit back and experience life.

Danny brought her one of those tablet doohickeys and tried to teach her how to use it. "Look how wonderful email is," he said. "Or texting."

"What's wrong with picking up the phone?" Rose wanted to know.

"Grammy, no one does that anymore."

Like talking to another person was a disease you didn't want to catch. Heck, the boy even tried to text her when he arrived at the house, standing there on the front porch like a nimrod while he waited. Finally, common sense struck and he knocked, then had the nerve to be annoyed that she'd left him out there so long.

The only time the gadget came out of the drawer was during family dinners or when one of the grandbabies came to call. She'd lived more than 80 years without one and she could damn well finish her life the same way.

Rose grinned as she finished her tea.

The coffee shop was starting to fill up, and Rose knew she should give up her table. It was the polite thing to do. In a minute. Right now she was still enjoying the warmth of the sun and the simple pleasure of people watching.

"Hi!" Someone tugged on her sleeve.

Rose looked down to see a little girl with light brown skin and bright red bows in her spongy hair. Little thing couldn't be more than three or four. Kaleb's age.

"Hello, baby girl."

"Sit with you?" The girl asked.

"Jayda, don't bother her." A woman in her late twenties with hair in cornrows and dressed in jeans and a patterned sweater put her hand on her daughter's shoulders. "That's not Meemaw."

"I know." Baby Girl placed her hands on her hips and gave her mother a haughty look. "Meemaw's old."

Rose chuckled.

"Jayda!" Her mama admonished.

Rose winked at the little imp, who beamed back at her.

"See?" Jayda challenged.

The mother shook her head. "I'm sorry, ma'am."

Before Rose could respond, Baby Girl had climbed into the empty seat beside her. Rose waved the mother off when she apologized again.

"She's welcome to join me and so are you."

"Well…" She hesitated a moment, then placed her bag, car keys, and coffee cup on the table. "Thank you. I'm Kimberly, by the way."

"Rose."

"I'm Jayda!"

"I guess we're old friends now." Rose smiled.

Kimberly returned the smile as she sank into her seat. She closed her eyes and drank her coffee, a peaceful look on her face.

"Mommy needed a moment," Jayda explained.

"Then we'll let her have it," Rose stage-whispered. "Do you know how to play I Spy? That was one of my favorite games when I was your age."

Jayda shook her head, red bows bouncing. Rose explained the rules. Jayda wanted to go first, but Rose thought it best if she guessed the first time in order to catch on.

"Okay," Rose said. "I spy something yellow."

"The sun!" Jayda shouted.

"A little closer to Earth, Baby Girl. Remember, it has to be something you can see."

"I can see the sun." Jayda pointed to the sky.

"Miss Kimberly, you've got a real bright little girl here."

"Tell me about it," Kimberly said in amusement. "She keeps me hopping."

"That car." Jayda pointed to the SUV parked in front of the store. "It's yellow. Is that what you spy?"

Rose nodded. "It is indeed. See, I knew you were smart."

"My turn." Jayda grinned. "I spy something green."

"Your mama's ring."

Jayda's mouth dropped open. "How did you know?"

Rose leaned in and whispered, "I'm smart, too."

The little girl giggled. "Can we play again?"

"Some other time, child." Rose pushed her seat back. "This old woman best be moseying along home."

"You're not old," Jayda insisted. "Old people are boring."

"Thank you, Miss Jayda." Rose placed a hand on the girl's head. "You be good for your mama."

"Did you walk, ma'am?" Kimberly asked. "We'd be more than happy to give you a lift home."

Rose shook her head. "Walking's good for the soul. Thank you, though, it was a kind offer."

"Maybe we'll see you here again."

"Maybe so. I'm here most Sunday afternoons after church. Goodbye, Miss Jayda."

"Bye, Miss Rose!"

Yep, a right smart girl there.

"Thanks for sharing the table," Kimberly said.

"You're most welcome." Rose gave a little wave and headed off.

As she walked the three blocks home, she thought about how Jayda said she wasn't old but thought her Meemaw was because she was boring. Maybe age really was a state of mind and only children saw the truth. Now that was a philosophy, and one the fellow widow lady could use, although Rose still had no plans to respond. Some things you just had to figure out for yourself.

Myra

The morning alarm woke me from a sound sleep. I couldn't remember what I'd been dreaming, but it put a smile on my face. I pushed Gracie off my legs so I could get up and make us both some breakfast. Despite her sad, soulful dark eyes, I resisted the urge to share my scrambled eggs with bacon and cherry tomatoes.

"I'll take you for a nice long walk later," I promised as I let her out into the backyard to do her business.

On Saturdays, the shelter preferred to have me in there early to clean and then help greet guests if I had the time. I enjoyed the interaction with the animals and the people, but it did leave poor Grace by herself for most of the day.

By the time I cleaned up the meal, she was scratching at the door. I let her come back in, then took a quick shower and threw on a pair of jeans and a purple T-shirt with the shelter logo emblazoned across the front. I grabbed a gold one as well, since the first one tended to get dirty during my first shift.

"Don't worry, love." I patted her sweet head. "I'll be home before you know it."

She whined in disagreement and flopped down in her bed by the window. Animals could lay on a guilt trip better than a religious mother.

I slipped my purse over my shoulder and headed out the door. The sun shone through the few clouds in the sky, which held the promise of another beautiful fall day.

"Can you give Maxine her pill?" Janet asked the moment I walked into the building. "She takes it better for you."

"Sure thing." I hung my things on the post. "Anything else?"

"No." Janet shook her head for emphasis. "Well, one of the new kittens was sick last night and Tracey hasn't had time to clean that cage."

"I'll start right after pilling Maxine," I assured the poor girl.

Tracey was the shelter director, and Janet was meant to be the manager. She did okay, but pawned the worst work off on the staff. I didn't mind. I just liked having somewhere to go, someplace people and animals needed me.

I rounded up a pair of gloves, the disinfectant, and the harsh paper towels and went to the feline isolation area to clean the cages. Most of them were empty, which I took to be a good sign. Empty cages meant the newest residents had passed quarantine and moved on to the kitten room, the adult cat room, or, if they were truly lucky, a foster or forever home.

After scrubbing the empty pens, I spent some time socializing with the few kitties left in the area. Miggy, a black and white cutie, mewed and pawed at me, so he received the bulk of my attention. I also spoke to Tito, a handsome gray fellow. He was too new and too scared to let anyone touch him, although his ears twitched back and forth at the sound of my voice.

"That means you'll relax soon enough," I told him. "And then we'll find a home for you. Just wait and see. I'll sneak you a treat later."

"You will do no such thing," Tracey said with a smile in her voice as she entered the room. "He's a big enough boy already."

"He's just fluffy. Right, Tito?"

Tracey laughed. "He's the man, alright." She moved to the back of the room where the washer and dryer were and started sorting clothes. "Listen, Joey has the flu. Can you man the front desk for a few hours by any chance?"

"Of course." I stripped off my gloves and shoved them in the appropriate canister. "Give me five minutes to get cleaned up and changed."

"You are a lifesaver."

One of the many things I'd learned working for a non-profit—the smallest favor you did was met with high praise, even if you didn't consider your contributions to be a big deal. Charities needed volunteers to function effectively, so I guess they figured if they showered you with appreciation, you'd stick around.

Getting to chat with people was by far the best part of being up front. I enjoyed seeing everyone come in, especially the families, with the expectant look in their eyes, and then seeing them again as they headed out, the grins and simple joy on the human and animal faces alike.

The downside of desk duty was the long, boring bits between visitors and potential adopters. I could always fold the shirts and other items for sale, or straighten the sign-in sheets and adoptions applications, or dust the bookcases and rearrange the literature. All of that took about twenty minutes, so the remainder of the time was spent watching the door.

Luckily, Saturdays tended to be fairly busy and the first guests arrived only moments after I sat down. A boisterous family by the look of them, mom and dad glancing around while their two boys, twins about six or seven, bounced into the building. They'd be here for a dog, no doubt.

"Hello there," The dad flashed a friendly smile.

"We're getting a new dog!" The boy in the yellow soccer jersey shouted.

"Inside voice," his mom said wearily.

"Are you going to take care of him or her?" I asked the kids.

Yellow Jersey nodded. His brother blushed deep enough to match the red jersey he was wearing. Oh, these two definitely needed a puppy. Or three.

"Use the hand sanitizer and then go on back," I instructed. "Susan will let you meet the different dogs and help you find a good one."

I'd buzzed the back room using the buttons at the desk so she'd know there was someone up front. I wished there was also a way to let her know the adopters were a family, though I suppose she'd figure that out soon enough.

"Thank you," the dad said.

"Good luck." I waved to them before they entered the next area.

Almost as soon as my butt hit the chair, the entry bell dinged again and a new person enter. Single woman this time. Mid-forties if I had to guess. Glasses. Kinda chunky. Ratty aqua sweater with designer jeans. She'd be looking for a cat.

"Hi," she said in a soft tone.

"How can I help you?" I smiled at her and stood.

"I'm here to see Helen." Her dark blue eyes took on a note of sadness. "She's expecting me."

Hmm….hadn't seen that one coming. Then again, she could've recently lost her pet and wasn't quite ready to commit to another one just yet. That's how Helen convinced quite a few people to drop by, or so Tracey had told me.

"Let me go check." I handed her a brochure. "I'll be a minute. Here's some information on our shelter. Read that and I'll get Helen."

I wasn't supposed to leave the desk, but I couldn't be sure who was still back there to respond to the buzzer. I found Helen in the kitten room, a bemused grin on her face. Spending time with puppies, kittens, or any other animal babies brought amusement and joy. If they weren't so damn cute, they'd never survive to adulthood with all their antics.

"Someone here to see you," I told her and quickly described the woman.

"My word, she actually came." Helen gently worked the tabby kitten clinging to her shoulder loose and handed her to me. "I'll go get Maureen."

The kitten mewed at me and tried to cling to my shirt. I placed it on the floor, where it was absorbed into a group chasing after a ping pong ball. Damn, but they were cute. I left the room before I got sucked in and headed back to the relative safety of the front desk. The woman was gone, replaced by a man not much younger than I.

"Well, how do you do?" He extended his hand and I shook it out of pure reflex.

"How can I help you?" I asked.

"Not sure."

His smile and body were relaxed, at ease even in an unfamiliar place. I wondered if he might have a background in sales or customer service. Something people-facing, at any rate.

"Are you looking to adopt a pet?" I asked.

"Not exactly. You see, I found a dog," he said. "Roaming my neighborhood. Poor fella seemed hungry, so I fed him. Now he won't stop hanging around the place and none of the neighbors want him or will own up to him being theirs."

Now we were getting somewhere. Rather than take a pet home, he wanted us to take the animal off his hands.

"Do you have the animal with you?" I wiped my hands on my jeans.

"In my truck." The man turned and glanced out the window. "Can I go get him? He's in the bed. I know better than to leave him in the cab in this weather."

"Has he been to the vet?"

The man blushed and shook his head. "He's not mine, y'see. He's a stray I happened to be feeding and I can't afford it. I'd like him to go to a good home. My co-worker said you guys don't kill the animals."

"That is true," I assured him.

"That mean you'll take him?" His eyes brightened with hope.

"Maybe." I held up my hand. "Let me call someone to come take a peek at him."

I used the phone to buzz the intake area and let the person who answered the phone know we had someone wanting to drop off a dog. Beth showed up a few minutes later and ushered the man outside. If the last half hour was any indication, this was going to be one busy Saturday indeed.

By the time I left the shelter, close to three o'clock, I wanted to go home and take a nap. But, since tonight was "book club" night, I stopped by the post office first to see if we had any new reading material.

"Holy Christmas!"

I could barely believe my eyes. The little cubbyhole was crammed full of envelopes. Plus we received three new emails this week, too. If this kept up, we were going to have to start having letter reading parties twice a week.

Even though my body and mind ached, I kept my word and took Gracie for a long walk once I arrived home. That was one thing I'd forgotten with owning a dog—the amount of exercise they required. I hadn't walked around my neighborhood this much in years!

Somehow, the simple joy of movement, along with Gracie's sweet face and wagging tail, managed to revive my spirit. When we got home, I decided to keep my T-shirt and jeans on and continue cleaning out the garage. Or I would have if the phone hadn't been ringing when we walked inside.

"Are you feeling okay?" June asked without preamble,

"Um, yes," I told her.

"Are you sure? You sound tired."

"I'm fine. Busy day is all."

She blew out her breath. "Well, we're all down with the crud here and Dolores just called to say she and Jim have it, too."

"Anything you need?" I asked.

"No, stay away," she said with force. "No sense you getting sick, too. But we're not gonna be there for the letter readings tonight. We'll have to wait a few days."

So that was what she was getting at! She may have been concerned about me catching something, but she really wanted to make sure I wouldn't read the latest batch of essays without her there. This from the person who originally shot down the idea. Guess you never know with people or experiments.

"I can wait a few days."

"I'll call you to let you know when we're on the mend. Take it easy so you don't get it, too."

"Y'all call if you need anything," I said.

"Got it. See ya."

Typical June, I thought as I hung up. She gets what she wants and forgets about anyone else. Which was an unfair statement in a way. June truly cared for people. She just had a hard time showing it, or saying it, but she was an absolute rock when you needed her to be.

I was a little disappointed not to be reading the next round of essays, though. The responses had taken off in the last few weeks. We'd read three letters and two emails last week, and we had another ten essays this week. Maybe we'd have a natural drop-off soon, but for the moment the experiment had exceeded beyond my wildest, wildest expectations.

"We really are going to have to get together twice a week," I told Gracie, who was curled up at the top of the stairs.

"You're useless to me," I kidded her. "Do you want to stay there and nap or come help me in the garage?"

Turned out she preferred to nap. That was preferable, actually, since I could get more done if she wasn't underfoot. She'd come get me when she got lonely, and that would be my sign to stop for the day.

In the last few weeks, I'd made significant progress in the inside rooms as well as the garage but found that working in the garage proved easier. The memories came, along with the mixture of joy and pain, just not with the same intensity. We stored what we no longer cared about in here, and the emotional ties were nowhere near as strong as they were with something I saw every day.

Take the workout equipment, for example. I uncovered three Thighmasters in one box, yet I cannot recall ever using one of them. Same for the weight set. Lee had high hopes for that one. Once you removed the dust, the set could have been brand new.

I kept a notebook and pen in my pocket as I combed through everything. If I felt someone else could use it, or might be interested in purchasing it, I wrote down the item and its location in the garage.

Once I'd completed my Herculean task, Betty's Jean was going to help me post items online for people to buy, and she promised to help me ship the item or to be here when they came to pick it up. I'd read too many stories of murder or kidnapping with these online exchanges to be completely comfortable having strangers dropping by, even if they were doing me the favor of getting rid of things I no longer needed.

Like the lawn mower. Lee bought the latest and greatest model about five years ago, but neither of us had used it since he took sick. At first, the guys would take turns coming over to cut the grass. Now, I paid a lawn service. I appreciated my friends helping out, but they had their own lives to focus on. The lawn service was a perfect solution for everyone.

All the old clothes I hauled off to Goodwill. I didn't even bother to look to see if I might want something. If they'd been relegated to the garage, there was no point in trying to work them back into regular rotation. I just hoped that the majority of pieces were in style or could be used for some other purpose.

The holiday decorations I set aside. Those I still used, but needed to do an inventory. I'd take care of that chore later, once everything else had been gone through and either kept, sold, or given away. Or maybe I'd wait until Christmas.

It truly is amazing how much you can accumulate in forty years of being in the same house. I wasn't quite ready to try the fancy new trend of "Swedish death cleaning". No, I just wanted to clear out the history, and some of the memories, and find out what I needed to go on with this life by myself.

The question of whether or not to sell the old place had occurred to me, even if none of my friends had mentioned it. The prevailing wisdom was not to make any major decisions for the first year after your spouse passes, and I believed that to be good advice.

I wasn't quite at one year. That dreaded anniversary loomed on the horizon, however. Each day seemed to get a little easier. I continued to dread the holidays, even though I'd successfully survived each one so far. But...Thanksgiving and Christmas weren't terribly far away, and I would need every ounce of my own inner strength, not to mention the love and support of my dear friends, to get through those milestones.

One step at a time.

I'd found old art projects (mine) and old collectibles (Lee). Mine were worthless and not very good. Why in the world had I even kept the darn candles and ceramic vases and knitted potholders? As proof that I wasn't totally useless in that area? No idea, and I happily tossed them in the garbage bins when I came across them.

Some of Lee's collectibles might possibly be of some worth. The sports stuff had already proven more valuable than I could have ever dreamed, and the shelter profited from this part of my husband's past.

The coin collection, the plates, and shot glasses would have to be appraised. Jean would do that research for me, since she already planned to help me sell the items online. What we couldn't find out using a computer, an in-person evaluation by an antique or collectibles dealer should give us some idea of worth.

I'd bet that the coin collection would be the only one that brought in any money. No one collected plates anymore, or at least you no longer saw them advertised on TV. And the shot glasses from all the different places we'd visited over the last several decades were sentimental to us. I couldn't imagine someone else wanting a shot glass from Mexico or Vancouver or any of the other places if they hadn't been there themselves.

Then again, you never could tell what people might consider valuable.

Grace poked me with her large head, bringing me back to reality. Had that much time really passed?

"Enough time in the past, huh, girlie?" I gave her a good pat. "Let's get both of us some dinner. What are you in the mood for?"

I gave her the standard kibble while I searched for my own meal. After the day I'd had, I expected to be hungry, but instead I didn't feel like eating. Or cooking, for that matter.

"What do I have that's quick?" I muttered as I searched the fridge and freezer.

I had bread, butter, and cheddar, so I could do a quick grilled cheese. I also had the chips to accompany the sandwich. As I was organizing the ingredients on the counter, the phone rang.

"Myra, that you?" Dolores asked.

Who did these women expect to answer my phone? They knew all too well that it was just me in the house these days.

"Listen, we're all under the weather here," Dolores said. "We're not going to make it tonight. You okay with that? You're not sick, too, are you?"

"June already called." I pulled the phone cord to allow more room to maneuver. "Tonight's meeting is cancelled. Y'all get some rest, feel better, and let me know if you need anything."

"Sounds good."

Dolores hung up. I returned my attention to preparing my simple meal.

With all the technology available today, couldn't June and Dolores somehow have communicated with the other that they were going to call me? I didn't really need to hear the news twice. I was, however, still disappointed at not seeing my friends and not getting the chance to read the essays.

Part of me felt like I actually could read the essays on my own first. After all, it was *my* experiment.

The more reasonable, giving part of myself knew better than to do such a thing. The curiosity might be overwhelming, but these women had shared in my idea from the beginning, before we even knew it would work, and they deserved the right to hear the essays at the same time I did.

"Fair's fair," I told Gracie.

She glanced up at me, then returned to her food. I loved the way she took her time with eating. Most dogs I knew wolfed everything down so fast you wondered if they'd even had the chance to taste it.

After I finished eating my grilled cheese, I washed up and decided I could use a good cleaning as well. My phone buzzed as I was undressing. Mabel, letting me know we weren't meeting tonight. Really?

I chuckled as I let her know I was well aware of the change in plans. Rather than get irritated, I decided to view this as my friends caring for me mingled with their own disappointment at not being here. Yup, that's what I was going with.

Liz

"Mom, have you seen my green shirt?" Brenda hovered in the kitchen doorway and glared at everyone.

"I want another piece of cinnamon toast," Cameron declared without looking up from his iPad.

"Me, too," Bethany said as she tried to steal the device from her brother.

"Cam, let your sister have a turn," Liz said automatically. "I'll make the toast."

After putting the bread in the toaster, Liz stared out the tiny window above the sink at the perfectly manicured lawn. Even with the trees losing their leaves, somehow the yard remained a perfect shade of green. Their landscaper deserved a bonus.

"I'll be late tonight." Charlie gave her a peck on the cheek. "Taking a client to dinner."

"Mom, my shirt," Brenda whined.

Liz stared back at her eldest. "Y'know, I think you're old enough to learn how to do your own laundry. I'll start teaching you this weekend."

Charlie squeezed his daughter's shoulder as he stepped past her and slipped out the door.

"Fine." Brenda sighed. "Can you help me find my green shirt now at least?"

"Check your closet," Liz suggested. "If it's not there, try your dresser. If you don't see it there, I'll help you look. Okay?"

Brenda rolled her eyes, but trudged upstairs to begin the search. With that request taken care of, Liz turned her attention to the little ones.

"More toast," Cam demanded again.

"No time." Liz picked up the plate and glass in front of him. "Go get ready for carpool. Mrs. Simmons is always early. Bethany, give me the tablet."

Liz ignored the groans and complaints as they scampered off. She slathered butter on the toast and bit off a piece. Brenda's triumphant shout of "found it" brought a secret smile. Liz knew the girl would find it, and she also knew it was high time her eldest washed her own clothes.

"Are you working today?" Brenda paused on her way out the door.

Liz nodded. "I'll be home when Cam and Bethany get dropped off. You can go out with the gang after band practice."

"Gucci." With a quick hug, she was gone.

Ten minutes later, Cam and Bethany were also on their way to school and Liz could think. Much had changed in the last few months, but the joy of a temporarily silent house still remained one of the best moments of the day.

Only now she had less time to enjoy it, and she was okay with that fact. After weeks of discussion, she and Charlie had agreed that she should take the job at the real estate agency. To her surprise, the kids had also been behind her. Especially Brenda.

"Mom can work and be here when the ankle biters get off the bus," Brenda pointed out. "It's no big deal."

Liz wanted to hug her daughter.

"Bethany's in school all day now," Liz had said when she and Charlie were alone. "And we're not planning on having any more."

"You don't *need* to work," her husband countered.

"I *want* to work," she insisted. "This is the twenty-first century, Charlie. Both parents work in most families."

"But I can take care of you," he insisted. "You know that I promised myself that my wife wouldn't have to work herself to the bone like my mom did."

He looked so confused she wanted to wrap him in her arms, but that would not help her case. Was there a way to appeal to the emotional side of her husband along with the lawyer side? She was certainly going to try.

"MaryEllen worked because she didn't have a choice." Liz kept her tone calm and even.

"And you do."

"Listen," Liz said before changing tactics again. "Your mother is an amazing woman and she was a great role model for you. I want to be that same type of role model for our kids. And I think showing them that I can handle a job and take care of the house and my family without wearing myself out will help them once they grow up and have lives of their own."

Charlie started pacing. That was the signal that she was wearing him down, so she pressed her point.

"Maybe seeing how competent I am will help Cam pick a strong partner," she said. "And my making the choice to work, even if it's part-time, will show Brenda and Bethany that they can balance a career and a family."

He stopped in his tracks and looked at her. "What exactly will you be doing again?"

"I'll be helping to manage the office. I plan to bring them into the digital age. They still keep actual files." She shook her head. "Getting them organized and efficient helps the office and their customers."

"You'll be able to here for the kids if they get sick?" He stroked his chin with his forefinger.

She nodded. "I'll even be able to take my turn as carpool parent."

"And what if something happens to my mom?"

"Charles Alan Dunleavy, your mother is sixty-five and in perfect health." Liz put her hands on her hips. "But *if* something should happen—God forbid—we will do whatever we need to take care of her."

"Okay, but—"

"Charlie, stop," she said in a gentle voice. "I love you, and I give you my word that everything will be okay. The kids are fine with me working. Your mom is fine with me having a job. I need you to be fine with it, too."

"Okay, okay." Charlie held up his hands. "We can give it a shot."

Liz threw her arms around him and squeezed him tight.

"I love you, too." He hugged back and placed a kiss on the top of her head.

That conversation had taken place two months ago, and the plan had worked beyond Liz's wildest hopes. Every day, she saw the kids off to school and Charlie off to work, then headed over to the strip-mall office.

She got a thrill every time she walked through the front doors and heard the keyboards clacking and people talking. The buzz of activity sent a shock through her—a good, energizing kind of jolt.

"Excellent. You're here." Bob gave her a big smile. "The copier is jammed and we're trying to get the booklets printed for the open houses this weekend."

"On it." Liz hung her purse on her chair and went to look at the copier.

Why did this big machine perplex everyone so much? The image on the screen displayed where the jam occurred. Following the directions, she had the pages spewing out again in a few minutes.

"You're a miracle worker!" Bob thumped her on the back. "Anna, finish putting those mini-binders together. I'm off to sign our next client."

Anna waved to her boss while Liz went to the front desk. With Bob out, visitors were unlikely, but he still preferred to have someone sitting and working there. Liz didn't mind—she would've worked in the coat closet if necessary.

In the short time Liz had been at the real estate agency, she'd made several improvements. She changed their group cell phone plan to save them money, upgraded the network, installed a postal meter in the mailroom, and set up corporate accounts at Staples, UPS, and the deli down the street.

While these things seemed like no-brainers to her, Bob and the rest of his staff were delighted. They were, however, fighting her on some of her plans to digitize the office. While they'd been using DocuSign for years in terms of signing contracts, they didn't see why it would be helpful to put their client information forms online.

"You can't have people entering their Social Security Numbers on an online form," Kathy, one of the real estate agents, insisted at the last staff meeting. "What if we get hacked?"

"You have people faxing or emailing them over now," Liz countered. "What if you left the forms in your car and someone broke in? It's much easier to encrypt the information instead of having it sitting out somewhere."

"Hmmm...is that expensive?" Bob asked. "Put a proposal together."

Liz was still working on that. Since the office didn't have a resident IT person, the work would have to be outsourced. Luckily, she knew a few people from her stints on the different boards who charged a fair price.

For the time being, she had Lara, one of the other part-time workers, taking information from the client files and entering it into Microsoft Access. Liz was going to bring The Bob Klopp Agency into the twenty-first century if it was the last thing she did.

Even with her time on non-profit boards, Liz forgot how much of a thrill it was to go into the office every day. Or from 8 until 2 five days a week.

Being part of a team felt good. With the board memberships, bringing everyone together could be difficult. It could in an office, too, although Liz found that with non-profits, everyone wanted to lead and, in an office, no one wanted to be in charge. After years of herding children and husband, plus dealing with all of the board egos, Liz had become a natural leader.

Bob's staff consisted of himself and two other agents, one dedicated to selling homes and the other dedicated to finding buyers their new house. The office also boasted three part-time assistants and Liz herself, the part-time office manager.

Although their agency consistently placed in the top one hundred for their region, Bob's dream was to move up to the top fifty. Liz adopted that as her goal, and even in the short time she'd been there they'd moved up one space. After six months or a year, she was sure she could help Bob meet or succeed that goal.

"Hey, Liz," Lara called. "Bob just texted and wants to know if you can email him a new client form? He forgot to bring one with him."

"Tell him he'll have it in two minutes."

And that, Liz thought, is why you need digital forms. You can pull it up on your tablet, complete it or have the client complete it, and save it to the network once you're done. Once she sent the document to Bob, Liz got to work on her proposal for the new system.

The hours flew by and soon Liz was done for the day. Working was both challenging and fun, but she enjoyed every minute of it. Even Charlie told her how much happier she seemed these days.

Since carpool wouldn't drop the kids off for another hour, Liz opted to swing by the library to drop off some books and visit with Corinne.

"Hey there, lady." Corinne hugged her. "We don't see as much of you these days."

"Less time to read." Liz breathed a happy sigh. "I can't believe I actually get to say this, but work keeps me hopping."

Corinne pumped her fist in the air.

"I know." Liz grinned. "I'm so happy you suggested me."

"Please." Her friend shrugged off the praise. "You were perfect for the position. Now, are you here for kids books or are you looking for something to read when you get a moment?"

"Both," Liz said. "Do you have the next installment of the LG Bridges series? *The Keepers*? Bethany can't get enough of those."

"She'll have to wait a few months, unfortunately." Corinne frowned, then brightened. "I have just the thing to keep her occupied, though. Oh, and the new fantasy book about Medea came in. I put that aside for you."

Liz waited while her friend went to retrieve the books. Once she returned, Corinne got called away before they could continue their conversation. They shared a quick hug goodbye, and Liz went to check out before heading home to meet the little ones.

"Mom!" Cameron yelled as he burst into the house. "Can I go play at Nick's? He has the new racing game."

Bethany followed her brother inside, dragging her purple backpack.

"What's up, buttercup?" Liz went over to her youngest and tickled her stomach. "Why so blue?"

"Buttercups are yellow."

"Mom, can I go?" Cam fidgeted from one foot to the other.

Liz sighed. "Yes, fine, go. Be back in time for dinner." She watched as he took off across the street. All boy, that one. "So, Miss B, what happened?"

When tears formed in Bethany's eyes, Liz picked her daughter up and held her while she bawled. What in the world could've happened? Bethany hadn't cried in her arms in a very long time, and not after school. Had someone made fun of her Halloween costume idea?

"Talk to me, love," Liz whispered as she lowered her daughter to the ground.

"Can I have cake?"

"Umm…sure," Liz agreed.

"Thanks!"

After wiping her eyes and running an arm across her nose, the child sat down at the kitchen table. Figuring that the sooner she brought the treat, the sooner she'd find out what was going on, Liz cut a slice of chocolate cake and placed it in front of her daughter.

"Can I have some milk, please?"

"Coming right up." Liz poured a glass of milk.

She let Bethany dive into the cake. Food shouldn't be the answer to life's problems, but the girl was only six. If she was hurt, let her take comfort in chocolate.

"Do you want to talk about it?" Liz smoothed back her daughter's silky hair and kissed the top of her head.

"Are you and Daddy getting a divorce?"

Talk about a kick to the solar plexus. Where in the world had her daughter gotten an idea like that? She and Charlie tried not to fight in front of the children, and other than the discussions about Liz working, they didn't have much to argue about. Charlie kissed her goodbye every morning and they often showed affection in front of the kids.

"Why would you think that?" Liz asked.

"Addison said her parents got a divorce after her mom started working."

"Addison's parents are still married." Or had something changed that she hadn't heard about yet?

"No," Bethany insisted. "Not Addison Connors. Addison Collins."

"Oh."

Jake and Marie Collins had indeed split up two years ago, but not because Marie went back to work. It was because of Jake's continued infidelities. Both Jake and Marie were high-powered attorneys and the divorce had been ugly. Their two children, Taylor and Addison, had not had an easy time of it. Maybe it was better to have Addison think her mother working was the cause rather than the truth.

"Your daddy and I are not getting a divorce."

"But Daddy didn't want you to have a job." Tears formed in Bethany's eyes again. "I heard him say so."

"He also changed his mind," Liz replied. "Daddy and I don't always agree, but we love each other and forgive each other. We're staying together."

"Promise?"

"Promise." Liz hugged her little girl. "Now tell me something positive that happened at school today."

"I knew all my spelling words." Bethany's face lit up. "I got a 100 on the test."

"Well done." Liz gave her another hug. "Now go play in your room or the backyard until dinner."

"I'll color in my room." Bethany hopped down from the chair and went upstairs, taking her bookbag with her.

With the crisis averted, Liz turned her thoughts to dinner. Her phone buzzed, distracting her. It was a text from Charlie reminding her that he was taking a client to dinner and would be home late. Maybe she'd stay up and wait for him the way she used to when they were first married.

Liz peered in the fridge to check her options for dinner. She eyed the ground beef, but wasn't in the mood for meatloaf or meatballs or meat anything. In fact, she wasn't in the mood to cook at all. They hadn't ordered Chinese for a while. Why not have it tonight?

The kids loved the idea when she ran it past them so Liz asked Brenda to dig out the menu from the junk drawer while she got her credit card.

"Hey, Mom?"

"Yes?" Brenda sounded hesitant and unsure, which got Liz's antenna up. "Can't find it?"

Liz turned to see her oldest child staring at a piece of paper and holding it away from her like a smelly diaper.

"What is it?" Liz asked.

"The letter," Brenda said in a hushed tone. "From that lady."

"What lady? Did you find the menu?"

"The lady wanting to know our personal philosophy."

"Okay." Liz couldn't see what the big deal was.

"I thought you tossed it," Brenda said accusingly.

"I guess I put it in the junk drawer instead by mistake. I'll throw it out now."

"No!" Brenda clutched the letter close to her chest.

"Fine. Keep it." Her mother nudged her aside. "I'll look for the damn Chinese menu myself."

The little ones came clamoring down the stairs, ready to tell her what they wanted. Liz finally dug out the menu from Crystal Palace and handed it to Cameron. He'd take forever to decide, then go for the shrimp in lobster sauce like always.

"I want to see," Bethany cried.

"You can't read it," Cam teased.

"I can so!"

"Let her see it," Liz ordered.

"I haven't decided yet," Cam whined. "She can have it when I'm done."

Liz should've just ordered and told everyone they were having Chinese food for dinner. Then her youngest two wouldn't be fighting and her oldest wouldn't be acting so odd.

"Do you know what you want?" Liz asked her.

"Beef and broccoli," Brenda said. "Do you think putting the letter here and me finding it is a sign?"

"Yes," her mother replied. "A sign that I'm losing my mind."

"I think it means we have to respond."

Where in the world was this coming from? Sure, teenagers could be screwy, but Brenda wasn't one to read horoscopes or tap the wall six times before getting dressed or believing in any of that superstitious or supernatural mumbo jumbo.

"And why should we respond?"

"Mr. Bradley told us today in English class that there are no coincidences," Brenda said. "He said there are connections in the world and sometimes we don't understand them until later."

"Mom, Cam won't give me the menu."

Almost absently, Liz stepped over, took the menu from Cam and handed it to Bethany.

"I thought you were reading *A Tree Grows In Brooklyn*."

"We started Shakespeare this week. *Macbeth*."

Ah, the weird sisters. They'd had an effect on Liz and her friends as teenagers, too. They'd read each other's palms and done tarot and held the clasp of a necklace above their wrists to let it predict the number and sex of the children each of them would have. She didn't remember the results, but it would be interesting to know if any of it had been correct.

Good old Macbeth. Brenda's behavior made more sense now. If she wanted to read something into the fact that her mother's forgetfulness meant they should participate in this lady's crazy experiment, so be it.

"Fine. We'll take part. Now, Bethany, what do you want for dinner?"

"Kung pao chicken."

"Thank you." Liz dug through her purse for her phone. "Now go do homework for the next thirty minutes, all of you."

"But I didn't say what I wanted," Cam complained.

"Shrimp with lobster sauce," Liz said. "Right?"

Cam nodded.

"Good. Now shoo."

After they scattered and she could think again, Liz ordered the food. She stayed seated at the table and opened the Facebook app. Way too much happening there, so she closed it again. As she started to go check on the laundry situation, the invitation caught her eye.

She read the letter. Well, they were certainly beyond the thirty day mark, but somehow Liz knew that wouldn't stop her daughter. That thought seemed to summon the actual person as Brenda came back into the kitchen.

"Done with homework already?"

Brenda shook her head. "I've been thinking."

"Good or bad?"

"Not sure."

Liz waited for her daughter to continue, but Brenda remained silent.

"Not sure if your thinking is good or bad?" Liz prompted.

"Yeah."

Talking to a teenager was enough to drive you crazy. One word responses, vague comments, and then if you got upset or asked for clarification, they looked at you like you were the lunatic.

"Why don't you tell me what you're thinking and I'll help you decide. We have time before the food arrives."

Or we should if you get to the point.

"I was trying to decide on what I wanted to write for my essay." Brenda pursed her lips as she chewed the inside of her cheek. "And I don't know what to say."

Essay? Oh, for the letter. Liz blinked. She hadn't really expected her daughter to take it so seriously.

"You don't have to decide tonight."

"So you don't know what your personal philosophy is either?" Brenda sounded surprised.

Liz smiled and put her arm around her daughter. "Honestly, I never gave it much thought. I was too busy living life and taking care of my family."

"Do you think Dad has one?"

"Why don't you ask him?"

And do it when I'm not around, Liz finished in her head. She loved the man, but he had an awful tendency of turning the most innocuous question into a lecture. When Cam asked him why he didn't get a new briefcase (the latch was sticking on the current one), his father expounded on the virtue of not wasting money for nearly twenty minutes.

"I'll ask him once I figure out mine," Brenda said.

"That's my girl." Liz gave her a squeeze. "Now, let's go take a look at the laundry and I'll start teaching you how to do your own."

Brenda rolled her eyes, but joined her mother in the utility room. Her bored expression as Liz explained the different ways of sorting clothes amused her mother. At least this subject got her off the last one, which was the real goal anyway. After the load of whites went into the washer, she asked Brenda to set the table.

Cam and Bethany came galumphing down the steps a few minutes later, so she asked them to help their sister.

"After dinner, you can wrap coins," she told them. "There's a 1% helper fee in it for both of you."

"Mom, they don't know how to do percents," Brenda said as she glanced out the window. "Hey, delivery guy just pulled up."

Liz went to pay the man, trailed by two of her little ducklings. The four of them were soon seated around the table, quietly enjoying their meal. Rather than try to get a conversation going, Liz opted to let them eat in peace.

For all their faults and the craziness they added to her life, she couldn't help but love them more every day. They were growing up, developing their individual personalities, and moving away from needing her all the time, but they were still her babies. And for now, she still had them all with her.

She smiled to herself as she watched them eat, marveling at how their personalities came out even while in the midst of such an everyday task.

Bethany sat on her knees for leverage, hunched over her plate as if protecting it from some unseen enemy. Cam shoveled in food so fast she wondered if he even had time to chew it. Charlie often chastised him and tried to make him slow down, but tonight Liz let her son be. He did everything with the same fierce energy, as if the world might stop if he did.

And then there was Brenda, staring moodily at her food and then into the ether, as if her thoughts were drifting somewhere in space. In reality, she was probably pondering how soon she could slip away to chat with her friends online.

"Mom!" Brenda waved a hand in front of her mother's face. "Aren't you going to eat?"

"Yes." Liz picked up her fork. "I was thinking."

"About Daddy?" Bethany asked.

"About how much I love you."

Cam gagged, Brenda rolled her eyes, and Bethany giggled.

"Will Daddy be here to tuck me in?" Bethany asked.

Liz hesitated.

"Dad's with a client," Brenda explained. "He's an important lawyer and can't be bothered to spend time with his children."

"Don't be saying things like that," Liz admonished. "It's simply not true. He tucked you in when you were little, and he'll be here to make sure this little monster is snug as a bug in a rug, too."

Cam pretended to throw up this time. "Can I go play video games? Yes, I finished my homework."

Liz nodded and sent him off with a flick of her wrist. Bethany soon followed, leaving the oldest with their mother as she finished her meal. Liz figured the girl wanted to have a talk about something, yet knew better than to rush her. Instead, she ate and waited, hoping the subject would be a positive one.

"Why did you and Dad get married?"

"Because we loved each other," Liz said.

Brenda shook her head. "I'm not a kid anymore, Mom. You can tell me the truth."

"I did." Liz sighed. Where was her daughter going with this?

"So it's that simple?" Brenda stared at her mother. "You're in love so you get married."

"For me and your dad, yes."

"How did you know he was the one? How did you know you wanted to spend the rest of your life with him and grow old together?"

My word. Did these questions come from reading *Macbeth* or had they moved on to *Romeo and Juliet*? Liz could understand that the Scottish play might have her daughter taking a coincidence as a sign, but not wondering about how and why her parents decided to tie the knot. And she doubted Bethany had expressed her fears with her big sister since the two rarely crossed paths. Which meant…

"Are you and Justin still just friends?"

Brenda aligned her fork and knife, straightening the utensils until they were perfectly parallel.

"Does he know your feelings have changed?" her mother asked.

Liz wasn't quite sure what she wanted the answer to be. Brenda had dated before, but nothing truly serious. The few boyfriends she'd had lasted weeks, although she and Justin had been friends since middle school. He was a nice kid, from a good family, and cute. Liz held her breath waiting for the response.

"Not yet," Brenda muttered.

Liz exhaled.

"Don't you tell him, either!"

"Why would I say something like that?" Liz stood and started collecting the plates.

Brenda hunched inward. "He wouldn't care anyway."

"Don't say that." Liz placed the dishes in the sink. "You're smart, funny, and pretty. Justin loves you and he'd be a fool not to go out with you."

"You mean it?" Brenda looked at her mother with hope. "You're not just saying that because you're my mom?"

Liz sent a silent message to her own mother, apologizing for ever having been a teenager.

"Fine. The truth is you're a horrible, ugly beast with bad breath and no man or woman is going to give you a second glance. Now hand me the silverware."

Brenda giggled. "Should I make a move on him?"

How did other women survive this stage? Liz knew she should be grateful her daughter still turned to her for advice, but walking the tightrope between being a mother and being a friend was treacherous. Damn those TV shows for making this shit look easy!

"Do your due diligence first," she advised. "Have your friends ask his friends to see what he says. It'll save you the embarrassment of him possibly rejecting you in person. Believe me, that stings."

Brenda wrinkled her brow. "So you don't think he likes me?"

"No, love, I don't know what he feels and neither do you." Liz gathered the forks and knives from the table. "I'm merely offering you a way to find out without getting hurt."

"Oh."

"Talk it over with your friends, but don't post anything online where other people can read it."

Brenda rolled her eyes.

"Or you can stay and help me clean up."

"No thanks." Brenda wrinkled her nose. "I'll ask Stefanie what she thinks. Ooh, I can tell her about the letter, too. We can figure out my personal philosophy."

Liz couldn't help but chuckle. What was that 80's song by The Style Council? *My Ever Changing Moods*? The writer of that song had either been or known a teenager because the name captured the life stage perfectly. She hoped Cam would be less dramatic, although she suspected boys brought their own set of trials.

Charlie walked in as the last fork was loaded in the dishwasher. His long face and drooping posture expressed more about his day than words ever could. Liz closed the distance from the kitchen to the foyer in two quick strides and pulled him close.

"That's more like it." He held her for several seconds.

"Are you hungry?" she tilted her head to look up at him.

"Had dinner with the client."

"Right. Cold glass of beer?"

"That I'll take you up on." He let her go and took a step back. "Let me decompress and shower first."

"It'll be ready when you are."

"You're the best." Charlie leaned in again for a quick kiss. "Are the kids still up?"

"Should be. You can check on them if you like. Save me the trip upstairs. Oh, and Bethany wants you to tuck her in."

He gave her a wink and a smile, which brightened both their moods. Married life might not be perfect, but these shared moments certainly helped make it special.

Brenda's Essay

This is so cool. I can't believe my mom agreed to do this, but how could she not? She put the letter in the junk drawer for a reason. I think we should get to read what each other has to say. Mom didn't like that idea, and I guess it is supposed to be anonymous and all. Still, she could at least tell me her philosophy even if I don't get to see the full essay.

I've given this lots of thought and didn't just write the first thing that jumped into my head. I didn't ask friends, either, although I really wanted to. I decided this was what I believed and if it really was to be personal, then I had to come up with something myself.

My personal philosophy is that you've got to roll with the changes. There's an old song that Mom plays on her phone sometimes, by The Speedwagons, and the song says you got to roll with the changes. When I heard that song again the other day, it was like a smack in the face. The song might be way old, but the words are still true.

Change is inevitable, or at least that's what my dad says. And if things are going to change, you might as well roll with them.

I can't even begin to list all the different times something changed in my life, it happens so often. I mean, I used to be the only child forever *and then Cam and Bethany came along so I had to adjust to being the big sister. Most of the time, it's nice being the oldest, until Mom or Dad asks me to share or take one of them somewhere or even stay in on a Friday or Saturday night to watch the kids while they go out.*

And school changes like every year, with new classes and new teachers. Sometimes new friends. Stefanie and I have been friends as far back as I can remember, and I hope we stay friends forever. Jenna and Sofia only moved here last year and we're like the Fantastic Four now. Julia moved away and we don't hear from her anymore, and Scott hangs out with the boys now.

Justin and I are still friends, and I'm hoping that changes slightly because I'm kinda into him lately. I don't want to lose the friendship, though. Some relationships start in high school and then people get married and stay together, so that could happen to Justin and me, too. Right?

We've had stuff change with Mom, too. She works now, which is Gucci. I haven't got to see her do her thing since she does it during the day. Maybe I can ask if I can join her on one of the teacher workdays or something, although she'll probably make me stay home and watch the rugrats. Doesn't hurt to ask, though, right?

This is so much more fun than writing papers for school! Here I get to say what I want and no one is going to grade me. I guess Mom was right that we shouldn't read each other's stuff because now I don't want her to read mine.

Dad had kittens when Mom wanted to go to work. At first, anyway. Now I think he likes it cause she's so happy.

That was another change we had to roll with, though. Mom not always being there when we wanted her. It's worked out fine, though. Even that time I fell in gym class and twisted my ankle, Mom was able to leave and come get me and take me to the doctor and everything just like she'd always done. Which only proves that Dad was being totally old-fashioned and needed to get with the times.

Hey, maybe Dad's the one who needs to learn to roll with the changes. I'll point that out next time he's around when Mom plays that song by The Speedwagons. Lol.

Or maybe he's grown old and doesn't remember what it was like to be young when things are always changing. I guess once you reach a certain age, things settle down, although I don't think that's ever possible, not really.

I mean, yeah, as an adult, you get more say, but you could still get divorced or lose your job or have to move or get cancer or something. Those would be changes you have to roll with, and it's better to roll with them than to fight them. That would be like that guy in that book Mom tells us about sometimes where he's fighting windmills.

I don't want to be like that guy. I want to roll with the changes, knowing that no matter how much something might suck at the moment, resisting is only going to make it worse and isn't going to make a difference.

This has been fun. I wish teachers assigned more essays like this where you have to think than the stupid things they normally assign. I'll bet you're having a blast reading what everyone has to say, huh?

Man, that makes me wish I could read them, too. Oh well, I get what anonymous means and with all the breaches and security stuff out there, I get why someone might not want to share if they thought the whole world would read what they wrote.

Liz's Essay

H as anyone who sent in an essay mentioned how intimidating it is to stare at a blank screen (or blank sheet of paper) and start putting words down? Even though you're the only one who's going to read what I have to say, the whole process is still daunting. However, the simple act of writing and sending this essay speaks to my personal philosophy, which is "don't lose faith in yourself."

I think the reason I chose that for my philosophy is that I've recently started living that belief.

And before I get to the meat of my essay, I do want to say that my daughter and I are very late in responding to the letter, but I'm thinking that will be okay. Not that I have a choice—my daughter found the invitation in the junk drawer and decided that the mere fact that I put it there instead of in the trash meant we were destined to respond. So here we are.

My life is quite different now than it was when we received the letter, although I don't believe one influenced the other. I probably would've had a different philosophy if we'd responded right away, though, so maybe there's something to Brenda's thought process.

Back in college, I'd wanted to do something special with my life, like manage people or teach school. Then I met Charlie and everything changed. Everything changed again when we had our first child, and my entire world became taking care of my family. That's still my number one priority, although I count taking care of my needs just as important as taking care of their needs.

I wouldn't have said that before, but that's because somewhere along the line I lost faith in myself. Not my abilities as a mother, or the way I took care of my husband. More like who I was and what I wanted out of life.

Change is not easy, and few people actually look forward to it. I'm a coward in that respect, although I knew I had to make a change or lose myself completely. What type of example would I set for my children if I allowed that to happen?

So I started working for a local real-estate agent. I can't believe how rewarding the job is, and how much of a difference it's made in my life and the life of my family. Even Charlie admits things are better now.

To be honest, I rediscovered my faith in myself and what I could accomplish. I will never, ever lose that faith again and if I see it happening to any of my children, I will take them aside and tell them everything I've learned by believing in and standing up for myself.

I wish I could tell it to everyone who's struggling in this way. It will take time and effort and energy, but it can be done if you have faith in yourself. That faith will show in your attitude, and once people know you believe in yourself, then they will believe in you, too.

I hope you haven't lost faith in yourself or, if you have, that this experiment and, more importantly, this letter, does something to start changing that belief. Because if you don't believe in yourself, who will?

At the end of the day, no matter how many people might be around you as friends and family, you are by yourself. And I don't mean alone. I mean by yourself. Answering only to yourself. Your thoughts, your moods, your beliefs. Remember that and remember that the most important thing you can do is to always have faith in yourself and who you are.

Mike

Mike looked at the clock. 11:16 AM. He should get up. But what was the point? No job to go to, no errands to run, no pets to feed, and no one who would notice or care if he stayed in bed.

Friends might check on him at some point. Family, too. All could be fooled over email and texts. The beauty of digital communication was that you couldn't decipher tone. Well, you could if you were really good at reading between the lines or the chat went on long enough, which is why Mike had perfected his ghosting technique ages ago.

Seven years he'd worked for the financial planning firm. They paid for his brokerage license and his designation as Chartered Financial Consultant. He got a thrill out of seeing ChFC after his name.

Well, he could still do that. And he could still help people plan their financial future. He knew plenty of solo planners, and plenty of independent agents, too. Maybe he could join their ranks instead of the ranks of the unemployed.

11:32 AM.

Okay, okay. Mike threw back the covers and sat up. He scratched at his beard, which was filling out nicely in this, his third week of joblessness.

"I wonder what Rick would think of it," he muttered. "Or Kaitlyn."

He pondered the idea of a threesome, and the thought brought a grin. The smile brought the feeling of dirty teeth, along with a dirty mind, and both thoughts propelled him out of bed and onto his feet.

"Mission accomplished."

Now that he was perpendicular, what next? A shower, to clean up and face the day? A shower, to further his fantasy of kissing Rick while Kaitlyn rubbed his—

The burring phone broke his dream.

"Goddammit!" He reached back to the nightstand. "What?"

"Dude, are you just getting up?" his brother Thomas asked.

Mike remained silent.

"Shower and call me back. I got news."

"Tell me now."

"I know better than to talk to you when you're half-conscious," Thomas said. "Shower. Call me back."

Mike stared at the blank screen. Fine, he'd follow instructions. Although he could go back to his nice, soft bed...

No, Thomas lived and worked nearby, and if Mike didn't phone him, he'd drop by. Plus he'd somehow know if Mike hadn't cleaned himself up. There was no point in crossing his big brother.

As the hot water streamed down his back, Mike felt almost hopeful. His mother used to say being clean made you feel better, so take a shower every day even if you were sick. She was right, but then she'd been right about quite a few things over the years. He was smart enough to keep that information to himself rather than share it with her.

Thomas hadn't said to get dressed, but Mike slipped on jeans and his lucky green polo before calling him back.

"What's the big news?"

"We're pregnant!" Thomas shouted. "Marty told me last night."

Mike could've done without the "we" since Thomas wouldn't actually be carrying the child, although he'd obviously done his part. That's what people said today, however. If Mike ever had kids, he was going to stay in the waiting room and let the woman do all the work.

"Congratulations," he told Thomas.

"Thanks, man. You know how long we've been trying. I was starting to think it wouldn't ever happen."

"Good things come to those who wait," Mike said. Another of their mom's favorite sayings.

"That's true in our case." Thomas paused. "It'll be true for you, too. You'll see."

Mike grunted.

"Listen, we're having a party Friday night at Ciao to celebrate. You're coming. Marty insisted."

"Friday? Yeah—"

"Rick's in Orlando," Thomas said. "Kaitlyn will be there. She's got a new boyfriend. Joel, I think. Don't make me sic my wife on you. She said you promised not to be a stranger."

"Okay, then," Mike agreed.

Kaitlyn he could handle. Rick…Rick was still too raw. And Marty was a strong woman he knew not to cross.

"Cool. I'll text the details." Thomas hesitated again. "Hang in there, man. It'll get better. And you can always stay with Mom and Dad if you have to."

"Thanks?"

Thomas chuckled. "Consider it motivation. Catch you later."

"Later, man."

"You made it!" Marty threw her arms around her brother-in-law and squeezed tight. "You suck at not being a stranger."

"Yeah, yeah."

"I like the beard," she whispered in his ear. "Tres sexy."

Mike grinned.

"You doin' okay?" She kept her hands on his shoulders and refused to let him look away. "Not bad. You're finding your way."

"Mikey!" Thomas joined them and slapped his brother on the back.

"Congrats, both of you," Mike said. "You'll make great parents. I'm happy for you."

Marty scratched his beard. "Thank you. Now go get a drink and mingle."

"Yes, ma'am."

"We'll talk later, bro," Thomas said.

Mike nodded and wandered off. As much as one could wander, although the private section at Ciao could hold close to fifty people. Only about twenty were there so far, so Mike got a Fat Tire beer from the bar and headed to the back corner to observe.

The dark lighting and white tablecloths gave the place an elegant ambiance. Only a few people sat at the tables. Most congregated in clumps around the bar at the front of the crowded room.

As many times as he'd witnessed the phenomenon, Mike still could not comprehend it. Why stand around holding your drink or food when you could sit comfortably in a chair and place your food and drink on a table? That people were sheep was the only reason he'd come up with, and he preferred to be a lone wolf.

He took a sip of beer and stretched his long legs out in front of him.

"Mingle," Marty mouthed at him before turning to greet her next guests.

His sister-in-law glowed in her mauve dress, or maybe that was the pregnancy. Either way, it suited her. She'd make a great mother.

No, a great mom. Thomas would be an excellent dad, too. The kid was lucky to be getting them as parents.

And speak of the devil…

"Sweetheart." His mother held out her arms as she floated over. "How are you, you poor baby?"

"Leave him be, Marie," his dad said. "He's not dying. The boy just lost his job."

"I'm fine, Ma."

"Fine? You can't even afford a razor. Are you depressed? I hear depressed people grow beards." She turned to her husband. "Isn't not taking care of yourself one of the signs? Look at him. He looks like a hobo."

Mike took a long pull from the bottle.

"And he's drinking."

"One beer." Mike felt obligated to point that out.

"So he grew a beard?" His dad shrugged. "It's not like he needs to shave for work every day. Who's going to see him?"

"Excuse me." Mike stood and pushed past his parents, leaving them talking about him to each other.

He finished his beer on the way to the bar and replaced it with a fresh one. He doubted there was enough alcohol in the building to get him through this evening. Convenient of Thomas to forget to mention the 'rents were coming, although he should have known they'd be here. Tom and Marie only lived three hours away, it was a Friday night, and this would be their first grandchild. Of course they'd be at the celebration party.

"Hi, Mike," a quiet female voice said.

He turned to see Kaitlyn standing there, her hand on the arm of the tall black-haired bruiser beside her.

Yeah, definitely not enough booze in the joint.

"It's good to see you," she said.

She'd cut her auburn hair in a bob, the lighter brown strands framing her heart-shaped face. The midnight blue blouse was new and brought out her eyes.

"Mike, this is Joel."

Thomas mentioned she started seeing someone new. Being told the news and being slapped in the face with it were not the same. He hoped this man would appreciate the jewel he had beside him. Kait liked funny cat videos, romantic comedies, and she smelled like strawberries in the morning.

"Mike?"

"Good to see you, too," he managed. "Nice to meet you, Jay."

"How's the job search?" Kaitlyn pushed her hair behind her ears. "Any luck?"

He shrugged.

"Well." She cleared her throat. "Maybe we can catch up later. It's a little crazy at the moment and I know you hate crowds."

"Sounds good."

Jordan led her away and they joined some of the other guests at one of the tables. Mike grabbed another beer. He'd survived the parents and Kait with her new boyfriend. Thank God Rick wasn't there, too. Two exes in one night. Not enough booze on the planet to get him through that encounter.

Mike stood off to one side of the bar, contemplating his next move. He didn't feel like joining any of the groups at the tables and the clumps of people standing around looked fully formed. He only recognized about half of them anyway.

Nice turnout, though, so good for Thomas and Marty. If they weren't the stars of this show, he'd be hanging with them instead of skulking in a corner by himself.

"Are you Mike?"

He gazed down at the intruder, a woman about his age with choppy blonde hair, green eyes, and a friendly face. For some reason, the word "pixie" popped into his head. The band or the mythological creature, he wondered, then decided it didn't matter.

"Who's asking?"

The woman grinned and he knew it was the creature.

"Marty said to tell you to get off your ass and mingle like she told you or she'll bitch-slap you to Toledo," Pixie said with a straight face.

"I'm standing," Mike said.

Pixie shrugged. "Same difference."

Mike had to laugh. Not only did the message sound like his sis-in-law, but the girl managed to capture the tone and intense posture as well.

"I'm Mona," Pixie said before he could ask. "Wait one sec."

Almost in spite of himself, Mike remained in his spot while Mona approached the bar. He couldn't hear the words, but it certainly appeared as if she was flirting with the bartender. Who happened to be a woman. After getting two Fat Tires, Pixie…er, Mona returned and handed one to Mike.

"I'm not done with this one." He shook the half-empty bottle. "And I think it's my third."

"Then I'll drink mine and yours." She shrugged. "Wanna sit?"

"Does that count as mingling?" He asked. "I'm not really in the mood to be bitch-slapped."

Her green eyes twinkled. "We'll make it work. It's better than you hulking in the corner like a pimple on a priest's ass."

Oh, he definitely needed to get to know this woman better. As he followed the enchanting creature, he wracked his brain trying to figure out who she was and how she knew Marty so well. Mike would've sworn he knew, had seen, or at least heard of all the key people in Thomas and Marty's social circle. After all, they'd pretty much shared that circle for the last decade or so.

"Stop looking like a lost puppy," Mona hissed when they sat down. "My job is to whip you into shape, not feel sorry for you."

"Job?" Mike finished his beer and placed the empty on the table.

She grimaced. "Poor choice of words."

Three beers didn't seem that many to him, but he couldn't keep up with this crazy chick. When the waiter dropped off some bread and butter, Mike asked for a water. And a menu. He needed food.

"Who are you again?" Mike asked.

"Mona."

"Mona?" Weren't old ladies named Mona?

"It's short for Ramona." She chuckled when he asked. "I have an older sister named Beatrice. Hand to God. And a younger brother Henry and twin sisters named Augustine and Ellen."

Mike gave her a blank stare.

"Seriously? Did no one ever read to you as a child?" She sighed. "Well, maybe boys don't read Beverly Cleary. My mom did, which is why we're all named after one of the author's characters. She even named the cat Otis and the dog Ribsy. The turtle was Seymour so I guess he escaped."

"Turtles do that." He was at a loss at how to respond to her outpouring of information.

"No, you big dumb ox. Seymour isn't called after a Beverly Cleary character. I thought you were supposed to be smart. Marty said you were."

Mike grabbed a slice of bread and slathered it with garlic butter. He loved the flakiness of Ciao's bread. Or any bread, really. He didn't indulge often because of the carbs, but tonight was a special occasion and it would help soak up the alcohol. He needed a clear head to wrap his head around the intriguing enigma before him.

"How do you know Marty?"

"It speaks!" Mona raised her hands in mock surprise. "I'm her hairdresser."

Marty invited the girl who cut her hair to a party celebrating her pregnancy? That seemed a little odd, even for his sister-in-law. Mike couldn't even recall the name of the guy who usually cut his hair. Steve, maybe? Or Stu?

"She hasn't mentioned me?" Mona winked.

Mike shook his head.

"Then you're at a disadvantage because I know buckets about you." She grinned mischievously, then sobered. "Sorry about your job. And your girl."

"Yeah." He pinched the bride of his nose and exhaled. "It is what it is."

Before Mona could respond, Marty swooped in. She flopped onto the seat next to Mike while Thomas stood behind her chair, his hand on her shoulder.

"I see you've met Ramona." Marty patted the side of his leg. "She got you to mingle."

"Or at least not stand in the corner like a total dork," Thomas said.

"Be nice," Marty said. "Your brother's going through a rough patch. We need to be supportive, not negative."

"I'm right here," Mike reminded them.

"Nice family." Mona took a pull from her beer and glanced at her phone. "Shit. Gotta go. Mikey, nice meeting you. Marty, congrats. Hugs."

In a flash, the pixie hairdresser disappeared. Mike gawked after her, but his thoughts did not bring her back. Was that good or bad? Good, probably, since there was no point in developing feelings for someone he'd never see again. Not to mention he had plenty of other things to occupy his time and thoughts.

Not that he was allowed much of either as his parents found them. Luckily, Thomas and Marty received the spotlight, at least for a few minutes. Thomas stuck out his tongue and rolled his eyes behind their backs, which caused his wife to bite her hand to keep from laughing. Mike pretended not to notice.

"You're coming to dinner Sunday, too." Mom jabbed her finger at him. "You're not taking care of yourself."

"The boy's fine, Marie," Dad said. "He'll land on his feet."

Mom grabbed his chin with her stubby fingers. "You need a woman to look after you."

"Or a man," Thomas quipped. "Rick should be back from Orlando in a few weeks when the project ends."

Marty smacked her husband hard on the back of his head. Dad found a fascinating spot on the ceiling and Mom pursed her lips. Thomas tried to look sorry, but the twitching corners of his mouth gave him away.

The fact that Rick was a man did not matter. His family had long ago come to terms with Mike's bisexuality. The issue with Rick resulted from his treatment of Mike and his need to be in control of all things at all times. The trait made him an excellent businessman, but a terrible boyfriend.

Still, Mike missed him. He'd tried to rebound with Kaitlyn and while that worked for a few months, it also cost him her friendship.

"I think I'm going to head out," Mike said.

"Did you drive?" Thomas asked. "Need a lift?"

"You can't drive in your condition, Mike," Mom said. "We'll take you home."

"I'll walk."

"Let them drive you," Marty suggested. "Or we can call an Uber."

"If the boy wants to walk, let him walk," Dad said.

"Guys. I'll be fine. My place is only about a mile from here."

"Be safe." Marty kissed his cheek.

He nodded. "No problem. No one's gonna bother me. I look like a hobo."

"Text us when you get home," Thomas said. "Marty will sleep better tonight if she knows you made it there safely."

"Will do," Mike promised.

He steeled himself for his mother's reaction, but to his surprise, she let him go with a hug and an order to be at dinner on Sunday. His father shook his hand, Thomas gave him a bro hug, and finally Mike wound his way through the people and into the fresh air.

The rather chilly air. His coat was back inside, but he'd rather freeze or buy a new one than go back in there. He started the long walk home.

"Yo Mikey," he heard his brother call before he got to the end of the short block.

He turned to see Thomas hurrying toward him, holding out his coat.

"Thanks, man," Mike said.

"Sorry about that in there," Thomas said. "I'll call you tomorrow when things are less crazy. Appreciate you coming. You sure you're okay?"

Mike nodded.

"Okay, man. Take care."

"Later."

The two men turned and walked off in different directions. Mike took a deep breath and let it out in a long plume of white. The booze had him feeling a little fuzzy, but the long walk home should take care of most of that.

Well, he'd gone to the party, done his duty, and survived. Having to deal with his parents wasn't half as bad as seeing Kaitlyn with her new guy, but he hadn't been forced to make too much small talk or deal with pitying looks and for that he felt grateful.

Mike moved along the city streets. Midtown had really come into its own over the last few years, and he'd been smart to get in early while mortgage payments and association fees were still reasonable. If he didn't find work in the next few months, though, that could change. What he really needed to decide was if he even wanted to stay in the financial planning arena or find a new gig.

As he ambled along, he looked around at the old homes interspersed with the brick buildings, the occasional tiny strip mall, and high rises. Even with the falling temperatures, other people were out and about. Couples strolled along the sidewalks, holding hands or hunched together for warmth. Students bounced along in packs or sometimes solo, joggers pounded past, and cars whizzed down the city streets.

Thomas and Marty had talked about moving to the suburbs, and now that she was finally pregnant, Mike bet they'd be in a new house in North Fulton by the time the baby arrived.

Let them go. Mike thrived on the energy of the city, of the people and all there was to see and do in Atlanta. He could not envision himself living anywhere else, although he supposed he might change his mind if he ever decided to settle down and get married.

"Not fuckin' likely," he muttered as he put his hands in his coat pockets.

"What's this?" Mike pulled a folded, plain white envelope from his right pocket. "Please don't let it be money."

He wouldn't put it past his mom or brother to slip him some extra funds, even if he had no need for it. No, the envelope was too thin to hold more than a piece of paper or two. A check, maybe?

He slit it open and pulled out the typed sheet. The light of the street lamps was enough to guide his way, but not bright enough to read by. At least it wasn't a check. He considered using his phone as a flashlight, then dismissed it. Whatever it was could wait.

Mike continued walking and let his thoughts wander. It was probably a note of encouragement from Marty. She liked to leave her boys—that's how she referred to Thomas and Mike—little notes now and again.

One of a kind, that Marty. She'd been Mike's friend at UGA first. When he brought her home for Thanksgiving the year she couldn't make it back to Wisconsin, she'd met Thomas and the rest was history. Not that Mike ever felt anything beyond friendship for Marty, but they remained close and he loved having her for a sister-in-law.

Mike's head had cleared by the time he reached the condo. He hung the coat, envelope still in the right pocket, on the back of one of the bar chairs. After taking a moment to text his brother as promised, Mike went into the bathroom to relieve his bladder and brush his teeth. He then moved in to the bedroom, where he shucked off his clothes, flopped onto the bed and went to sleep.

Mike stumbled into his stainless steel and granite kitchen. He started the coffee and opened the fridge. Sour milk, moldy bread, and expired eggs.

"Ugh."

Time to do a better job of taking care of himself. No self-respecting man or woman would want to be with him, or hire him, if he was a total fuck-up. He tossed all of the bad food-stuff, then grabbed the trash bag and headed for the door. The fact that he only wore a pair of plaid boxers dawned on him before he stepped into the hall.

"Jesus. Fucking idiot."

Mike left the trash by the door and went to get dressed and freshen up a bit. By the time he managed to wash his face and dress himself in a pair of jeans and his Atlanta United jersey, the coffee had brewed.

"Gonna take more than coffee," he said after the first cup. "Great. Now I'm talking to myself, too. I need food."

The little breakfast place two blocks down was packed, and the coffee house had a line coming out the door. Okay, so he could deal with the crowd, stand in line, or get something from the convenience store. What to do, what to do…

"Atlanta!" A guy yelled.

"United!" Mike called back instinctively.

He put his hands in his pockets to check his phone and pulled out the strange envelope from last night instead.

"Crap."

His phone must still be in the condo somewhere. He really was starting to fall apart if he forgot his phone. At least he had his keys so he hadn't locked himself out. Well, best to do takeout from the breakfast place and head back. Mike read the letter while standing in line.

"The hell?"

"Bad news, bruh?" The hipster guy behind him asked.

"No, just weird."

"I feel ya."

Okay, no more talking aloud on the street. Apparently it gave other people permission to join the conversation.

Mike read the letter again. Who in the world would give him something like this? And why? He dealt with numbers, not words. English had always been his least favorite subject, for good reason. No one wanted to hear what he had to say.

Deciding to attack the problem with logic, he started with the "who" portion of the equation. As the line inched forward, he ran through various options. Thomas could be eliminated. No man would do this shit to another man. No, a woman was behind this scheme.

Mom? Maybe, if she thought it would help or motivate him somehow. She'd want credit for it later, and she'd talk through it and insist on knowing how he responded, which went against the rules. So, not Mom.

Kaitlyn? Odds for Kait were better, but somehow Mike couldn't make himself buy it. He doubted she had the opportunity. If they were still dating, sure. Now, it looked like she'd moved on and therefore could be eliminated.

"Dude, move up." Hipster Guy nudged him.

Mike complied.

Marty? Now that was a real possibility. He could easily see her slipping the letter into his pocket. Marty had the means and the motive, and her husband had been the one to make sure he wore his coat home. Yes, Marty was the culprit.

Wait...what about Mona? They'd only met last night, but the pixie chick was out there and he believed her capable of such an act. Then again, she was Marty's friend and had only talked to him because his sister-in-law requested it of her.

His brain was starting to hurt.

"Sir, what would you like?" The cashier asked.

"Breakfast Bowl #2," he said and handed her a ten. She gave him a receipt with his order number in return, and he went to join that line.

So, Mona? A definite possibility, and not just for the letter carrier. Would Marty give up her number? She'd been the one to make sure they met, so perhaps. He could use the pretense of wanting to talk to the pixie about the strange note in his pocket. That would give him a good indication of whether or not it was Mona or Marty. His sister-in-law tended to be a terrible liar.

As crazy as it sounded, Mike was suddenly looking forward to dinner with his parents. Yes, this outing could prove quite interesting indeed.

Five minutes later, he headed home with his breakfast bag in hand. Now that he was well on his way to figuring out the person who gave him the letter, he needed to decide if he wanted to participate in the crazy widow lady's grand experiment.

Before he got canned, he never would've considered it. Circumstances had changed and he needed something to focus on besides being unemployed. So...what to do next was tell this old bag what his personal philosophy was. And get Mona's number. Marty owed him that much.

"I can't believe I'm doing this."

Mike got a Diet Mountain Dew from the fridge, sat at the counter, and instead of scrolling through the news while eating breakfast, he thought about his personal philosophy.

The breakfast bowl and soda were gone and he still didn't know what he wanted to say. Maybe he didn't have a personal philosophy. He'd bet no one else would respond with that answer. His essay would stand out.

Yeah...did it really need to? This wasn't a contest, just a way for this lady to feel less lonely. Mike could certainly relate to that.

His phone buzzed. After a brief search, he discovered it on the coffee table in the living room.

"You're up!" Thomas sounded surprised.

"Not only awake, I've also gone for a walk and eaten breakfast," Mike said. "What's going on?"

"My wife asked me to check on you."

Mike smiled. "Tell her I'm fine."

"I did. She still made me call."

"Good thing she's knocked up. The kid'll give you guys someone else to focus on. Mom and Dad, too." Mike paused. "Hey, listen. So Marty's hairdresser seemed interesting."

"I'll have the ball and chain send you that chick's number." Thomas chuckled. "She said the two of you would hit it off."

"Does she also know anyone in need of a financial planner?"

Another chuckle. "You really want to get back into that racket? Why not go for something new while you have the opportunity? You were bored long before they canned your ass."

"Been thinking about it," Mike admitted.

"Good. I better report in to the wife."

"Later, man."

If you'd asked him two days ago, Mike would've said that while he was friends with his brother and sister-in-law, they didn't know his deepest thoughts. But here Maty had picked out a great option for a potential girlfriend and Thomas knew he'd been considering changing careers for some time now. Maybe he should ask them what his personal philosophy was since he couldn't figure it out himself.

Nah. He'd get there eventually. And he'd figure out the job situation on his own, too. He had time on all counts.

Mike's Essay

My life has been pretty tough lately. Lost my job and my girl dumped me. Add my truck breaking down and my dog running away and I'll be a country song. Except I don't own a truck or a dog. But you get the point.

Still, I'm not ready to just lay down and die. I've got decent savings. I'm young, good-looking, and I own my own place. I can find another job in a flash once I discover what I'd like to do with my life.

Yeah, I should have figured that out before now, but some people work their whole lives and never find out what they truly want to do when they grow up. I don't think I'm going to end up like that. No spouse or kids to speak of, at least not at the moment. The only person I have to feed, clothe, and shelter is me.

What does all this information about my life have to do with my personal philosophy? Well, maybe what it is explains that.

I believe that you never know what's waiting around the corner.

Sometimes what's waiting is bad, like losing the job and the girl. Sometimes what's waiting is good, like a new job or running into an old friend. You won't know until you get there, and that's the fun of the journey.

Okay, Word tells me that I've only written 226 out of the 500 to 1,000 that the assignment calls for so I guess I'll keep writing. Not sure what else to say.

How do all those writers churn out those massive novels? Hell, I can't even write 500 words of an essay. I guess that's why I got such crummy grades in English. Numbers speak to me, not words.

Some people are afraid of what's waiting for them around the corner, and some rush around without much thought to what's coming next. I really don't see the point in either way, to be honest. I mean, what's waiting for you will find you regardless of your fears, and being scared of change is just plain stupid. It's going to happen anyway. If you go too fast, you won't see the crash coming.

That's starting to sound like "stop and smell the roses," but that's not how I want to sound. Just look at life with wonder and joy and deal with the good and the bad when they come. The highs can be super high, and the lows really low, but you can't ever truly prepare yourself for either one. And sometimes the middle is a good place to be, where things settle for a bit.

Okay, that got me to 444, so I'm getting there.

Umm….I know. When you're headed to the corner, sometimes you make the turn yourself and sometimes the turn just happens. What's waiting for you after the turn is unknown, but not always bad. Kind of like this essay, right?

So, yeah…my personal philosophy is that you never know what's waiting for you around the bend.

Hope I did okay.

Myra

My new routine was set—mornings at the shelter, afternoons cleaning out the house, evenings relaxing with a good book or good friends. I still missed Lee something fierce, and still talked to him every day, but the tidal waves of grief were receding. Now when I thought of him, I was more apt to smile than cry.

Tonight was letter reading night, but instead of preparing the house I found myself looking into Lee's empty study. All the sports knick-knacks had been carted off, even the framed items from the walls. That left the personal photos and souvenirs from our various trips.

I played with the miniature Eiffel Tower, then replaced it on the desk and picked up the tiny Liberty Bell.

"Remember that funny couple we met at that Greek restaurant in North Philly?" I asked out loud. "What were they celebrating again?"

A new job, came the response in my head. Even though I knew I supplied the answer, part of me liked to believe it came from Lee.

Grace whined and butted the side of my leg. "I know, girl," I told her. "Gotta tend to the living, too."

With a sigh, I turned from my husband's study and went back upstairs to get everything ready for tonight. In between cutting up cauliflower and carrots for the crudité, and making the cinnamon white chocolate chip cookies, I placed a different essay on each person's chair. Even with that, we had enough for each of us to read multiple essays. The experiment was going like gangbusters and I had no clue how or if I even wanted to stop the momentum.

To help me decide, I posed the question to the woman once they were all here and situated in their usual spots.

"Why would you want to stop?" Dolores asked. "We're having a blast!"

"I keep expecting to see something about it on the news," Mabel said. "Y'know, like the painter guy or the person who leaves a hundred dollar bill as a tip in those sketchy restaurants."

Betty nodded. "I thought the same thing. I had Jean look online, but she couldn't find anything."

Whether I wanted to admit it or not, my grand experiment had matured beyond me. Beyond all of us, really.

"I still think you should do another round," Susan said as she piled veggies on her plate.

"Another round?" I gaped at her.

"Like we talked about before." Mabel leaned forward. "Only this time ask them to tell us about their first love, or maybe the one who got away. Or something deeper, like do they believe in God and why."

Now that they mentioned it, I could recall discussing this idea before...and shooting it down.

"Myra doesn't need another essay topic." June scoffed.

"I don't need another hobby, either." I bit into a cookie. "I've got plenty to keep me busy and you know it."

From the look my best friend gave me, lips pursed and head tilted to the side, she disagreed with my last statement. I swallowed the cookie and steeled myself for what she was about to say.

"The essays aren't a hobby anymore." June held up a hand to silence the others before they could speak. "It started out that way, but now it's just like book club. You collect the responses and we read them and talk about them. None of us, including Myra, has actually given anyone an invitation in months."

Huh.

While everyone else argued with each other, I dropped back in my chair, absorbing June's words. She made an excellent a point. I handed out the first invitation more than six months ago. The responses continued to come in—we seemed to get more each week—so the experiment was more successful than I ever dreamed it would be.

But…the real hobby that had come out of it was volunteering at the shelter. And taking care of Grace. I liked my routine and didn't feel like changing it just yet, although eventually Lee's office and the garage would be cleaned out.

"Myra, what do you think?" Mabel's high-pitched tone brought me back to the conversation at hand. "Should we do another round?"

I shook my head. "No."

She wilted in her chair and her lower lip jutted out. "But this has been so much fun. I don't want to go back to reading books."

"Me neither," June said.

"Oh, you never read the books anyway and you know it," I told her, then looked at Mabel. "We'll keep reading the essays we do get, and when those dry up, the experiment is complete."

"So what are you going to do next?" Susan asked me.

"Keep living." I shrugged. "Good lord, why are y'all so interested in my life? Don't you have enough going on in yours?"

You'd think I'd know not to ever ask a question like that to these women. Mabel and Susan glanced at each other, then away.

Dolores looked at Betty, who blushed and looked at the carpet. June suddenly found the ceiling an intriguing spot to study.

"Okay, someone say something." I put my hands on my hips. "I'm not mad, you know, just curious."

"It's just that you're the first of us," June said. My confusion must have been plain because she explained further. "The first one to lose a husband."

Oh. That I understood all too well.

"I'm the test run." I sat back down. "I see."

"Kind of," Dolores jumped in. "I mean, we all know how this ends, and no matter of thinking or planning prepares you for the reality of it."

Susan placed her empty plate on the coffee table. "I've talked about it with Sal, especially after Lee got sick," she said. "You have to talk about it, even when you don't want to. And with you being the first of us to lose their spouse, we want to help you and at the same time plan for our own futures."

"Plus we all have kids and grandkids to consider," Betty added.

"We need more cookies." I took the ceramic bowl with me to the kitchen.

No one was going to be brave enough to follow me after that outpouring. I doubted anyone would even speak until I returned.

I guess I always knew the push for me to get a hobby so I wouldn't slide into depression was about more than my friends wanting to take care of me. Oh hell, who cared about the reason behind the experiment anyway? We'd all learned something from it—me, my friends, and everyone who responded—and that was enough for me.

All five women kept their eyes on me when I returned to the living room. I put the cookie jar back on its place on the table, took one for myself, and lowered myself onto the poufy chair.

"Why don't we continue reading the essays?" I sat as straight as possible. "Mabel, why don't you start us off?"

She gladly complied. The emailed response seemed to be from a young man or so I gathered from the tone. I guessed young from the philosophy of not knowing what was waiting around the next corner, and man since he said his girlfriend dumped him.

"He sounds lost." Dolores sighed.

Mabel and Susan nodded.

"Not lost," June put in. "Young."

"Just because you're young doesn't mean you're lost," I felt obliged to add. "Overall, I'd say his philosophy is positive. Why don't you read the next one?"

"Are we done with this one?" Betty asked.

Had I jumped ahead too quickly? When I asked if anyone else had an opinion they wanted to share, no one spoke up. I briefly wondered if maybe my wanting to move ahead caused their silence, then changed my mind. These women were not shy.

"Okay." Betty unfolded her letter. "Here goes."

We spent the next hour dissecting the responses and trying to guess the gender and ages of the respondents. I hadn't done an official count, but I'd gather that more women than men had sent in letters.

I know it sounds sexist to say it in this day and age, but women are more in touch with their feelings and more willing to share those feelings. Men are getting better, no doubt, and that's a good thing. We all benefit when we share. The experiment had proven that much even among my group of old friends.

"Hey, Myra," Mabel said, bringing my focus back to those friends. "After reading all these responses, I'm curious. What's your personal philosophy?"

Her question stopped me in my tracks. Pamlineta had asked that same questions months ago, near the beginning of this crazy journey, and I hadn't been able to answer her. I doubted I could answer Mabel's question now.

"I'm the instigator." I clutched my glass of water. "You don't need to know how I would respond. None of us submitted an essay."

"So you don't know," June challenged.

"Oh, you hush," Betty frowned, then turned her lips around to a smile. "Wait a minute. Why don't we all share our personal philosophies? We could send in a response and then read them along with all the others."

Mabel whooped. "That's brilliant!"

I wasn't quite sure I agreed with that assessment, and from her sour-lemon face, June was on my side. Mabel, Susan, Betty, and Dolores felt differently and started talking over each other in their excitement. Hmmm…better to wait them out than try to change their minds.

"Oh, I can't wait to get my thoughts down on paper," Betty gushed. "And I'm not going to tell you which one is mine when we read it aloud."

"I'd say that's fair," I said before anyone else could interject.

"But I want everyone to know mine," Mabel whined.

"Then let's leave it up to the individual," Dolores said. "If you want to tell us which one is yours, you can. If not, don't say anything."

Mabel's face grew stormy and she crossed her arms over her chest. June's eyes glinted with amusement, although she did not add to the conversation. Since the majority of women agreed with Dolores's plan, it was adopted.

Good lord, that meant I really would have to come up with my own personal philosophy even if no one else knew it was actually mine.

"I'm sorry, ladies, but I've had all the fun I can stand for one evening." June stood and gathered her things. "Am I seeing everyone at my house next week for Thanksgiving?"

"Sal and I are going to see Little Susie and her brood in Charlotte," Susan said.

"Are your girls coming?" Betty asked.

June shook her head. "They can't make it. They'll be here for Christmas, though. I can't wait to see them and the little ones."

"Well, Jean's girls are spending this holiday with us so we'll bring them along." Betty patted June's arm. "That'll help some."

"Always good to have children around." Dolores slipped into her pink and white windbreaker. "I'm waiting to hear from John on his plans."

"Let me know." June held her keys in her right hand. "Myra, you're coming?"

I was impressed that sounded like a question rather than an order. "Yes, ma'am," I said. "Grace and I are coming."

"Very good."

We shared hugs and then all the women dispersed back into their own lives, which meant it was time to face my own. I gathered all the plates and glasses and put them in the kitchen sink. I fed Grace, then finished cleaning and putting leftovers away. When I was done, I stretched out on the couch with Grace curled up next to me.

"We're all a bunch of crazy old ladies, huh?" I scratched her ears. "Bet you're glad you only have to deal with me."

Grace yawned in response and put her head on her paws.

"What's your personal philosophy? That it's good to have a forever home?"

No reaction this time. Well, that's what I got for talking to a dog. I had to come up with something. I mean, it was only fair after asking all those people to tell me what they believed. And I was more than old enough that I should know that kind of thing.

I'd ponder on it over the next several days. Maybe I'd have something by Thanksgiving, even if I didn't share it with the others. That meant two things I was going to have to figure out—my personal philosophy and what I wanted to do next with my life.

Thanksgiving Dinner

Thursday came before I was ready for it. Even though I looked forward to the event. June goes all-out for Thanksgiving and I knew she'd been up since long before the sun to make sure everything was perfect. She didn't mind others hosting book club or wine tastings or any other group activity we did, but holidays were her specialty.

"You ready for this, Gracie Grits?" I asked as I snapped on her leash.

Her liquid brown eyes peered up at me and her pink tongue lolled out of her mouth. After a pat on the head, I opened the door and we headed out.

No need for Henry to come pick me up for this gathering. June had no doubt I'd keep my word this time and be there smack dab on time. She didn't consider asking how I'd get there, so I decided to walk the mile there and back.

"This way we get peace before and after," I explained to Grace, who sniffed at the ivy by the neighbor's mailbox. "Well, I think it's ingenious."

I took a deep breath of the cool November air and let out a pleasurable sigh. The sky held that perfect shade of blue only seen in fall. The trees had dropped leaves of golden yellow, stark red, and light orange. We crunched through the ones not yet raked up, bringing back fond memories of previous autumns before Lee became sick.

This had always been Lee's favorite time of year. Spring was for celebrating another year together. Summer was for new adventures, whether to domestic or international destinations. Winter was for planning. But fall, that was for revisiting nearby favorites—nearby meaning within a day's journey—to remind us of all the reasons we loved living in Georgia.

Last year, Lee's cancer kept us home-bound, although we did manage to take a drive through the mountains to see the leaves changing color.

"Beautiful," he'd said, squeezing my hand to let me know he meant more than just the trees. "Simply divine."

I stopped walking and wiped at my eyes, overcome with emotion. Why couldn't this wonderful man be here to experience another autumn with me? Fifty years simply was not enough time together.

"Myra, hello there," someone called.

Mary Robey waved to me from her front step before scurrying down to give me a holiday hug. After exchanging pleasantries, she hesitated.

"Listen." She ducked her head, then placed a splayed hand on my upper arm. "My mother's friend lost her husband a couple months ago and she's having a real hard time of it. No kids or family nearby to help out." She paused to take a deep breath. "Would it be okay if she called you just to talk?"

I stepped back, stunned to silence by the question. My goal throughout the entire grieving process had been to avoid counseling or group sessions. I didn't need or desire to listen to other people's grief when I had a tough enough time dealing with my own. Not to mention I had no special wisdom to share.

Then again, I'd been lucky enough to have friends to see me through the first several stages of mourning, and even to kick me in the butt when I thought I was doing fine. Hmmm. Maybe it *was* time to share how I'd coped, how I was continuing to manage. Not everyone was lucky enough to have a ready-built support group.

"Sure," I told Mary. "You can pass along my number."

"Thank you." She gave me another big hug and allowed me to move on. "Tell June and them I said Happy Thanksgiving."

"Will do."

I tugged gently on Grace's leash and we continued on our way. Hopefully everyone else was inside chowing down on turkey or parked in front of the television watching football so I could avoid another request for a favor.

For the next few blocks, I noted all the different decorations. Most people had a wreath or cornucopia on their front door, and several had ribbons on their mailboxes. June went all out. She had a wreath with gold, maroon, and brown ribbons on her mailbox, a line of purple mums lining the walkway, and a large horn of plenty on her front door.

I'd barely knocked when she flung it open and dragged me inside. Grace barked and I placed my hand on her head to let her know everything was okay.

"What in the world?" I asked as I shrugged out of my peacoat.

"Mom!" The younger of Jean's daughters shouted. "Dog!"

Grace shook herself and gazed up at me. She hadn't been around many kids since I'd adopted her, but she obviously wanted to play. I unhooked her leash and she happily wriggled her way over to the girl.

"Where have you been?" June demanded, arms akimbo. "Everyone else has been here at least an hour."

"You said two." I moved toward the kitchen. "And unless I miss my guess, we won't eat for at least another hour."

She harrumphed.

"Myra, get in here," Betty called. "We need someone to chop celery."

I looked at June, who indicated I should lead the way into her kitchen. If hosting was going to stress her out so much, why bother?

Because she needs to be in charge. I answered my own question as soon as I asked it.

Betty handed me the celery and a knife. "Your dog might not be coming home with you," she said. "Lily's been asking for one forever."

"Like Jean would ever let that happen." I grinned. "Do you mind if I say hello to the menfolk before KP?"

June and Betty both waved me away. Mabel nodded from her spot chopping pecans, and Dolores didn't even look up from the recipe book.

The men, as expected, had taken over the living room and were watching the football game. I knew better than to even ask what was happening since I wouldn't understand it even if I tried to care.

"Happy Thanksgiving, fellas," I said from the doorway before stepping into the room.

Most of the men uttered some type of greeting in response. Roy mentioned that I could have brought fresh snacks, but he and Henry did hoist themselves off their designated spots to come give me a hug.

"You gonna sit with us?" Roy's eyebrows went up and down. "More interested after all that money sports got you?"

I chuckled. "No, I'm merely here to say hello."

"Well, it's good to see you," Henry said. "Even if it's only for a moment."

"How soon do we eat?" Jim asked. "This game'll be over soon and that leaves an hour until the next one."

"I'm not falling for that." I shook my forefinger in his direction. "Two minutes can last thirty with football. Lee hasn't been gone long enough for me to forget that fact."

The men laughed, proving my point, so I left them to it and tried to slip back into the kitchen. No such luck—June handed me the knife and vegetables I'd left on the counter. I'd finished two pieces of celery when Jean's girls came barreling into the kitchen,

Grace a stride behind them. A second later, Jean appeared and gave me an apologetic look.

"Miss Myra, can we take Gracie into the backyard and play?" The oldest girl asked.

I nodded. "Don't wear her out too much," I said. "I don't plan on carrying her home."

The girls giggled, and then the two of them, once again followed by Grace and Jean, hurried out to the backyard. I shook my head and smiled, pleased to have done my small part to keep everyone happy.

"You walked here?" Mabel's voice scaled up from her spot at the table.

"Yeah." I shrugged. "It's not that far and it's a beautiful day. Lee and I used to walk here and back all the time."

That seemed to be enough to satisfy her and before I went back to chopping celery, I took a moment to inhale all the other wonderful scents—the sweetness of pumpkin pie, the tang of gravy, and the simply heavenly turkey. I had to agree with my husband. This really was the best time of year.

After the celery, June handed me two tomatoes to slice for the salad. I obliged, concentrating on the task and letting the conversation wash over me as much as possible. Mostly everyone talked about TV shows and movies I hadn't seen, so I wasn't able to contribute much. I waved at Henry when he came in for another round of beer for the guys.

"Your team winning?" I winked.

"Got no dog in the hunt." He smiled. "Jim's been cursing a blue streak, though, and Roy said as long as the point spread holds he'll make some serious coin."

"Very good." I wasn't quite sure what else to say.

The girls came back inside. Grace, poor thing, had her tongue hanging out, but she looked happy. I gave her ears a good scratch when she walked over to me, ignoring June's shout to get her away from the food.

"You better wash your hands before you touch anything else," June said to me. "Girls, take her into the front room and play."

Ah, the joy of spending the holidays with loved ones. I followed directions, though, and then she directed Dolores and I to set the table. I gathered the silverware while Dolores reached for the plates, and we took the housewares into the dining room. June already had her ceramic turkey as the centerpiece along with smaller turkeys holding the name cards.

"She goes all out, doesn't she?" I asked Dolores.

"You doing okay?" She placed dishes at each seat. "This was always Lee's favorite holiday after Halloween."

I nodded, a little surprised her words did not bring tears. Did that mean I was getting better? Maybe. Maybe it meant that I'd learned how to let the love of friends take away some of the pain of loss. And could enjoy the memories.

"Good," she said.

Should I tell her what Mary Robey asked me on my way here? Was it better to wait until the six of us wives were together before bringing it up? I needed to think on it more before sharing.

After the table was set, it seemed like everyone started getting antsy. A small argument broke out between Jean's girls, although their mother stepped in and smoothed things over right quick. The game ended, so the men stretched their legs by walking over and getting in our way, which sent June into a tizzy.

"Why don't we go ahead and eat?" Henry put an arm around his wife's waist. "Is everything ready?"

"Yes," Betty said.

"No," June said at the same time.

Mabel cleared her throat. "Give us five minutes to get all the fixin's on the table," she said. "June just took the bird out of the oven and it's ready to carve."

The hostess glared at her friend, even though she'd spoken the truth. Henry went to carve the turkey while the men stood around and us women scurried from kitchen to dining room with the corn, stuffing, sweet potatoes, mashed potatoes, gravy, and cranberry glaze as well as several other side dishes. The heavenly smells and the buzz of activity brought Grace and the girls as well.

"Everyone sit." June made pushing motions with her hands.

"Let's eat," Henry announced.

By the time we were all stationed around the table, I'd ended up by Betty, Jean, and the girls. Grace plopped down in the corner by me, far enough to be out of the way yet close enough to pounce should a miracle happen and something fell on the floor.

I automatically looked to my left, where Lee used to be. Oh, this was going to be bad. I steeled myself for the surge of grief, and I was not disappointed.

"Henry, say the blessing," I heard June say from a distance.

At least when I shut my eyes, everyone would think I was praying rather than breathing through the pain. Lord, we better not go around the table and say what we're thankful for. Better to skip that particular tradition this year.

"Myra, you okay?" Betty whispered.

I nodded and opened my eyes. She handed me the green bean casserole and I scooped a little onto my plate. Almost by rote, I added the turkey and other dishes as they got passed around.

Everyone else dug in while I hesitated. I remembered Easter and not being able to eat a thing and Henry having to carry me home. This time, I knew the pain would pass. I'd gotten much better at riding the grief waves over the last several months.

"Myra?" Betty whispered again.

"I'm fine." I reached for the gravy boat and dribbled some on my turkey and mashed potatoes. "See?"

She narrowed her eyes, but let me be. I tried a small bite of food and it tasted wonderful. I took another mouthful and turned to Jean.

"When do you finish nursing school?" I asked.

"Another six months, Miss Myra," Jean said.

Betty relaxed and started in on her own meal. Jean and I kept up the conversation, eventually including her parents and the girls. Mabel gave me a smile and a subtle thumbs-up, which brought a smile to my face. It really was nice to have good friends to be there for you in the worst and best of times.

I think the same thing every year, but I don't know how we all ate so much. After dinner, the men returned to watch the next game. Mabel, Betty, and I divvied up the leftovers in various types and sizes of plasticware. June and Dolores cleared the table and filled the dishwasher.

By halftime, everyone was clamoring for dessert. June had outdone herself with pumpkin pie, pecan pie, cherry pie, and cherry cheesecake. Not to mention vanilla ice cream and homemade whipped cream for on top.

I helped pass out the slices, and then decided it was time for me to mosey on home. As expected, this announcement was met with complaints.

"Don't go just yet," June said. "Henry can drive you back."

"Yes, please stay," Mabel added. "We can talk more about what you're planning to ask people to write about next."

Friends can also drive you crazy when they don't listen.

"I told you," I said gently. "No more essay topics."

"So what are you going to do next?" Dolores asked. "Helping out at the animal shelter is all well and good, but you need more in your life."

"We'll see." I patted my pants pocket to check that my keys were there. "For the moment, I'm good so y'all should be, too."

This comment was met with well-intentioned grumbling, but they relented and let me leave. Well, after making sure I had all my leftovers, including pieces of cherry pie and the cheesecake. With more containers for the ice cream and whipped cream even if it might not survive the journey.

I waved to the men, pulled Gracie away from the kids, and started the middling walk home. Unlike on the way to June's, several people were also out and about. Family clusters moved along the sidewalks—kids in front with the adults a little ways behind, taking the time to enjoy being outside under the pretenses of working off the big meal.

While I nodded or occasionally waved at folks, for the most part Gracie and I managed to keep to ourselves. When I passed the Robeys, I thought about Mary's request to have me help her recently widowed friend. And Dolores and my other friends telling me I needed more than spending time at the shelter to keep me busy.

"Meddlesome women, huh, Lee?" I asked.

No response that anyone else could hear, but I felt him smile his approval at my using one of his pet phrases.

"What if they're right, though?"

Much as I hated to admit it, June's forcing me to get a hobby had helped me deal with losing my husband. Her suggestion led to the grand experiment, and to me adopting Grace, and even to my work at the shelter. I wasn't giving that up. Too much fun, and they counted on me to be there.

My presence made a difference, not just in the lives of the cats and dogs who stayed or who were adopted, but also in the lives of the people who visited or ended up taking a new pet home with them.

What if Mary's friend helped me at the shelter or what if she took a pet home? That would certainly help ease her grief, as long as she loved animals.

As I continued along, another thought struck me. If talking to me really did help Mary's friend, maybe I could also talk to other folks who recently lost a spouse. Men grieved, too, after all, and I was living proof that you could survive the pain of loss even when there were days you didn't think it would be possible.

"What do you think, Lee? Should I do it?"

No response. Then again, I didn't need one when I was so filled with love and a feeling of peace that I knew his answer regardless.

"Okay, then." I grinned. "Won't the girls be happy to know I've figured out the next chapter, too?"

When we got home, I put all the leftovers away and filled Grace's water bowl while I made myself some tea to go along with dessert. I went to sit at the dining room table and had to move the latest round of essays, which reminded me of my friends wanting to know my personal philosophy.

Even though I'd begun the experiment, and a few folks had asked about my philosophy, I didn't really know what I believed. I'd read lots of good ones, and several resonated with me, but they weren't mine.

And then it hit me. I did know after all. It had been right in front of me all along.

Myra's Essay

F unny when you think about it, but when I started the grand experiment, I didn't know what my personal philosophy was. Not that I needed one since the purpose was to find out what other people believed. And I wouldn't even have done that much if it weren't for my lifelong friends.

I'm over the moon that people responded to my invitation, and I can't put into words how much joy I've gotten out of reading the essays. So many amazing thoughts, so many different ways of looking at the world.

For me, however, it comes down to this: love will see you through.

I don't mean romantic love, at least not exclusively. My nearly sixty-year relationship with Lee, fifty of those years as his wife, is the strongest and most meaningful kind of love I will ever experience. He was my rock, my anchor, and he remains my inspiration and the great love of my life.

But I've had the privilege of experiencing all different kinds of love. The bond you have with a pet, as one example. I know it's temporary each time, and although it would take me some time to count all the dogs and cats who have shared their lives with me over the decades,

287

I can still picture each and every one of them. I've outlived them all, but they each have a special place in my heart.

I never did get to experience the love of a child, although I did get to love a child ever so briefly. And I've seen that connection between parent and child, and even grandparent and grandchild, many times over. I know how strong that connection can be.

Lee and I were both only children, so we missed out on those familial ties. I've witnessed enough sibling battles second-hand to both be thankful and sorry for that lack. I do find it fascinating how brothers and sisters can be at each other's throats one minute and the best of friends the next.

And speaking of friends, I've survived those knock-down, drag-out fights with friends, too. Somehow, we always make up and sometimes I think the relationship is stronger for it. I wouldn't have started this experiment without the guidance of friends. Even when I resisted when they told me I needed a hobby after Lee died, in the long run I knew they were right.

So love comes in all shapes and sizes. Family, friends, spouses, pets, and even co-workers or neighbors. And that love, that connection, will see you through.

I survived losing Lee because my friends cared for me enough to help me past the first and hardest stages of mourning. I also survived because he loved me so much that I knew I had to carry on for him, which may or may not come down to loving myself.

Even in my darkest hour, I found a way to keep my heart and my mind open to the possibilities of love and life. Friends got me started down that path, and along the way I adopted Grace, my latest and wonderful dog, and I began the grand experiment.

I've learned so much about myself, about strangers who I will probably never meet face-to-face even though they've shared some of their deepest thoughts with me, and even about my friends. People who have been in my life for thirty, forty years or longer.

And it all started because they believed in me enough to kick me in the butt and get me moving forward with my life, and because I loved them enough to listen. Not much more you can ask for than to love and to be loved, and I have been so very very lucky in my life to have the best of both sides.

In closing, I hope that all the people who have received the invitation, whether or not they sent in an essay, are blessed with that same experience.

Philosophies

Dawn: You make your own happiness

Joe: did not respond

Pamela: Never stop learning

Carol: Just keep going

Brad: Don't be afraid to take risks

Maureen: Trust your inner voice

Rose – did not respond

Liz: Don't lose faith in yourself

Brenda: Roll with the changes

Mike: You never know what's waiting around the bend

Myra: Love will see you through

Book Club Guide

1. Which character did you relate to the most and why?

2. If you received the invitation, would you respond? If you did respond, what would your personal philosophy be?

3. Why do you think Myra's friends were so interested in making sure that she found a hobby after her husband's death?

4. What did you think about Myra's decision to start volunteering at the animal shelter? And her choice at the end of the book to start counseling other widows?

5. How did you feel about Myra? Were you able to relate to her character?

6. Do you think Myra would have a different experience if she had been a young widow instead of an older widow?

7. How did you feel about Myra's friends? Do you have a similar group of friends you can count in good times and bad?

8. Did you like the format of the book—getting to see Myra's story, but also the stories of some of the people who received the invitation?

9. What did you think about getting to read the essays that the various characters submitted? Do you feel this added to the story's appeal?

10. Which character surprised you the most? Which character surprised you the least?

11. If you were faced with a similar circumstance to Myra, what hobby do you think you would choose?

12. Did Myra's story ring true to you? What about the stories of the other characters?

13. If you were to devise a similar experiment, what question would you want people to answer?

14. How do you think this book would be different if set in another country or time period?

15. How would this book change if the story were told from a man's point of view?

About the Author

Kathleen Walker lives in north Georgia with her two cats and too many books to count. This is her first novel.

Made in the USA
Columbia, SC
05 September 2019